Dedication

This book is dedicated to Edwin Garcia Junior. Junior, as we all called him, was the owner of a bar called, "Tavern at the Creek." The bar was located in Orlando, Florida. I walked into his bar one afternoon after work and met Junior's dad. Everyone called Junior's dad; Pop. Pop and I became good friends over time. The bar was something special because it reminded me of my days in the music business and almost every bar that I played in as a musician while living in the northeast. Over time, I became a regular at Junior's place and over time also became friends with Pop, Junior, and many regulars at the Tavern. It was at the Tavern where I would sit, relax, and quite honestly just think. From the time I walked into Junior's place and right up until the time Junior closed his bar, I had written and had released two books. Junior gave me a place to relax, a place to unwind. It became a sanctuary for me as both a musician and a writer. By the time I was nearing the completion of this, my third book, Junior had fallen ill, and was battling cancer. Junior told me before he passed away that he wanted to write a book of his own. He never got the chance to do that. But I have the chance to honor him in my book's dedication. Edwin Garcia Junior created a legacy in the businesses he started. I dedicate this book to Junior because without Junior's vision, I would have never found that perfect place to create this book. The characters, Junior and Jayde in this story were created with the specific purpose of honoring my friend, Junior and his wife, Jordan. He was a great person, and I do miss him. This book is dedicated to him.

PROLOGUE

When walking the figurative tightrope in my mind, I sometimes look down and realize the end is closer than I thought. With sanity ahead at one end of the rope and the past behind me, I do my best to maintain balance eager to reach the other side while knowing I am always just one misstep away from losing it all. I often wonder: if something lies ahead of me, behind me, and below me, then what exactly is above me? Well, that, my friends, is my personal conflict.

As I begin writing this book, I struggle with the reality of what has happened to my family, my friends, and my life. I suppose everyone wants their story told to share their experiences with others. There was a time when I felt confident I would know what to say, how to express myself, how to present my version of the events. But right now, I'm not so sure. This story is a tangled web of confusion and deceit. I find myself searching for a place to begin. I hesitate to share it because doing so will shine a light on me that may make you dislike or even despise me. I offer no excuses. I have no logical explanation for what I am about to reveal.

When passion enters your life, it can drive you to do things you wouldn't normally do. In this story, we'll walk through those moments and expose the most incredible and unbelievable circumstances, showing that sometimes, the connection between two people truly takes on a life of its own. No matter the reality surrounding them, their personal world is all they can see. Everything else remains in their peripheral vision never coming into focus.

This is not just a love story it's an unusual love story. In fact, it's a story of more than one love. A story that involves murder, deceit, passion, and lust. A story that may hold you in its grip right up until the very end. These are the characters you're about to meet.

I'm Paul Turner, and you'll be getting this story through me. I'm a 5'9" man with dirty blond hair and a thin build. I'm a musician, a salesman, and I'd say I have an average level of intelligence. I have a personal conflict with faith and struggle internally with several weaknesses drug use, alcohol, and my attraction to Leah. I love my wife, Pam, and my sons deeply. I'm an honest man with real inner battles, searching for guidance through this chapter of my life.

Pam Turner stands at 5'6", with dirty blond hair and a great figure. She's a librarian type intelligent, professional, and the kind of woman most men dream of being with. She loves her family and works hard to balance home and career. She's passionate about her work and has two very different sides to her. Most of the time, Pam is steady, composed, and nurturing especially with her family. But she also struggles to balance her professional ambitions with her responsibilities at home. Over time, her career begins to take precedence over her family, becoming the catalyst for my fall and for the weaknesses I had managed to keep mostly under control until now. I don't blame Pam for everything that happened, but I can't ignore the role she played in my unraveling. Pam has a dark side one I never saw coming.

Tony Santos is tall 6'0", well built, with dark skin and dark hair. He loves to boast about his success and his business ventures. But Tony is a criminal, running fraudulent schemes through his so-called rehabilitation center. He and Leah have posed as husband and wife in the past a lie and as boyfriend and girlfriend, which is also false. In this story, they're pretending to be in a relationship again. Tony works closely with Pam, and that working relationship creates distance between her and me.

Leah is close with her mother, but seems distant from her twin sister.

Leah Kessler stands about 5'4" and weighs around 110 pounds. Her usual attire includes jean shorts and a snug, low-cut black t-shirt. Her hair is brown, her skin is tan, and she has no idea how attractive she really is. Leah is vulnerable, caught in the struggle between her dreams and the painful sense that they may be out of reach.

She and I talk often and grow close as we discover how much we have in common. Leah is a singer with an incredible voice. We share musical interludes our way of coping with the chaos in our lives. Leah and I also share a darker bond: our addictions to drugs and alcohol, which at times consume us.

Leah seems deeply dependent on Tony. But when things between them begin to unravel, she turns to the one man she believes truly desires her. She plays the role she feels she must doing whatever it takes to escape the complex web of life she built with Tony. That man is me. Leah and I share a very real connection in this story.

Junior and Jayde Garcia are what some would call the perfect couple. Like Pam and me, they met in high school and later reconnected. Junior, a former police officer, now owns Junior's Tavern in Jamesport. Jayde, who looks like a model, is both his partner in life and in business. I first met them as a salesman visiting their tavern. Over time, Junior and I developed a friendship, and eventually, Pam and I became regulars at their place for dinner and drinks.

After Pam and I got married and moved into our first home, we saw less of Junior and Jayde, but our friendship endured. Junior was always a reliable source of advice. Though we lose touch for a while in this story, we reconnect again near the end.

Now you know a little bit about some of the people in my life. If you were to ask anyone what kind of man I was, you'd get different answers from every person you interviewed. In the end, you have to understand: when everything that matters is taken from you, all you have left to live for are the memories of what once was. Desperation drives people to do things they would never imagine themselves doing.

CHAPTER 1

Pamela, my wife, looked as lovely as ever. It was mid-May, nearly summer, and we were getting ready to take the kids out for dinner. Life was going really well. The kids were doing well in school, Pamela and I were in a good place financially, and our marriage felt strong.

I say *felt* because at the time, I truly believed it was. It's a powerful thing to feel like a man who has it all. And at that point, I really did. I had everything a man could ever ask for. Life was everything I'd once dreamed it could be. I truly believed that.

Let me start from the beginning.

My name is Paul Turner. I see myself as a musician an ambitious songwriter with average intelligence. I'm deeply passionate and tend to question everything in life. I've always struggled with faith, likely because I overthink and overanalyze everything. My emotions often get the best of me. Still, in my younger days, I was just an ordinary guy chasing the same things every young man wants. Pam and I met when we were both teenagers in high school. We grew up in Connecticut. She was something else back then very popular. A solid ten.

Me? I was into music, already playing in a band and trying to be a rock star. I wasn't much to look at, but I could fake it as well as anyone. I was softspoken, a hopeless romantic, and somehow, that always got me by.

Pamela and I met in homeroom and became friends in 11th grade. She stood about 5'6", usually wore her blonde hair in a Pamela Anderson style, and had a fantastic figure. She was attractive in that librarian kind of way smart, reserved, and confident.

The first time I really noticed her, it was winter. She was wearing blue jeans and leg warmers. My God my heart would race just seeing her walk down the hall. I was so drawn to her that everything else around me just faded.

I wanted more than friendship, but I never had the nerve to tell her. Maybe it was meant to be that way. I'd wake up excited to go to school just to see her. The moment I walked into homeroom, I'd scan the room to see if she was there yet.

We were sixteen. I didn't fully understand what I was feeling, but I knew one thing: Pam made me feel something I couldn't explain. When she was near me, I felt strange. When she got close, it was even more intense.

Pam was a goddess in my eyes. But I had no idea how to approach this goddess. No matter how many times I thought about it, I never worked up the courage to walk up to her and say what I truly felt. It stayed that way all through high school. Every time I was near her, I froze.

In my mind, I knew exactly what I wanted to say. But somewhere between my thoughts and my mouth, the words would hit a roadblock. If I tried to speak, I'd stutter.

So I stayed silent most of the time Pam was around. That became the norm for the rest of our high school years.

It didn't matter that we went to the same parties, the same places, or hung out with the same group of friends. The nervousness I felt around Pam never left me. It was something I never learned to overcome.

I remember more than one occasion when Pam and I ended up alone at a party. We'd exchange a few words brief conversations that never led anywhere. No matter how many chances I had, I could never thread the needle. I wanted her more than any girl I'd ever laid eyes on, yet I never had the nerve to just ask her out.

That evil form of adolescent torture lasted all through high school. I could kick myself even now so many moments when I could have just said something, but I never did.

It wasn't until after high school, when we both ended up at the same college in New Hampshire, that I finally found the courage to tell her how I'd felt all along. Pamela was still incredibly beautiful and just as smart. She was majoring in sports medicine, and I was studying criminal justice and law enforcement. We were opposites in every way, yet somehow, we fell in love.

Again, we found ourselves in the same places, making the same kinds of friends. It was like we were drawn to the same circles without even trying. Don't ask me to explain it I still can't. But when I looked at the big picture and how I felt about Pam, it all kind of made sense. This time, I wasn't going to let her slip away.

I finally worked up the courage. I walked up to her in the courtyard one afternoon. We started talking about classes, laughing about high school and then it happened. She mentioned homeroom. There it was: my opening. "Pam," I said, "I've always found you attractive and honestly, I've always been intrigued by you. I was wondering if you'd like to go out sometime. I'd really love the chance to get reacquainted."

She smiled. "I'd like that."

I did everything I could to contain my excitement. We set a time and place.

I went back to my dorm that afternoon, and man let me tell you I was *stoked*. My heart was pounding like Bonham's bass drum in "The Ocean."

After all this time, the girl I'd been crazy about in high school was suddenly within reach. All I could do was pray I wouldn't blow it.

Then came our first date.

Pamela looked absolutely stunning. Me? I was just doing everything I could not to mess it up. Some girls just look incredible in a summer dress but Pam? She may have been the most beautiful girl I'd ever seen wear one.

She stood around 5'5", with dirty blonde hair, and she couldn't have weighed more than 100 pounds soaking wet. She had the kind of figure that could've made her a model. And her smile? When she looked at you and you made eye contact man, it felt like the start of a roller coaster ride. That feeling in your gut, the rush? That's what it felt like just looking at her.

Now you can probably understand why it was so hard to ask her out. But somehow by the grace of God there we were.

Our first date was dinner and a movie. We went to this Italian place "Vinnie's," or maybe it was "Vincenzo's." It closed down not long after, but I think it reopened as "Massimo's" or something like that. We were just two college kids, living life. And honestly? I think we fell in love that night.

After dinner, I leaned in to kiss her. Her eyes lit up she wanted it as much as I did. That first kiss was electric. It sent me falling into love faster than I ever imagined.

Later, we headed to the theater to see *Memento*. The movie was good, I think, but truth be told, neither of us was really paying attention.

I had fallen for the girl of my dreams in high school and now, here we were in college, falling in love for real. That night was magic. And the goodnight kiss we shared set the stage for everything that followed.

I went home after our date, and I'd be lying if I told you anything other than this I knew Pam was the one. As I drifted toward sleep that evening, just before slipping under, I remember seeing her face. Her eyes. Her smile. I could still feel her aura. And with that, I fell into a deep sleep.

The next morning, I woke up feeling like I could take on the world and taking on the world was exactly what I had in mind, with Pam by my side.

We went on several more dates, and just like that, we were a couple. Our conversations shifted toward the future. We started talking about building a life together. Over time, we grew even closer. Despite having very little in common, we loved being together. What we *did* share was a dream a shared vision of the future. And that was enough.

Honestly, it all moved so quickly. Time flew by. Before we knew it, life came at us full force. We decided to get married. It wasn't really a surprise. After the last few years, we both knew it was inevitable.

Pam threw herself into planning the wedding. And I? I just wanted to make it as special for her as I could. Don't get me wrong it was special for me, too. But when it came to this part of our life, Pam had the vision. She made it our reality. And I was more than okay with that. Honestly, isn't that how it's supposed to be? I like to think it's what God intended.

It was 2003. The country was still reeling from the 9/11 attacks just a few years earlier. Planning a wedding during such a devastating time wasn't easy. Both of us had lost people in the towers, and we were deeply patriotic deeply affected. President George W. Bush was in office then, and we both felt he handled the crisis well, considering the weight of what had happened.

Even though the world felt chaotic, we pushed forward. When love finds you, passion drives everything and that's exactly what happened for us.

Our wedding was phenomenal. Pam planned every detail perfectly and executed everything flawlessly. It was held at Samuels in Port Jefferson, on Long Island, with around 150 guests. We had a live band "So Close" also from Long Island. They were

fantastic and kept the music going all night. I'd
known a few of the guys from years earlier when I
played with them for a while, and I'd stayed friends
with them. So when I asked if they'd play our
wedding, they were all in. It was perfect. That was
my only job, and I think I nailed it.

The magic of the ceremony and the thrill of the
celebration carried us through the evening. Pam was
wildly popular, and her side of the guest list was
full of family and friends. I came from a smaller
family and tended to keep to myself, so my side was
much smaller. But none of that mattered. It was a
beautiful day.

As the night came to a close, Pam and I climbed
into our limousine and said goodbye to everyone.
The doors shut, and just like that it was us.
Champagne. Music. The sound of the night fading
behind us. The wedding may have ended, but our
private celebration was just beginning. That night
turned out to be the best night of my life.

The love I felt for Pam was something I couldn't
explain something beyond words. Our life together
was just beginning, and both of us were full of
emotion and excitement, our veins humming with it.
We believed with everything in us that we had
found the love of our lives. Each other. And with
that belief, we hit the ground running. Our journey
had just begun.

CHAPTER 2

To her credit, Pam insisted on finishing college. I, on the other hand, decided to go into sales and play music as a solo act on weekends. I played gigs whenever I could get them mostly 70s and 80s rock. The music always went over well, and I loved performing, so naturally, I took every opportunity to play.

Between my sales job and the bar gigs, I was making decent money. Eventually, I made the decision to leave college and honestly, it turned out to be the right call. Pam went on to become a physical therapist, and I stayed in sales specifically restaurant sales. I spent a lot of time in bars and restaurants, and for a while, life was really good.

We both made a decent living and eventually saved enough money to start looking for a house out on eastern Long Island. Pam received an offer to join a private practice in Greenport, and it was an opportunity she couldn't pass up. As for me, I took a sales position with a seafood company. It turns out, I had a real knack for it. I was good with people sales came naturally to me. And truthfully, I loved the business.

My job took me all over the island and into the city. On Long Island, seafood is king nearly every bar or restaurant serves it so I met a ton of people and made some great business connections. It was a great fit, not just for sales, but because it also allowed me to network with places I could potentially play music at on the weekends. That lifestyle sales by day, music by night became my rhythm for a while.

Pam eventually landed a position at the rehabilitation center she'd been aiming for. It was privately owned and located just a few miles from our new home on the fifth floor of a large medical building. Looking back, that period of our life was one of the best. We were incredibly happy. Life felt full of possibility, with nothing but bright lights ahead.

We were both content with our choices, and before long, we bought our first house. After saving diligently, everything just seemed to fall into place. The house was a few blocks from the Long Island Sound exactly what we'd dreamed of.

We found the place through my friend Junior, the owner of a bar called Junior's Tavern in Jamesport. We'd become close after I played a few gigs at his place, and he also did business with the seafood company I worked for. Junior had this great spot that I visited often sometimes for business, sometimes just to sit and talk. He was a voice of reason in my life, and we shared some truly meaningful conversations.

One day, he mentioned that a friend of his was selling a house in New Suffolk. It looked perfect for

Pam and me. And just like that, everything aligned. New jobs, a new home, and a new chapter.

A new life is what we started.

Closing on our house was a huge moment for us. With each passing day, Pam and I could see our life taking shape right before our eyes. I think every married couple goes through that time in their relationship when they're so in love elated, hopeful, and excited about what lies ahead. That was us. Just the two of us, building a life together.

We planned to wait a few years before starting a family. We wanted to get settled we had a plan. But let me ask you something: how often do those carefully made plans ever work out exactly as expected? Pretty much never, right?

Did you know a girl can get pregnant even while on birth control? Yeah, we didn't think so either. But it's true. Pam was pregnant, and just like that, our lives changed.

We started preparing for the baby talking about nursery colors, furniture, names if it was a boy or a girl. Pretty typical stuff, right? But a few months later, the sonogram revealed something we hadn't expected: twins. Yep twins. We were definitely not ready for that.

Pam worked nearly all the way through her pregnancy. And then came the day the day when she gave birth to our beautiful boys, just minutes apart. Our family life had officially begun. We named them Chris and Brian. From that moment on, everything changed.

I remember feeling completely overwhelmed after they were born. So, I headed over to Junior's Tavern for a little perspective. I needed a voice of reason, and Junior was always that guy. The idea of being a father a father of twin boys, no less had me on edge.

Junior and I sat and talked for a while. Like always, he helped me find my footing. He had this way of calming me down, helping me see the path forward a little clearer. That's one of the reasons I loved going to his place. Junior's Tavern felt like the perfect bar. The décor, the vibe, the staff it all felt like home. Everyone who walked in felt like family.

His wife, Jayde, was just as impressive. She helped run the tavern and was always warm, sociable, and full of good energy. Pam and Jayde really hit it off. They'd chat over coffee whenever we were there, and over time, their bond grew strong. Junior and Jayde became our closest friends after we moved out there. We visited their place often, and every time I left, I felt better.

Pam, to her credit, was a total trooper. She was an incredible mother. She took time off work to stay home with the boys and handled it all like a pro. I worked extra hours to help make ends meet and honestly, I didn't mind. That's what I felt my role should be as a father.

I was gone a lot. Sales meant travel. And during that time, Jayde and Pam grew even closer. Jayde would often stop by, and the two of them would sit, talk, and support each other. I was so grateful for their friendship especially since we were still new to the area.

At that point, life was good. We were proud of the choices we made. We had a beautiful family, a home we loved, and a strong bond between us. Even though it wasn't easy it was a lot of work we made it work. Pam is an amazing woman. She practically raised our two boys on her own during that time, and in the end, it all paid off.

When you're in the thick of life, time really starts to speed up.

It's crazy how much goes into a day's work. One day bleeds into the next, and before you know it, weeks turn into years. But we were young, energetic, and up for the challenge working hard and raising kids, day in and day out. Looking back now, that time in our lives feels like a blur. It went by so fast.

Pam and I were still very much in love. We had passion, and whenever we had the rare chance to be alone together, we cherished it. We held onto those moments as tightly as we could, never wanting them to end. And yet, of course, they always did. Life resumed, and the daily grind continued.

Sometimes we'd visit Junior's Tavern on those free nights. Other times, we'd head to the beach in the evening. We both loved the Long Island Sound. It might not sound like much grabbing drinks at a bar or walking the beach but when you're raising a family, those simple moments become everything. They were our oasis, a way to reconnect and remind ourselves who we were to each other.

Looking back, those nights helped keep our love alive. Our relationship stayed strong because of those small but meaningful things.

Time flew by, and before we knew it, the boys were teenagers. Chris and Brian already over fifteen. It's hard to believe. More than fifteen years gone in the blink of an eye.

Pam was back at work. I was still selling seafood up and down the East Coast restaurants, clam bars, oyster joints. And once a month, Junior and Jayde let me do my acoustic set at the tavern. I loved playing music again, and the crowd was always welcoming. The extra income helped, too.

We worked hard really hard to pay off the house and save for the boys' college. And we were getting there. It felt like our goals were within reach. Pam and I made a great team. Our life reflected that in nearly every way.

Whenever I had time off, I'd spend it with the boys. Even though they were twins, Chris and Brian were completely different. Chris was the thinker focused, sharp, and always up for a good debate. He thrived on challenges and loved anything that pushed his brain.

Brian, on the other hand, was the romantic. He reminded me a lot of myself at his age. He wore his heart on his sleeve, played guitar, and loved music. He was confident, outgoing, and always had a girlfriend. I still don't know where he got that boldness not from me, that's for sure.

I genuinely loved spending time with them. Despite our differences, we got along really well. I say "oddly" because teenage boys and their dad don't always mix, and Chris and I are especially different. But somehow, we connected.

What meant the most to me was that they trusted me. They talked to me about everything. That trust that openness made our bond so strong. I found myself constantly proud of them and excited to hear about their lives. It's the kind of relationship most parents hope for, and somehow, I was lucky enough to have it.

The boys were becoming young men each forging his own path, each full of drive. The three of us were tight, even as they started pulling away to form their own lives. That's how it goes. Kids grow up.

I embraced every moment I had with them. And when they were busy which was most of the time I'd do chores or swing by Junior's Tavern to catch up. Spending time with Junior always grounded me.

On this particular day off, I decided to take care of a few things around the house starting with organizing the garage. I slept in a bit but finally got moving around 11 a.m. While I was outside, I noticed a moving truck a few houses down. Curious, I looked in that direction and saw a man fit, well-dressed, and probably in his thirties unloading boxes.

Naturally, I waved, just being friendly. The man waved back and started walking toward me. As he got closer, he extended his hand and said, "Hello, I'm Tony."

I shook his hand. "Paul. Looks like we'll be neighbors. Welcome."

"Thanks," he replied. "I'm from New Jersey."

"Well then, welcome to Long Island."

Tony went on to tell me about the rehabilitation facility he owns in town. He had run a practice back in Jersey and recently decided to start fresh out here on the East End.

"It's about two miles from here," he said.

That's when it clicked. "Wait are you *the* owner?"

"Yeah," he nodded.

"My wife is Pam."

"Paul! Pam's husband great to meet you! She talks about you all the time. Your wife is amazing with our patients. She's a huge asset to the team. Honestly, she's holding down the fort today. I'm lucky to have her on board."

As Tony and I were chatting, I noticed a young woman walking toward us from the distance.

"Tony!" she called out. "If you want unpacking to go smoothly, you need to help me get these boxes sorted!"

She had a thick Jersey accent. And my God she was beautiful.

She stood about 5'4", maybe 110 pounds. She wore jean shorts and a snug, low-cut black T-shirt. Her brown hair was tied back in a ponytail, and her skin was sun-kissed. I felt my heart skip a beat. My stomach dropped like I'd just gone over the first hill of a roller coaster.

Tony turned to me and said, "Paul, this is my girlfriend, Leah."

"Hi, Paul," she said. "Nice to meet you. Now come on, Tony we've got work to do."

Before they left, I asked Tony, "Did Pam know you were moving into this neighborhood?"

He shrugged. "She knew I was looking, but I doubt she knows the address."

"Well, she's going to be surprised. What a coincidence!"

Tony and Leah walked off, and I stood there for a moment, trying to wrap my head around the encounter. Both were attractive like movie-star attractive and they seemed friendly. Pam and I hadn't really made many friends in the neighborhood. A lot of folks came and went seasonal types so this felt like a good change.

But Leah… there was something about her. Something more than just her looks. She was magnetic undeniably alluring. I chalked it up to the fact that she was stunning. It's a natural reaction, right? Any guy would feel a flutter meeting someone like that. Still, I had a gut feeling that being around her might be… difficult. Not because I'd act on anything but because she was the kind of beautiful that makes you nervous to speak. The kind of beauty that makes you stutter like an idiot.

Anyway, I couldn't wait to talk to Pam not about Leah, of course, but about her boss becoming our new neighbor.

When Pam got home from work, I asked, "Did you talk to Tony today?"

She shook her head. "No why?"

"I met him earlier. Right in our front yard."

She looked confused. "Wait, what?"

"Tony bought the house a few doors down. You know, the one that's had the For Sale sign up all year? He's our new neighbor."

She smiled. "Did you like him?"

"He seems like a good guy. I met Leah too, briefly they were still unpacking."

"I really like her," Pam said. "She stops by the rehab center a lot. We've become friends. Paul, did you notice how beautiful Leah is?"

Now, how does a married man respond to *that* question?

I smiled cautiously. "Leah is very pretty… but not as pretty as you."

Pam rolled her eyes and laughed. Women. How do they always know when we're lying or trying to save ourselves?

"Let's have them over for dinner when they get settled," Pam said. "I like her. I think we'd all get along."

"Sounds good," I replied. "You make the plans. My first impression was a good one."

As Pam walked into the other room, I stood there, thinking. I knew she'd picked up on my reaction. She caught me. Now she'll be watching me like a hawk when we eventually have that dinner. Maybe I'm overthinking things. I just need to calm down. Take it in stride.

CHAPTER 3

We spent our time off doing all the things a typical family does errands, housework, catching up, and just living day to day. The boys were older now and had their own friends, their own lives. Pam and I spent whatever free time we had going to dinner at Junior's place or walking along the beach in the evenings. The Long Island Sound is especially tranquil at night. We both loved our home and the town we had chosen to settle down in. Life was good really good.

Our house was just a few blocks from the Sound, so the boys could walk home easily after hanging out with friends. But for Pam and me, the beach became our place a quiet escape at the end of the day. Even just thirty minutes of walking along the water could ease the stress of an entire week. Something about the soft rhythm of the waves and the shimmer of moonlight over the Sound calmed us, body and soul.

Often, we'd walk in silence, soaking in the serenity of the moment. On other nights, we'd talk for hours about life, the kids, our dreams. Those conversations were some of the most intimate moments we shared. They reminded us of how far we'd come, and how much we still loved each other. These nights were sacred. Amid the chaos of raising a family and juggling work, these walks grounded us. They gave us space to reconnect, to breathe.

Tonight was one of those nights. We lost track of time, as we often did, completely enveloped by the peace around us. By the time we returned home, we were both ready to sleep. I kissed Pam goodnight, and we crawled into bed, physically exhausted but emotionally content.

But as I lay there, waiting for sleep to take me, something unexpected happened. Leah's face drifted into my mind.

Why is this happening?

I didn't want to admit it even to myself but I found myself thinking about her again. I wasn't proud of it. There was just something about her I couldn't shake. Her image her voice lingered.

I didn't *want* to be fantasizing about her, but there it was, uninvited and vivid. I told myself it was just a reaction just a married guy encountering someone new and attractive. A fleeting infatuation. That had to be it, right?

But something about Leah was different. I'd seen attractive women before. I'd worked in bars and restaurants, for God's sake. Leah had even crossed my path before bartending at a few places I did business with but I'd never really noticed her like this. Not until I saw her up close. Not until she moved onto our street.

And now… she was in my head.

I told myself it was just a fantasy. Just curiosity. Just something passing. I'd never act on it. I loved Pam. We had a beautiful life. But I couldn't help wondering: why was Leah still in my thoughts?

Hopefully, by morning, it would pass. I closed my eyes and tried to let sleep take over.

CHAPTER 4

The sound of the alarm clock jolted me awake, and I immediately recognized that another day had begun. Another workday but we had plans for later this afternoon. You guessed it: Tony and Leah.

It had been a few weeks since Tony and Leah moved in, and we'd started spending time with them pretty regularly. We even introduced them to two of our friends, Junior and Jayde, and the five of us often hung out together, just talking and enjoying each other's company.

We love Junior's Tavern it's become one of our favorite hangout spots. Honestly, just knowing we'd be spending the evening with friends made the day feel more bearable. Pam and I had built a solid friendship with Tony, her boss, and his girlfriend Leah, and we were growing closer as friends. We really enjoyed their company.

Tonight, we were having dinner with them again. Time flew by, and before we knew it, the evening had arrived.

Leah, who bartends at a few places around town, had looked familiar to me from the start. I later realized it was because I'd sold to some of the bars where she works. That connection made our friendship feel oddly natural, even from the beginning.

We'd started going out with Tony and Leah about once a week. This night was special Pam had just been promoted to manager at the rehab center. We were out to celebrate both her promotion and Tony's continued business success.

Naturally, we chose Junior's Tavern. Junior has a surprisingly great food menu for a bar, and everyone loves the place. It was the perfect spot to celebrate.

Tony runs the rehab center and has been Pam's boss for a while. Now, with Pam managing the center, she'd be helping him with patient scheduling and rehabilitation plans. It's a big facility, and her organizational skills would definitely be put to the test. Pam's great at what she does, but we hadn't really talked about how this might change things for us.

Tony is the kind of guy who's easy to talk to and often funny. Leah is quieter, a little shy, but incredibly attractive. When we're all together, she's comfortable. Over time, Leah and I found ourselves talking more and more, especially when Pam and Tony got caught up in work talk.

I guess that's how Leah and I really became close friends. We were often nudged into our own conversations while they discussed business. Neither of us seemed to mind. We discovered we genuinely enjoyed each other's company. Those evenings out turned into something we both looked forward to.

Pam and Leah also became close over time. I'm sure they share their own stories about Tony and me. The four of us shared a great dynamic we truly enjoyed our time together.

But tonight was a little different. The conversation turned to the recent string of murders in the area. Four men killed over the last four months. The media called it the work of a possible serial killer. All four victims worked in the hospitality industry.

It was unsettling. Things like this don't usually happen on eastern Long Island. It hit especially close to home since Leah and I both work in the same industry and we indirectly knew three of the victims. It was chilling.

The authorities believed it was the work of a serial killer, but so far, there were no leads.

Even though we talked about it that night, none of us seemed to take it too seriously. Maybe because we didn't think it affected us. Still, we were curious.

Junior, a former cop, joined our table during the conversation. His background gave him a unique perspective, and he had some fascinating theories about the case. We talked for what felt like hours.

Junior believed the murders were connected but possibly driven by more than one motive. He said the pattern was scattered there didn't seem to be a specific type of victim or consistent method. I agreed with him.

Eventually, Junior got a phone call and stepped away.

I realized I was the only one at the table who seemed truly interested in the murders. The others just weren't as engaged. That struck me as odd.

I mean, people were being killed. That should be a big deal, right?

But I guess that's how people are. We get caught up in our own routines and distractions even something as horrible as a killer on the loose can get buried under the weight of daily life.

Still, I kept following the case. It became a habit. I'd check the news regularly and even stop by Junior's to hear his latest take.

Despite all the media coverage, there wasn't much new information. That made the whole thing even more disturbing.

As the evening wrapped up, the four of us said our goodbyes and called it a night. Once Pam and I

were settled at home, lying in bed, I asked,
"So, what kind of hours will you be working now
with this new position and all?"

Pam replied, "I'm not sure, but I expect longer
days."
She paused, then added, "Does that bother you?"

"No," I said. "I was just wondering. I know you're
going to be great in your new role."

I smiled. "Anyway, thanks for a great night."

I leaned in to kiss her goodnight, and she kissed me
back deeply, passionately. The night ended just as
beautifully as it had begun.

As I drifted off to sleep, I couldn't help but feel that
I was the luckiest man in the world. Pam is an
amazing woman. We have wonderful friends and a
beautiful life together.

As Joe Walsh said, *"Life's been good to me so far."*

CHAPTER 5

Another workday.

I'd started noticing that my sales numbers had leveled off over the past few months and in some recent weeks, they'd even slipped. My boss thought it was the economy; overall numbers were down across the company. We were all trying to strategize, looking ahead and thinking about how to boost sales.

The problem was fewer people were going out to eat. A clear sign people were pulling back on spending in anticipation of a possible economic slowdown.

With fewer sales came lower commissions. I started making less. I was also coming home earlier and more often because I had fewer appointments and leads.

Pam, on the other hand, was working longer hours. Three or four late nights a week, sometimes weekends too. The shift in our schedules changed everything. We hardly saw each other anymore. I had more free time than I knew what to do with.

At first, it was fine. I used the time to work on music, play my guitar, write a little. I kept telling myself things would change eventually. But for now, this was our life.

The boys had their own lives. They were out all the time young adults doing their thing. I hardly saw them either.

That just left me.

Me, by myself.

Lately, the boredom had started to set in and with it, a nagging anxiety. I began writing music again, mostly just to fill the empty hours. I also found myself obsessing over the killings. I'd watch the news constantly, trying to keep up with every new development.

The victimology was confusing. No clear pattern. Junior might be right: there could be more than one motive behind the murders.

Too much time on my hands is not good for me. I hate moments like this when the anxiety creeps in, and I find myself longing for anything to break the monotony. A conversation, a distraction, anything. I could only play so much music, write so many lyrics, and scroll through so much news.

Another late night for Pam. No surprise it's what we expected. So why was I starting to feel so angry about it?

I didn't know how much more of this I could take.

I felt like I was going stir-crazy. I couldn't stand another night in this house, alone. I was tired of waiting. Tired of feeling invisible. Tired of being bored and lonely.

Maybe I just needed to get out. Clear my head. Do something for myself.

I decided to go see Leah.

The bar wasn't far just up the road. She was working tonight, and I figured maybe being out would help ease this loneliness. Even just for a few hours. I'd never gone to see her at work before, but she was a friend. It felt harmless enough.

The place was called *The Rock n Roll Bourbon Café*. A local spot. She usually worked weeknights, and it was a short drive from the house. I really needed the break.

Pam was working late. The boys had their own lives. They didn't need me.

Happy hour was quiet. The bar was nearly empty. Just Leah behind the bar.

I paused for a moment, wondering why I came. Maybe because Leah and I just… connect. She's undeniably attractive, but it's more than that. I enjoy being around her. She has this magnetic energy like staring up at the stars and realizing the sky is full of silent, dazzling beauty. That's Leah. Quiet, glowing. Beautiful inside and out.

Seeing her behind the bar made me question whether coming here was the smartest thing to do. But I needed to get out. And she's a friend.

Leah's usually quiet and a little shy. She's about 5'4", maybe 110 pounds. Most nights, she wears jean shorts and a fitted, low-cut black T-shirt sometimes a variation, but always that same casual, eye-catching style. Brown hair. Tanned skin. An alluring smile. Red and white painted nails. She wears her hair down sometimes, other times in a ponytail. However she wears it, she turns heads.

Me visiting Leah alone like this this was new. We'd talked plenty when the four of us were out, but never one-on-one.

Well, not exactly. When Pam and Tony drifted into their usual work conversations, Leah and I often ended up in our own little world. We'd talk about our dreams. Our creative ideas. The kind of people we wanted to be. The places we longed to go.

I don't think Pam or Tony ever noticed how close Leah and I had become.

In our conversations, I mostly listened a rarity for me. Leah's a passionate soul, and when she speaks from the heart, she gets completely lost in her thoughts. I always noticed that. And honestly, I couldn't look away. Her vulnerability made her even more captivating.

Over time, we'd become completely at ease with one another. That comfort was inevitable. She listens when I talk. Really listens. She's genuinely interested. And that means a lot.

Pam, on the other hand… Pam doesn't really want to hear me anymore. If I repeat myself tell the same story twice she gets frustrated. She'll cut me off mid-sentence. It feels like what I have to say doesn't matter to her. Or maybe I don't matter. At least, not in the way I used to.

We barely see each other these days. We share a house, that's about it.

Maybe that's why I came to see Leah tonight.

With Leah, it feels different. When our eyes meet, I can feel it this honesty, this calm. A rare moment of soul-to-soul connection. It's like we're two kindred spirits, stumbling into the same quiet place in time. That's what makes these moments with her so special.

I needed a friend. And I found one in Leah.

She listens not just to my words, but to what I mean. And that makes me feel seen. Sometimes, that's all anyone really needs. To feel like they matter.

So here I am.

And there she is.

Leah was on the phone when I walked in, so I hung back for a few minutes. I could hear a little of the conversation it sounded like she was talking to her mother. It seemed intense.

When I saw Leah get off the phone, I walked over and said, "Hey, stranger."
She looked genuinely happy to see a familiar face. "Hey Paul! Glad to see you! What brings you here?"

"Pam's been working late a lot," I told her. "And my own work's slowed down. I had some free time and thought of you, so I decided to stop by. Hope that's okay."

Leah leaned forward, her smile softening. "Paul, I'm so glad to see you. Tony's hardly ever around either, and even though I love tending bar, this place is never busy anymore. I'm not making much, and it gets lonely."

"Was that your mom on the phone?" I asked.

Leah nodded. "Yeah, she's something else."

She started talking about her mom, and it was clear how much she loved her. There was a warmth in the way she spoke a closeness that was hard to miss.

Once she vented a bit, I decided to change the subject.

"Leah, have you heard anything about the killings?" I told her I'd been following every news report I could get my hands on.
"This is crazy. What the hell is going on? We need to be careful this seems like someone in our industry. Are you concerned?"

"I am," she said, "but life is already so full of everything else. I think I'm too busy to let it get to me."

"Want a drink?" she asked.

"Sure. I'll do a Stella and let's do a shot together."

"I better not," Leah said, laughing. "You know how I get when I drink."

"C'mon, Leah. Just one shot! You know I won't stop asking until you say yes."

Leah smiled. "That's what I'm afraid of."

"Listen, it's just you and me. Let's take a break. We deserve one. I won't tell if you don't."

We both laughed, and she agreed. One shot of Jim Beam and a beer chaser later, we were talking again. The bar was still empty, just the two of us.

"Leah," I said, "have you ever felt like you just need someone to talk to?"

"All the time," she replied. "I used to talk to my sister Lydia a lot, but we don't really keep in touch anymore."

Then she surprised me.
"Paul," she said, "we've been friends a while, and I think we're both happy at least, I think we are but... if you weren't with Pam, and I wasn't with Tony, do you think we'd be interested in each other?"

The question hit me hard. I hadn't expected it. There was something thrilling about it, but also unsettling.

I'd never said anything to Leah about how I felt. I thought I could keep those feelings buried forever. But now, with her words hanging in the air, I realized maybe I shouldn't have been surprised. We had spent a lot of time together even if usually in the company of Pam and Tony. We had built something.

"Leah," I finally said, "you're a beautiful person. And yes, I find you very attractive. Any man would be lucky to have you. I get the loneliness I feel it too. So I get the question. And honestly? I wouldn't hesitate for a second if things were different."

I paused.

"But can we just stay friends for now? If things change, maybe we revisit this. It's just not our time yet. But if that time ever comes... ask me again. You have my word."

Leah smiled and laughed. "Paul, it's not surprising you're a salesman."

I laughed too. "No, I suppose it's not."

"How about another shot?" I asked.

To my surprise, she said yes.

We took another. We paused.

Then I said, "Maybe this question should stay our little secret."

We were both a bit buzzed. Emotions stirred between us unspoken until tonight. We talked more. We drank more. We got closer.

At one point, we were face to face. That kind of intense eye contact the kind you can feel. We were seconds away from kissing.

Instead, I gently kissed Leah on the cheek.

"Will you be okay if I go?" I asked.

"I'll be fine," she said. "I always am."

"I should get going. The boys are probably home. Pam will be back soon too."

"Take care, Leah. I'll see you soon."

Just before I left, Leah called out with a hint of sarcasm.
"Tell Pam I said hello."

There was something in her voice that felt... less than sincere.
But I understood the moment, and the weight of it.
So I just nodded and walked out.

That was far too close. I still can't believe how near I came to kissing Leah something I didn't want to do, yet something I deeply wanted in the moment. The pull I felt toward her was sharp, magnetic, almost dangerous. I'm relieved I had the will to walk away.

But what is it about her that hooks me so completely? Leah is wrapped in mystery. There's an unspoken depth to her, a secret I can't name, and maybe that's what keeps drawing me in. Still, I know I must avoid being alone with her again. The temptation was too strong, and if I'm being honest with myself, I doubt I'd resist her twice.

I made it home quickly the bar is only a few blocks away. After settling in, I flicked on the TV and let it play in the background. Around 10:30 PM, Pam came in. She greeted me softly, saying she wanted nothing more than a shower and bed. She's been working herself to exhaustion lately. She loves her job, which probably makes the long hours easier to bear, but still… it's taking a toll.

Pam always showers as soon as she gets home. I've never asked why what reason would I have? She emerged from the bathroom, kissed me goodnight, and went straight to bed. That's become the routine, Monday through Friday without fail.

It's wearing on me. I've kept my growing restlessness hidden, trying to be supportive, but she must know this can't go on forever. Love doesn't erase loneliness. It doesn't quiet neglect. And right now, I don't know how much more of this I can take.

CHAPTER 6

Another slow day at work, with nowhere to go and nothing to do. As the clock neared 5:00 PM, I knew Leah would be at the bar. The thought took root and wouldn't let go. I decided to head there again.

Even as I drove, I couldn't control the pull. I knew instinctively that if I kept seeing her, I'd eventually give in to this attraction. Part of me urged caution, told me to turn around and go home. But another part of me was insatiable, craving the same rush I'd felt the last time I was with her.

Pam would be working late again. That meant hours empty hours I could fill with Leah. This is how harmless intentions become stepping stones to inevitable, and less-than-innocent, outcomes.

Against my better judgment, I kept driving. When I arrived, I parked and walked inside. There she was, behind the bar, talking to someone. I made my way over slowly, smiling, offering a casual hello, and waited for her to take my order.

She looked incredible like always. Leah had the kind of beauty that seemed staged for a magazine cover, as if she were seconds away from a photo shoot. Maybe that was part of her magnetism.

When she finally noticed me, she stepped out from behind the bar, hugged me, and kissed me on the lips. "Paul," she said, "I'm so glad you're here!"

It caught me off guard. She smelled intoxicating. I fought to steady myself, to push back against the attraction clawing at me. It was wrong I knew it was wrong. But knowing I shouldn't be there wasn't enough to make me leave. Not yet.

Leah leaned in with a smile. "Let me introduce you to my friend Eric. Paul, this is Eric. Eric, Paul."

I extended my hand. "Hey, Eric. Nice to meet you."

Eric grinned. "Man, Leah is something else, isn't she?"

Without hesitation, I replied, "Yes, she most definitely is." Then, curiosity nudged me forward. "So, how do you know Leah?"

He leaned casually against the bar. "I'm in the hospitality business. Worked with her at another restaurant a few years back, over in Blue Point, Long Island. We actually dated for a while until Leah figured out she could do much better than me."

Leah and Eric both laughed.

"Seriously," Eric continued, "her next boyfriend swept her right off her feet, and I was history. But I got pretty lucky. Ended up dating Leah's sister, Lydia."

I tilted my head. "Why's that lucky?"

Eric's grin widened. "Because Lydia and Leah are identical twins."

That caught me off guard. Leah had never mentioned her sister not once in all our conversations. My curiosity sharpened.

"Well," I said, "nice to meet you, Eric. Any friend of Leah's is a friend of mine."

We kept talking about Leah and Lydia for a bit. Eric turned out to be a genuinely easygoing guy, and we were getting along well. Then, almost casually, he pulled out a photo from his wallet.

"Here, take a look," he said, handing it to me.

The resemblance hit me like a wave Lydia could have been Leah's reflection in a mirror. For a moment, I couldn't look away.

Shaking it off, I smiled and asked, "Eric, can I buy you a beer? Leah, could you get us two Stella drafts?"

She smirked. "Sure. When you two stop drooling over my sister, I'll bring them right over."

A few minutes later, Leah returned with the beers, and the three of us drifted into conversation about the hospitality business. We shared plenty of stories turns out all of us were in the industry before the topic shifted to the recent murders.

Eric and I were immediately engrossed, swapping theories about the killings. They'd been going on for some time now, and still, there was no explanation from the authorities. Leah, though, seemed distant barely contributing until she murmured, "I hope they catch this person soon."

I'd noticed this before: whenever the murders came up, she seemed to pull away, as though the conversation left her somewhere far from the room.

Eric and I speculated for a while longer. I even shared some of my friend Junior's theories. Eventually, Eric drained the last of his beer and stood.

"Well, time for me to head out," he said, giving Leah a quick hug. "Great meeting you, Paul. Hope we cross paths again soon."

"You too," I said. "Be safe."

And just like that, Eric was gone.

Nice guy, Leah, I said. "Leah," I asked, "are you doing alright?"
"I'm fine," she said.
I pressed, "Fine as in you're really fine, or fine like... not fine?"
Leah cracked a sarcastic smile and said, "Why don't you stick around and find out on your own?"
That sarcastic smile reminded me of a little girl who knew exactly how to get her way and that you were helpless to stop her. I think she enjoyed that a little too much.

After a pause in our exchange of words and subtle body language, I asked, "Do you want to do a shot?"
"Sure," Leah replied.
"Our usual?" she asked.
It was hard to believe we already had a usual.
"Of course," I responded.
We had a shot of bourbon followed by a beer chaser.

A few moments later, our conversation picked up again. Once more, we were the only people in the bar.
This isn't good for happy hour it's just a sign of the times.
But for Leah and me, it was perfect. It gave us time to talk, to help each other get through what we were feeling about our significant others.

Leah and I spoke for a while, once again drawn into an intimate conversation.

We talked about our love of music and our lives in general. The conversation ran deep much deeper than last time.
I felt the emotions intensify between us. Our communication had just reached a new level.
Our eye contact was intense, making Leah even more desirable with every word she spoke.

We connected as two souls yearning for kindred spirits finding in each other a rock to lean on. Two people who seemed to have arrived at similar destinations, now alone together.
Our emotional connection was real, reflected clearly in our body language. We had so much in common that the emotional and physical bonds felt undeniable.

What came next seemed inevitable like two friends discovering a new level of intimacy.
We kept things proper for the moment, but both of us recognized that being together was inevitable.

We kissed goodnight nothing romantic, just a friendly kiss filled with anticipation and desire for what might come next.

"Well, Leah," I said, "I've got to go. I'll see you soon. Are you working tomorrow?"
"No," Leah responded. "I'm off, but I do work Thursday."
"Paul," she said, "can you stop by Thursday? It's been so slow, and I really enjoy our conversations."
"Of course," I said. "I'll see you then."

Leah blew me a kiss, and in that moment, I knew I was making a mistake.

How could I fall for someone this hard while being married to Pam the love of my life?

Maybe sex and love really are two separate things for some people.

Maybe this attraction will fade over time. Then again, maybe not.

Now, I may be out of my mind, but there's something about this girl that draws me in. Part of me would never take this any further, yet another part can't help but want to. Leah doesn't make things easier she always seems to be flirting with me. I don't think it's intentional, but either way, she's hard to resist. Trying to rationalize my decisions and behavior has become a full-time job. Something has to give. The question is, what?

Realizing how much I have to lose by making the wrong choice didn't deter me. Instead, it did something strange it dared me. It became a rush just to be in a position where I had to face such a decision. I'm not going to lie. This situation made me feel alive something I hadn't felt in a long time. Something that lifted me from loneliness into excitement.

It's getting harder to resist this feeling this thing I can't name, but that's pierced my heart and soul, captivating my entire being. These feelings are real, and honestly, I don't know if I have the strength to resist her.

When I got home, I watched the news something that's become a regular habit. No new updates on the murders tonight. That's good news. After that, I decided to head to bed. I fell asleep quickly, which sometimes happens when I drink. No complaints here I really needed the rest.

CHAPTER 7

Another murder on the news this morning. Pam and I were watching television during breakfast when the newsman announced yet another killing. The victim was a man named Eric, found dead in the parking lot at the beach. He was discovered in his car, and once again, the police said they had no clues. Then it happened Eric's picture appeared on the screen. I was silent. It was Eric from Leah's bar. Eric was the ninth victim.

Pam stood up and said, "Eric Sanders! He was one of our patients! This is crazy." Leah and I work in hospitality so did Eric. Pam added that Eric was a patient at the rehab center. A knot formed in my stomach as a strange feeling washed over me. This was too close to home, and the first thing I wanted to know was if Leah knew. Leah and I had been with Eric just last night!

Of course, Pam doesn't know I've been spending time at the bar with Leah. Telling her wasn't something I was ready to do. This killing sent chills down my spine. I'm not sure if it was because I was so close to this murder or because of the uncertainty of the whole thing. After all, it could have been Leah. It could have been me.

Eric had shown me pictures of Leah's sister, Lydia. Eric and I got along well, and seeing this on the news this morning was awful. Somehow, I have to wrap my head around the fact that Leah and I were

with Eric just last night and that Pam remembers
Eric as a patient at the rehab center. I had to stop
myself from saying it out loud, but what the hell is
happening right now?

CHAPTER 8

Alone again at the house the phone rings.

"Hello, Pam."

"Yes, I know. I'm glad you're still busy. No new leads for me, but I'm working on it. I've been making calls and may have a few appointments set up soon. I figured you'd be late again. Don't worry I got dinner for the boys! It's not like I'm new at this. I love you too."

"When do you think you'll be home?"

"No, that's okay. Ten is fine. I may be sleeping, but if I'm still awake, I'll see you then."

You know, what really bothers me about all this is that I can't even tell Pam how I feel. She'd just get mad at me. I feel trapped in a life that's no longer mine. Another night. Same story. I feed the boys, clean up, and sit down to watch the news.

As I sit and listen, the reporter announces that victim number ten has just been found another killing. This one in Patchogue. Another man, found in the parking lot of a pub off Route 112 near Sunrise Highway.

I'll tell you; these killings are really starting to get to me. Again, the reporter says the police have no leads. How can this be? How is this person getting away with killing people so easily? There has to be something somewhere somehow.

Once again, I found myself with the urge to get out of the house. So, where else would I go? "The Rock n Roll Bourbon Cafe" to see Leah.

Tonight, I walk into the bar. There's Leah, with two girls at the bar. A couple of guys are playing pool, but otherwise, the bar is pretty much empty.

"Hey Leah, how are you?"

Leah looked up and smiled. "Paul, so glad to see you. Let me introduce you to Kim and Amber, two good friends of mine from college."

"So nice to meet you. How long have you known Leah?" I asked.

Amber grinned. "Seems like forever! We went to high school together, then college."

"Kim, how long have you known Leah? What's your name again?" she asked.

"Paul," I said.

She nodded. "Okay, Paul, Leah and I also go way back to high school."

"So, what brings you to town?" I asked.

Leah shrugged. "She called us and just wanted some company. Things have been slow here, and she regrets leaving Jersey. We're just here for support."

I paused. "Actually, I am too. I know things have been dead around here for a while. Leah is a great friend, and I come to keep her company and for the great conversation!"

"So, what do you girls do for work?" I asked.

"We both work for Hartford Hospital in Connecticut," they said together. "We're nurses. We take the ferry to Greenport and visit Leah every once in a while. She seemed so down last time we spoke that we decided to come over and maybe lift her spirits."

I had to ask, "Did you major in healthcare in college?"

Amber and Kim nodded. "Yes, actually, we both did."

Then I asked, "What did Leah major in?"

They paused, then replied, "Leah, believe it or not majored in computer programming."

"Can you imagine that?" I said. "I can't see it. Leah doesn't come across as the computer geek type."

On that, the three of us agreed.

"I think it's great you're here for Leah. Can I buy you ladies a drink?" I asked.

"No, we appreciate that, but we really should go," they replied. "We're doing dinner with our friends, but we may come back later to see Leah."

"Well," I said, "it was nice to meet you both. Have a great time with your dinner guests."

"Alright, Leah," Amber said. "We'll see you later."

"Later, Kim. Later, Amber. Later, Leah," I added as they left.

I have to say, Leah has some pretty attractive friends.

"So, Leah," I said, "can you tell me something? Are all your friends as beautiful as you?"

Leah laughed. "Most of them," she replied. "Now stop messing around."

Then I asked Leah about her computer skills, and she just laughed it off.

"Paul, can we please change the subject?" she asked.

"Why?" I asked. "I knew you were beautiful and smart, but not geek material smart."

Leah seemed annoyed at that comment, so I let it go.

After a few minutes, I tried again. "How about a drink? Shot of Jim Beam and beer chaser?"

Leah smiled. "Alright."

Now that was fast! No hesitation. I wasn't expecting that.

Meanwhile, the two guys playing pool came to the bar, and Leah took their drink orders.

"You guys from around here?" I asked.

"Yes, we're in town from Farmingdale for a weekend getaway with the wives," one replied. "We just had to break away from the girls to shoot some pool and have a few drinks."

This is a pretty cool bar. You guys picked a great place to come to.

"I'm Paul, I live in New Suffolk, and Leah, the bartender, is a good friend of mine. Glad to meet you both," I said.

"I'm Mike, and this is Dennis. We're just here for a few days, you know, to get away."

"Is it always this quiet here?" Dennis asked.

I replied, "It didn't used to be, but lately, it has been."

Mike and Dennis told us they were both in town for pleasure but also for therapy. They had read that the rehab center on the North Fork was the best place for therapy after surgery. Apparently, there are specialized therapies the rehab center offers that can't be obtained in many other facilities.

I explained that my wife Pam works at the rehab center, and both Mike and Dennis immediately recalled speaking with her. They had nothing but great things to say about Pam.

Our conversation continued for a while.

Leah, Mike, Dennis, and I had a few drinks and shots, spending a few hours talking about just about everything.

The conversation then turned to the recent killings in our area. Mike and Dennis had been following the news, but outside of the area, coverage was very light.

Mike and Dennis are from Farmingdale, and there was little mention of the killings in their hometown. Mike said they first heard of the killings on the news when they got into town a few days ago. There's not much news coverage outside of eastern Long Island.

"Really scary," said Mike. "Hard to believe someone could kill so frequently and without leaving a trace."

Dennis chimed in, "I really can't believe there are no leads yet!"

"I know," I said.

Right about then, we all finished our drinks.

"Well, we have to get back to the wives," Mike said.

Dennis added, "Yup… we've been out a while, and we really don't want to drink too much and then drive back to the hotel."

"Where are you guys staying?" I asked.

Mike replied, "We're staying at the Soundview on Route 48."

"That's a cool place," I said. "I used to stay there sometimes on business in between stops."

"It was nice to hang with you both. Be safe," I added.

Mike and Dennis were leaving, and on their way out, they looked back and waved.

"You two, take care," Mike said.

I just remember thinking to myself that these were two really nice guys.

So, now it was back to just Leah and me alone in the bar.

"Leah," I asked, "when you get out of here, do you go straight home, or do you stop anywhere?"

"Why do you ask?" Leah replied.

"Well, I'm just concerned. I have to leave early enough to get home before Pam, but leaving you alone for hours has me worried."

Leah just looked at me and said, "Don't worry about me; worry about everyone else." That took me by surprise. I was tempted to ask what she meant, but I also realized it might be better to leave it alone. It was an incredibly intriguing statement. I wanted to ask her to expand on it, but before I could, she spoke...

"Paul, do you ever just daydream? I mean, just wish you were someone else, somewhere else?"

"Leah," I said, "I think everyone dreams. Some dream during the day, some at night, but we all have dreams."

Leah looked at me, then said, "Paul, I dream because I want to get away from myself, my life.

I'm sad and lonely, and I'm having a hard time right now."

"Leah, I think emotions are normal. Many people, including myself, go through this kind of emotional uncertainty."

Leah put her hand on my shoulder, looked me in the eye, and said, "Paul, you don't hear me. I don't want to be myself any longer. I'm hurting. I want something else out of this life."

"Paul, I want you," Leah said, locking eyes with me, leaving me no escape nowhere to run from this head-on collision between her and the extreme attraction I had developed toward her.

One thing that took me by surprise was that this incredibly attractive girl couldn't see how amazing she was. Leah hugged me and started to cry. What could I do but hold her? I felt bad for her and, at the same time, was really turned on by her. Leah had basically just told me she wanted to be with me. I really needed to get a hold of this situation.

"Hey Leah, why don't we just stay here and talk a while?"

Leah wiped the tears from her eyes, looked at me, and smiled. "Okay," she said.

We started talking, and it seemed to lift her mood. She smiled and laughed, and I just stared at her in wild wonder. She's such a cool chick. I started to realize she might have a few ounces of crazy in her. But then again, don't we all?

One thing Leah didn't know was that I was hurting too. I didn't know how to tell her, nor was I sure I wanted to. Leah didn't know how much I really wanted her.

Our conversation flowed for hours as we talked about almost everything. I wasn't sure, but if I didn't know better, I think we were falling for one another. Were we falling for one another, or just feeling like we'd found someone who could help us through the rough feelings we both had in two very separate yet incredibly similar situations?

The afternoon went on, and I found myself staying much longer than I really wanted or should have. But there we were, and Leah wanted to talk so she did.

Leah began telling me how, when she was little, her dad used to take her to the park. How she loved the monkey bars and really missed him. Leah's dad had passed away about ten years ago, she told me. They were very close.

As we continued talking, Leah shared her dreams and ambitions. She really wanted to be a singer. She loved music and hoped someday to sing with a band.

I told her it's never too late. She was still young enough to do it. Her eyes lit up when I said that.

"Do you really think so?" she asked.

"Absolutely," I replied.

Then I said, "Leah, there's no one here. Why don't you sing for me?"

"What do I sing?" she asked.

"Anything your heart desires," I said.

Then it happened. Leah looked right into my eyes and started singing "If I Close My Eyes Forever" by Lita Ford and Ozzy Osbourne. She really got into it, and I have to say, not only was she good, she was also captivating and sensual.

All I could do was stare at her with a blank expression. I was amazed and simply unable to react. It was like I was engulfed in a sea of astonishment.

What was I feeling? What was I doing? I could feel myself falling for Leah once more. As she sang, I became more and more enthralled with the whole package the way she looked, her eyes, her body, her voice.

It was time for me to go before I fell in way too deep.

Her choice of song concerned me a little because of its suicidal lyrics. But she was amazing and sounded great. Being a musician and songwriter myself, I could appreciate the raw talent Leah possessed.

Of course, my fantasies expanded from being Leah's lover to being Leah's musical partner.

After a few moments of paralysis, I had to respond. My response was enthusiastic, heartfelt, and sincere.

"That was amazing! I had no idea you were that good. Where did you learn to sing like that?"

Leah glanced at me and teased, "You're just being nice."

I looked her in the eyes and said, "No, Leah, you're amazing. I've always loved music and admired people who sing with such emotion. You have serious talent. What else are you good at? You keep surprising me every time I come see you."

In that instant, I realized my last question was a double entendre probably out of line but it just slipped out as a reaction to what I had just witnessed. I wished I had filtered it before blurting it out. Too late to take it back. I hoped Leah didn't take it the wrong way. Who was I kidding? It came out exactly how I meant it, though only I was supposed to hear it. My mouth had betrayed me. Uh oh...

"Paul, you're married to Pam. Why are you here? Why are you spending time with me? Why am I even letting you spend time with me?" Leah asked suddenly.

I was lost for words. She had asked the hard questions. I answered, "Leah, I think I'm feeling very lonely right now. And you're beautiful inside and out. I'm attracted to you. I'm captivated by your presence."

Leah smiled and said, "Paul, maybe I should be asking myself why I want to stay here with you. It's just you and me, alone. Do you want to kiss me?"

"I promise I won't tell," she added playfully.

I stood frozen, like a deer in headlights, unsure what to do next. This time I really paused to think. What was I doing? I had to stop this before it got out of control. If I didn't know better, I'd swear Leah was leading me on. She wanted me to kiss her.

It was hard to wrap my head around. I have a wife, and Leah has Tony. I struggled to find a good enough reason to resist her. I felt like Pam had emotionally abandoned me, and it was so hard to justify defending my marriage to her. My heart still loved her, but lately, I felt like I'd dropped to the bottom of her priority list.

Even though I was tempted to give in, I decided to pause and think clearly. Right then, walking away was the best choice.

I looked at Leah and said, "Hey girl, I think I better go. I'm so tempted, so attracted to you. But I just can't..."

"You sounded amazing tonight, but it's late and I have to go."

"Are you sure you'll be alright?" Leah asked.

"Yeah, I'll do my best," I smiled.

I thanked her, blew her a kiss, and said, "Thanks for being a friend. See you soon." Then I got up and walked out the door.

As I walked away, Leah called my name: "Paul, I know you'll be dreaming of me tonight."

I looked back at her standing in front of the bar and said, "Yeah, I'm sure I will. Goodnight, Leah."

Walking out, I reflected on what she said. Leah was right I probably would be thinking about her all night. Saying that felt odd, but the feeling faded quickly as I replayed my time with her this evening. Tonight was different.

Surprisingly different.

Yet, somehow, I escaped what felt like an inevitable crossing of a dangerous line.

The question was how much longer could I hold out?

Another night passed, and another part of my life felt uncertain. My heart and soul were tangled up in my encounters with Leah.

Truth be told, I was elated. Spending time with Leah lifted my spirits and made me forget my troubles. For the first time in a long while, I felt relevant.

I was walking on air slightly buzzed and feeling great. Maybe I just needed an ego boost. It felt good that someone else found me interesting. Maybe the loneliness was finally catching up to me.

As I thought about what was said tonight, two things echoed in my mind Leah telling me not to worry about her, and her asking if I'd be alright. Maybe I shouldn't overanalyze it.

I got home, slipped inside quietly, and started getting ready for bed. Pam was already asleep; I doubt she heard me come in.

I climbed into bed, kissed her gently on the side of her head, and fell asleep. Pam didn't stir or react.

I lay there for a while, staring at her, memories flooding in how we met, our first date, the birth of our sons, and how deeply in love I once was.

What happened to us?

Is this what time does to people?

As I lay there waiting for sleep, my mind raced, circling around all the ways we might have changed our path what we could have done differently.

Part of me didn't want this to end. Another part felt trapped, longing to escape, seeking refuge in the arms of someone who truly wanted me as much as I wanted her. And then I thought wait a minute. Isn't that how Pam and I started? Isn't that what we both wanted? Is love just a feeling that lures you in, only for time to wear it away? So many questions.
Maybe I'm the problem. Pam works so hard. I should be ashamed.

Yet, these feelings of emptiness and dissatisfaction haunt me.

As I drifted off, those questions lingered how to fix this, what to do next, and whether I could ever find peace again.

CHAPTER 9

The morning arrived, and we began our day. Pam was getting ready for hers, and I was preparing for mine. My days seemed to be growing shorter, while Pam's appeared the same or even longer. We kissed goodbye as I planned to leave early, eager to get a jump on the drive to Nassau County. I had a meeting with a restaurant owner at eleven a genuine lead, my first in weeks.

Putting on my most confident attitude, certain I would land this account, I got into the car and set off. The mornings between Pam and me had become so routine. We barely talked anymore; we had both become so self-involved that we were like living, breathing pieces of furniture to each other.

Driving west on the Long Island Expressway toward my appointment, I had a long stretch ahead. Sometimes, I do my best thinking during drives like this.

I began to imagine what it would be like if Pam and I could go back in time to when we were both truly happy. Looking ahead down the highway, I pictured better days. It hadn't been that long ago we were so content. What happened?

As I struggled to make sense of it all, my thoughts drifted to Leah. Were my feelings for her just a reaction to the emotional emptiness at home? Had I overreacted? Was this connection with Leah real, or were we both simply seeking company to fill the loneliness inside our relationships with Pam and Tony?

Life can be incredibly rewarding, and when it's good, it can be really good. But when things go wrong and challenges arise, it becomes confusing hard to choose the right path forward. Well, here I am. It's not like I would ever leave Pam, but that doesn't change the fact that our relationship is strained right now. It feels like everything was so good just a short time ago.

I started thinking about how fast time has flown. The boys are already getting ready to head off to college. It's crazy I flash back to the sonogram, that moment when we found out we were having twins. That instant changed both of our lives. Driving sometimes does this to me; I drift away and reflect. That one moment when Pam and I learned what we were about to embark on was something special a pivotal moment for both of us, individually and as a couple. When my mind races like this, time just evaporates.

That two-hour drive went quickly. Well, here goes nothing! I got out of my car and walked to the front door. The place was Anthony's. I tried to open the door it was locked. I peeked through the glass and saw no one inside. The place was closed.

I called Phil Casso, the owner and the man I had the appointment with. It rang. "Hello," Phil said.

"Phil, it's Paul with Harbor Seafood," I said.
"Oh Paul! I forgot to call you. I have to cancel," he said.
I was so distraught. "We had to close the restaurant for a few weeks' rodent issues. I'm sorry I forgot you! There's been a lot going on, and this whole thing was a surprise. The county shut us down until we get the place treated. When we're ready to reopen, I'll call you. Again, Paul, I'm so sorry."
"Phil, I understand. Good luck with everything. Take care."

Back in the car, heading back to eastern Long Island, I felt disappointed but understood. These things happen, and the last thing anyone remembers is a sales appointment. I left the house this morning hoping a new client and account would lift my spirits. Now I was heading home feeling like a loser. I told myself it was just an unlucky break. Usually, I bounce back quickly after getting knocked down. But this time, I felt crushed, defeated. I drove in silence, listening to the voices in my head the whole way home.

It's amazing how time sometimes evaporates so quickly. But when things don't turn out as hoped, time can be healing and yet, a thorn in your side when you have too much time to dwell on things.

I returned home early this afternoon because my appointment with Phil was a bust. I really felt like having a beer. I grabbed one and turned on the TV to catch the news. Turns out economists are predicting an economic downturn. Watching it, I kind of already knew, but now it was official. This could change lives for the worse. Hell, it already seemed to be hurting us financially. I had to stay informed. I admit, I was nervous. What about our jobs, our lives, our family?

You have to admire newspeople. One minute, they're telling you what you already know and feel about the economy, and the next, they seamlessly switch to a serial killer and the latest victim. Is it any wonder most people can't stomach the news?

Yes, another murder. This time, a man was found dead in his car in Cutchogue. It's amazing how fast these reporters pivot from one subject to the next, void of all emotion or compassion for the victims. It's just like the song "Dirty Laundry" by Don Henley. I had to turn off the TV I'd seen and heard enough.

Right now, I feel like I'm standing on the edge of a cliff, looking down and wondering whether to jump. These murders are deeply troubling. It's hard to believe someone is killing people without leaving a trace. Needless to say, I worry about our family and friends since the killings are mostly in Suffolk County, the North Shore, and eastern Long Island.

With everything going on, I better get my act together.

Well, the economy did, in fact, slow down, and it wasn't long before I was out of a job. I kind of saw it coming with how slow things were getting. Pam was still working, but her facility was also facing challenges. Every night at home was stressful. It started taking a toll on our relationship. We were both angry much of the time. Before long, we were hardly talking. The boys were in their own world most of the time, both absorbed in computer games. I'm not even sure they noticed what was happening between their mom and me.

Pam spent a lot of time on the phone with her sister, Jessica. They were very close, and whenever Pam needed to talk, she called Jessica and Jessica did the same. I noticed that after Pam and I got married, she and Jessica grew even closer. They talk frequently. Me? I tend to self-counsel and self-medicate when I face challenges. I guess you could say both Pam and I were really feeling the pressure right now.

How can two people so deeply in love become strangers so quickly and abruptly? We seemed to fight constantly, and most of the arguments weren't even about money. They mostly stemmed from the stress we were both feeling at work and home arguments over the dumbest little things. It felt like we started to irritate each other almost every time we were together.

I still loved Pam, but honestly, a part of me began to hate our lives. It felt like we were becoming different people than when we first started dating.

We had both changed, but the changes hadn't been so evident until the stress hit. I know she sees it too, but the question is how will we overcome it?

Pam would get up in the morning, make breakfast for the boys, and head off to work. Me? I was looking for work. The sales business dried up. No one had disposable income to go out to restaurants, so things in my line of work were very slow. Overnight, a great economy turned into a nightmare, and the new president and administration didn't look promising.

That's the thing about politics and real life the politicians are so good at creating division to keep you distracted enough to elect people who don't have your best interests in mind. Pam started out as more of a left-leaning person, which was expected since she was pretty much indoctrinated in college. Me? I maintained a certain level of common sense that didn't let me accept the lies fed from either the left or the right.

Politics is one of those subjects everyone fears to discuss and tries hard to avoid. But I find politics revealing because a person's true core shows when you know where they stand politically. It's not so much about the party or politician they support, but what their support directly or indirectly endorses.

I know that sounds rough around the edges, but think about it. Are you someone who really cares about people? Or are you someone who just wants others to see you as caring? There couldn't be more contrast between these two.

When someone asks you who you are, which will you be? Pam is someone who really cares about others, but somewhere along the way, she was brainwashed into believing lies that make no common sense. Someday, she'll see those lies for what they are.

I noticed her views began to shift after we had the boys. Having children has a way of sobering people up to reality. Very little liberal ideology is based in reality, which is why I understand how she's evolved on most of her positions. That's how most people are. As a person matures, it's hard to remain fully liberal especially after 30. People grow up. People mature. That's a good thing. But not everyone does, and that's how we find ourselves in the current situation.

Poor leadership has caused the economy to slow. People like Pam and me just want the opportunity to earn a living. Sorry to vent so much, but my mind is racing. I don't know what we'll do if the economy doesn't rebound. I guess all middle-class people feel this way right now.

The president and his party have always talked a good game about the working class, but when you look at what they've done compared to their promises, they fall way short. Well, all us little people can do is work hard and pray. That's why I say never put your faith in politicians. Put your faith in a higher power.

Which leads me here: I've been praying a lot lately. Frequently, I find myself praying that God heals Pam and me, and guides me to make the right choices. But as an imperfect human being, I feel helpless against my weaknesses and addictions. Still, I keep trying.

I tried talking to Pam whenever we had time together, but she had become very cold toward me. She reacted to this stressful time with anger and sometimes resentment. I wasn't sure why, but she hardly talked to me. This was something I couldn't figure out. Was it something I did or said? I had no idea. For weeks, we went on like this. I was becoming so lonely. I had no one to talk to, and I felt useless. Being out of work took a toll on my morale.

I kept reflecting on the nights I had spent at the bar with Leah. The more stressful our marital situation became, the more I thought about seeing Leah again. Leah became my escape from my life. It felt like Pam was driving me right into Leah's arms. I had to remind myself that Pam, Leah, Tony, and I were all friends. Any action would be a bad idea, yet I couldn't stop thinking about Leah. She was like an oasis for me as I wandered aimlessly through this desert of absolute loneliness and confusion.

Then, just when we thought we couldn't face any more challenges, more bad news arrived Pam's office cut her hours. We had bills to pay and our boys to take care of. It was clear we were in over our heads. We wouldn't be able to afford the mortgage. How could we put food on the table? The boys' college? Now, we were both at home together, and the arguments got pretty heated at times. I had to leave sometimes just to get away and let us both cool down. We had never fought like that before. The stress was what I think really changed our relationship.

I mean, we still loved one another, but now we were so angry so much of the time. Pam told me the layoff was temporary and that Tony wanted her back soon, but he didn't offer a timeframe, and Pam didn't know when she would return to work. Tony had offered to pay Pam on the side to help with some restructuring of the facility. Pam was technically not working but had agreed to help Tony until he reopened. She told me they were going to downsize the facility. This meant layoffs, and Pam thought that once the restructuring was complete, she would have better hours when she eventually returned. But for now, Pam would be home.

One bad day led to another. The boys were starting to see what was going on between Pam and me. It was that obvious. It seemed like we were headed toward a divorce. I asked Pam if that was what she wanted, and for the first time in weeks, she spoke to me and said… no. She didn't elaborate or explain her answer. She just turned on her side and went to bed. That was enough for me. I was feeling alone, depressed, and angry. One thing was sure I had to get out for a while.

CHAPTER 10

When I was at the end of my rope, I always went out for a drive. That always seemed to get me through. At this point, I was upset and confused. I couldn't sleep. I decided to go for a drive to clear my head. It was late, but I just didn't care. I needed to get out. I got in the car, turned on the radio, and drove away. "Running Down a Dream" by Tom Petty was on the radio, and I cranked it up and went for a ride.

Eastern Long Island is pretty desolate in the late evenings. I turned onto 25A and headed east. As I was driving, I had to clear my head. I needed a release, someone to talk to or be with. For the first time in a long time, I was very lonely. That Petty song is a great song to drive to. I was feeling a little revved up and finally felt my emotions let loose.

The next song that came on the radio was "No One Like You" by the Scorpions. It was like the music on the radio was exactly what the doctor ordered!

Then, it happened. I thought I saw someone walking along the road in the distance. I had to look again. Then I was sure I saw a person walking along the side of the road. As I got closer, I noticed the person was a lady. It was close to 11:30 in the evening. She looked confused and maybe a little startled as I pulled over to see if she was alright.

Normally, I wouldn't be out at this time, and I certainly wouldn't stop for a stranger. But on this night, things would be different. I rolled down the window and said, "Are you alright?" No answer. I asked a second time, "Are you alright?"

She looked right at me and said, "I am now." It was Leah! Man, I was surprised! What the heck was she doing out here this late? Obviously, I had questions, but then I just decided to let this play out. I had to wonder why she was out walking the streets, all alone. Was this destiny? I was about to find out.

Leah was wearing shorts, a half-shirt, sneakers, and her makeup was running from what appeared to be tears. I asked her, "Where are you going? Do you need a ride?"
"Yes, I do," she replied. I asked her to hop in. She did, and at first, it felt awkward, but then it felt a little exciting. Right then, I noticed she looked shaken up. She had been in an altercation. I asked, "What happened to you?"
She replied, "Tony hit me."

There was an obvious pause in our conversation. What did I just get myself into? But she was so afraid extremely frightened. It was clear she had been shaken up. I was not in the right frame of mind at that moment. I thought to myself: this was not good. But there we were. There she was.

"Leah," I said, "What happened?"

Leah spoke softly and said, "He hit me. Tony hit me." She explained, "I left before he could hurt me again. Tony came home after they cut Pam's hours, and he had been drinking. Our business has slowed, and Tony has become very stressed lately. We argued for a while about money, and he lost his temper. He hit me hard, Paul. He hit me more than once, and I just left. I started walking and haven't looked back."

After feeling so alone, with a wife who basically treated me like I didn't exist or matter, I found myself in a position that would be hard to reverse. I was with my friend Leah, in my car. I could have and probably should have just taken her home or asked if she wanted me to drop her off somewhere, or take her to the police station, but I didn't. Instead, I felt excitement. I felt alive. I wanted to comfort her. I decided to let this play out.

"Leah," I asked, "What happened?"

Leah wasn't willing to tell me more than the fact Tony hit her. She didn't want to discuss it further. As I drove, we decided to park. There was a parking lot close to the Long Island Sound, and no one was there at this time of night. We started talking. She really opened up about herself and genuinely wanted to know about me.

Leah started saying how possible it was that this night was already written in our stories. Destiny, she said. We had talked like this before, but this was different. I could see the emotion in her eyes. Leah really meant it.

We were in my car, all alone, in a very desolate place. I told her what had been happening with Pam and me. I expressed concern for her situation and asked what she planned to do about it. She didn't know and had no immediate answers.

"Paul," she asked, "Do you remember when we were alone in the bar a few weeks ago, and I asked you if you thought we'd be together if I wasn't with Tony, and you weren't with Pam? Do you remember that night?"
"I do," I said.

"Leah, let's just talk for a while. We both could use someone to talk to."
"Okay," Leah said, and then she started talking.

Leah loved to write poetry, and she loved music. We started talking about bands we liked and songs we loved. We talked about dreams we had and fantasies we dreamed of. This was much like our previous conversations at the bar.

We started to talk about her and Tony, and Pam and me. Through all these exchanges, we found ourselves becoming really engaged with each other's personal feelings. We had so much in common, and we were both hurting and struggling emotionally.

We connected once again, only this time, there was more than just conversation. There were clearly feelings growing between us. We were really connecting. The emotional magnetism we both started to feel was undeniable, and the momentum felt like it couldn't be stopped.

I wanted to learn even more about her. For the first time in a long while, I was genuinely interested in having a conversation with someone. All I really ever wanted was to feel engaged and relevant. I wanted to feel alive. After all, it had been so long. When she was talking, I was captivated by both her words and her body language.

"Leah," I asked, "If you could do one thing right now, anything to get your mind off what just happened, what would it be?"

Leah replied, "I just want you to hold me. Is that okay?"

I responded with body language of my own, pulling her toward me and resting her head on my shoulder.

"Leah," I said, "It will all be okay."

I could feel her embracing the closeness I offered, and I knew this closeness would lead somewhere. But as much as my mind knew better, my wounded heart and strong physical attraction to this girl wouldn't lose this battle the battle I was having within myself. I felt the momentum slowly pull me in the direction, and the rest just kind of happened.

As one thing led to another, before I knew it, we started to kiss. I couldn't resist her. She was so attractive and so vulnerable, and at the same time, she became aggressive. I don't know what got into me. I don't know what got into Leah. Every moment fully aware that I was cheating on Pam. Still, I couldn't stop myself.

Leah let me kiss her neck, then her shoulders, and then I was kissing her breasts. She was really into it, and I kept going. Leah pushed me away briefly but then started kissing me very passionately again. I knew at that moment there was no coming back.

It didn't stop there. We embraced one another and started to make love right there in the car. We made love for about half an hour, and when we were done, we just held each other and watched the water along the Sound. I had to roll down the windows because they had gotten all fogged up.

Now it was about 2 AM. I had been away for hours. I had to start thinking about what to do, what to say when I got home. There was Leah, with her head on my shoulder. I wasn't sure what to do or how to handle this. What have I done?

Still, Leah was amazing. I wasn't sure what to make of what had just happened. The guilt was overwhelming, but so were my emotions and feelings for Leah. I was in some kind of shock. Yet, we talked for a while, and when it was over, we knew what we had done, and we both made the decision to call it a night.

The weird thing, though, is that I think we both understood what had happened, and yet neither of us seemed to feel much guilt. At least not at that moment.

Leah kissed me, and then as she got out of the car, she said, "I will see you around. This was really nice." Then she walked away.

"Leah!" I yelled, "Please let me drive you home."

She just smiled and walked away.

"Paul," Leah replied, "Our day is coming. Be patient, my love."

I wasn't sure what to make of this, but she already had a hold on me.

Me? I could never forgive myself for being unfaithful to Pam. But I was. What should I do about this? I felt horrible, but at the same time, I felt alive. Leah found me attractive, and I just had sex with my friend, my neighbor, my wife's boss's girlfriend!

Wow. I'm not sure what to do other than go home and hope Pam is asleep. What have I done?

So, I managed to get into the house, into our bed, and go to sleep without anyone hearing me. Before I went to bed, I had to get into the shower and clean up, as I was sure Pam would know I was with another woman. I rushed through the shower. That worked out, and now I was lying in bed, my heart pounding because I knew I had betrayed the only woman I had ever loved.

I kept trying to justify it in my mind. Pam had been distant, ignoring me, and treating me badly. Still, the guilt was eating me alive. How could I go to sleep like this? I worried and anguished throughout the remainder of the morning until I finally fell asleep. Leah told me Tony hit her. This was about as insane as it gets. I just hoped I could get through the next few days until things became clearer.

It was not difficult to fall asleep. My mind was racing, but my body was tired and my heart felt gratified. Still, I was thinking about everything in rapid succession. Much of the frustration while I lay awake waiting to fall asleep came from the fact that I really couldn't say or do anything about this situation. Any attempt to stand up for Leah would surely reveal what the two of us had been up to, which was completely out of the realm of possibility.

Still, all I could think of was Leah. Lying there next to Pam, a woman I really believed with all of my heart and soul would be my one true love forever. I started to drift away to sleep, but as I was floating on air and finally falling asleep, I paused for a moment and just before dozing off, I felt a release.

I finally just let go and realized that what is, is, and what will be, will be. I think I convinced myself it would all be alright in the end. Well, that remains to be seen. Until tomorrow, I slowly and eventually found peace and was able to sleep.

CHAPTER 11

For some reason this morning, I woke up before Pam. Something that rarely happens, but today, it did. Pam was still asleep when I walked out of our bedroom into the living room. I went to turn the light on, but it did not come on. Maybe a circuit breaker tripped or a light bulb was out. I then turned the light in the hallway on. It worked just fine. So, I decided to head down to the basement and check the breaker box. Sure enough, the breaker had tripped. I turned the breaker back on. Our washing machine and dryer are in the basement, and I noticed that the washer was on the same breaker as the living room light. There was clothing in the washer that I think Pam intended to wash but, because the breaker tripped, it was still dirty.

For some reason and don't ask me why I looked at the clothes in the washing machine. On one of the garments, I saw what looked like a dark red stain. It appeared to be a pair of Pam's pants. I looked further and then saw the same type of staining on one of Pam's white shirts. Not sure what to make of this, and without even thinking about it, I just went ahead and started the wash. When Pam wakes up, I will ask her about those stains, but until then, I figured restarting the washing machine was the best option.

I started up the stairs and went into the kitchen to make some coffee. With a lot on my mind, I peacefully sipped my coffee while sitting at the breakfast nook, just staring out the window. This was about as peaceful as it gets silence and solitude, just the environment I needed to gather my thoughts. I started to drift away a bit, into a place that was tranquil and peaceful. I was embracing this moment of solitude and really just soaking it all in. Finally, some time to think. Time to reset my mind and process all that has happened recently. For just a moment, I was at peace and in control. It started to feel essential. So needed to regain my sanity.

Then, the next thing that happened was unbelievably shocking. It was a moment that I will never forget.

Suddenly, there was loud pounding on the door. "Open up! Police!" the voice yelled. I went to the door and opened it. In came the police, guns drawn, pointed directly at me. Pam came walking out of our bedroom and just stood there in the doorway as the officers then pointed their guns toward her. Pam looked at me with confusion, and I looked at her the same way. Several other officers walked in and handed me a warrant. Pam and I did not resist; we complied with the orders given by the police. They walked right past me and approached Pam.

The officers proceeded to arrest Pam. As they read her rights, I was dumfounded and confused. Pam looked confused as well, and she looked extremely angry. After they read her rights, they explained that she was being arrested for co-conspiring in the murder of at least nine individuals. As the officers placed handcuffs on Pam, I just stood there shaken up and overwhelmed.

With all this turmoil swirling around us in real time, the phone rang, and everything felt confusing and disorganized. I picked up, and it was Leah. She told me that Tony had just been arrested. He was being taken away, and she asked me what to do. The police had just entered their home with a search warrant. I calmly explained to Leah that Pam had just been arrested too, and that the best thing for us to do was to wait a little while, collect our thoughts, and then try to learn more about what had happened. There was little for either of us to do other than go down to the police station to find out more, so that's what we decided to do.

I tried to get the boys ready to go to Pam's sister's place, but at the moment, they wanted to stay with me, go to the police station, and see what we could do to help their mother. I can't imagine what they were feeling right now after watching all of this unfold with their mother. As I talked with Leah on the phone, I told her that we would get her, and together we would go to the station and see what was going on. This was crazy!

I asked one of the cops what had happened, and he told me that Pam and Tony were persons of interest in a case involving a series of local murders in the area. They believed that the two conspired together to murder the victims in the rash of killings that had taken place in our eastern Long Island community.

This couldn't be real. It was too much to process, and I don't think me or the boys could really come to grips with the reality of what was happening.

The boys had so many questions, and since they love their mother, many of those questions were incredibly hard to answer. I wanted to believe Pam was innocent, but I also knew the police don't come to your house and arrest you without probable cause. I had to think fast. Who could I call to help us?

Then it hit me I had restarted the washing machine in the basement, and before I did, I had seen unexplained stains on Pam's clothes. By now, those stains were history, but I knew what I had seen, and I now had to wonder what those stains were from. Right now, I needed some guidance.

I called Junior and asked if he could help, and if he knew anything about this. Junior is friends with the investigators working with law enforcement on the murder cases. He told me he had just found out about this late yesterday evening. He hadn't called me sooner because he couldn't. He apologized profusely, but I stopped him right away. "Junior, I understand," I said.

He told me that DNA evidence had linked Pam and Tony to several victims in the string of recent murders on eastern Long Island. I was dumbfounded. I hung up and headed to the police station.

Sitting with two detectives assigned to the case and listening to what they had to say left me and the boys in a state of shock. Leah was with us, and we all received the information together. Leah looked as if her emotions had frozen, her eyes glazed over. She sat quietly and stared in my direction, looking past me.

One of the detectives asked if we had any knowledge of the crimes, and naturally, we all said no. I asked the detectives, "So what happens next? Are we under arrest?" The taller one replied, "No. We have your statements. Pam and Tony will be processed and detained until their arraignment. They will both be provided with a public counsel if they do not have or cannot afford an attorney."

We all stood as the detectives left the room. As I was leaving, my phone rang. It was Junior. He told me he had a close friend, Gabriel, who would help Pam and me. Gabriel would be in touch. Junior assured me that Gabriel was top notch the best. I just thanked Junior and went through the motions with my sons, all of us still in shock.

Leah, the boys, and I left the police station in a state of disbelief. We all climbed into the car, and not a single word was spoken. The drive home gave us the rare luxury of silence, a quiet space to gather our scattered thoughts. We headed to Pam's sister Jessica's house, about 45 minutes away in Deer Park. The boys understood they would be staying with Jessica for a while until things settled down.

After dropping them off, we stood outside the car before going to the front door. I asked the boys if they were okay. Chris and Brian opened up about their feelings how upset they were, not only about the situation but also about how Pam and I had been distant lately. Their reluctance to talk was clear, but we all recognized that we felt the same way, a shared pain binding us. It was with that understanding that we were ready to call it a night.

Then, Chris suddenly changed the subject, asking when Aunt Jessica got her car. It came out of nowhere, but I thought for a moment and remembered: Pam and I had bought our car at the same dealership. They had promised us a deal since Jessica had bought the exact same model just a week earlier. So yes, Chris, Aunt Jessica, your mom, and I all have the same car. I had completely forgotten about that. Brian stayed quiet, still processing everything.

It was time to wrap up. I hugged both boys and told them I'd do everything I could to help their mother. I think that gave them some encouragement, even if it didn't erase their worry. Walking the boys up to Jessica's door, she answered quickly. We embraced, and I thanked her for taking care of Chris and Brian. One thing about Jessica she truly loved her nephews. This was the first time in a long while that Jessica and I were alone together.

Jessica knows how deeply I love Pam, and I know she understands how difficult all of this is for our family. I am so grateful for her. She has been like a sister to me for years. I'm thankful she's helping, especially with the boys, because right now, I can't give them what they need. Thank God for their aunt.

Jessica invited us inside, and we stood in the foyer for a few minutes, talking. I hugged her again and thanked her for her support. I expressed sympathy, knowing how much she loves her sister. We talked a little longer, and Jessica said she's always known how much I loved Pam how she believes I have always loved her.

We hugged again, both of us realizing we wanted the same thing: to stand together and get through this. Jessica seemed hopeful, which I thought was important for the boys. They need that positivity, especially given how confused and worried Chris and Brian must be after everything that happened in just a few hours.

I told Jessica I should get going Leah was waiting in the car. Before I left, Jessica said something that caught me off guard: "Paul, my sister needs you. Please tell Leah I said hello, will you?" I wasn't sure what to make of it, but I promised I would.

As I walked back outside, I was distracted by her words and, for a moment, walked to the wrong car. How strange, especially since Chris just mentioned the cars were the same. Where was my head? I shook it off, redirected myself, and climbed into the right car.

I looked over at Leah, who seemed a million miles away, distracted and distant. I chalked it up to the events of the day. The drive back home was quiet; neither of us spoke much. I wished I knew what she was thinking or feeling, but Leah seemed unwilling or unable to discuss it.

Neither of us could fully process what we had just witnessed. I understood the silence. We were both emotionally confused, carrying our own broken pieces. Our lives both of our relationships were unraveling right before our eyes, like a car crash happening in slow motion.

Leah and I both had strong feelings for one another feelings we couldn't deny or control. There wasn't much to say. We both felt incredibly lost. I asked Leah if she'd mind stopping at the beach on the way home to try to wind down. I needed time to absorb everything. She agreed, saying, "Sure, we both need to think. Let's just take a walk, just the two of us."

We were both so disoriented by everything that had just happened; we truly had no idea how to feel or what to think.

At the beach, Leah and I walked for a while. Not much was said, but there was a sense of peace and comfort amid the immense turmoil swirling around us. Even through it all, we felt comfortable with each other and shared a sense of commonality. We were going through what felt like hell a real-life nightmare. It was fortunate to find that level of comfort in each other.

After our walk, we got in the car. I drove Leah home and dropped her off. We kissed goodbye not a romantic kiss, but the kind you share at a funeral, arriving or leaving the services. We had both been through so much.

I headed home. It was still early afternoon, and I was reeling from the day's events. I could hardly believe what had happened.

At home, I grabbed a beer and sat on the couch, seeking solitude and searching for answers. Time passed slowly as I sat in a meditative, reflective state. Pam and Tony were being held, with a bail hearing set for tomorrow morning.

One hour crept into the next. When I felt lost in the past, I'd pick up my guitar and play. It had been a while since I'd wanted to play, but the guitar had always been my best friend. Today, she would be that again a soothing presence, guiding me down a winding path into the depths of my soul.

As the afternoon wore on, one drink became two, and one song idea led to another. I picked up a pen and started writing down my feelings. Years ago, when I got into this creative flow, words would come faster than I could keep up. Today, I found myself drifting back to a time when I could bask in solitude while swimming in tranquility.

Finally, I reached that place the place where, no matter how complex life became, my mind separated me from reality, creating a space where I wasn't reachable by the chaos around me. I had landed in that perfect place.

As I wrote and played, I should have been consumed by what happened to Pam. Instead, all I could think of was Leah. She had become the muse inspiring the music I created in that moment. That didn't surprise me, but the emotions she stirred inside me were confusing. For years, Pam had been the love of my life. Yet right now, Leah was the passion driving me she was the fire inside.

It's hard to contain emotions that break through their metaphorical barriers, yearning to be free. That's exactly what I was feeling. My feelings for Leah were like a tidal wave that could no longer, and would no longer, be contained. No wall was strong enough to hold this passion.

In my mind, I kept asking: What have I done? Why do I feel so strongly for this woman?

It was still early, and the day had been crazy. Drinking alone wasn't the answer.

I stepped away from my escape when the phone rang. Answering, a man said, "Paul?"

"Yes, this is he," I replied.

"This is Gabriel, Pam's attorney. Did Junior tell you I'd be calling?"

"Yes," I said. "He did."

"Thank you. Do you have a minute?"

"Yes, please go ahead."

Gabriel continued, "I wanted to fill you in on some things. Do you understand why they arrested Pam?"

"No," I said. "I tried to get answers from the police, but they wouldn't disclose anything when they came to our home this morning."

Gabriel said, "There was an anonymous tip to law enforcement that led them to look at your wife and Tony, her boss. That tip directed them to the rehab center where they both work. All of the victims were patients there. From there, Pam, Tony, and the entire staff became persons of interest."

I asked, "How did they come to that conclusion that Pam and Tony did this? It still makes no sense to me."

Gabriel continued, "Each victim was tested for trace DNA. They collected DNA samples from all of them. Then, they obtained a warrant for the DNA of everyone who worked at the rehab center.

Somehow, the two matches they found were from both Tony and your wife, Pam."

"But Gabriel," I said, "this is so hard to believe. This just can't be true."

Gabriel replied, "Pam maintains her innocence. I believe her. I called you because it's important you remain part of this process. Your wife is being held without bail, and she may be detained for some time."

"Gabriel," I asked, "what can I do?"

He said, "Visit her first thing tomorrow. She's going to need your support."

"Okay," I answered. "I plan to be there in the morning."

Gabriel continued, "I'm representing both Pam and Tony. Could you reach out to Leah and relay this information? Let her know Tony is alright."

"Yes, of course," I replied.

"I'll call you again later or update you tomorrow with more information. Leah could visit Tony as well; the two places are pretty close."

"Okay," I said. "Thank you, Gabriel. I appreciate the update."

As soon as I hung up, I called Leah. After a few rings, she answered.

"Leah, are you okay?" I asked.

She answered emphatically, "Yes!"

She sounded surprisingly upbeat given everything that had happened. Then it dawned on me the last interaction between her and Tony hadn't been good. She was relieved and welcomed his absence.

"Leah, would you be alright spending the night at my place?"

She asked, "Why?"

I said, "Because the boys are at Pam's sister's, and I'm all alone. I don't think I'm in a good place right now, and I could really use the company."

Knowing full well this might not be the best idea, I was willing to do it anyway. I needed Leah. We were still friends first. No matter what, she was the only cure for how I was feeling.

Leah arrived a few minutes after we ended the call. Her and Tony's place was just a few houses away. I saw her walking up the driveway.

She knocked at the door, and I answered almost immediately.

I let her in. She took off her coat and was wearing jean shorts and a t-shirt.

I hugged her, a hug between two friends who hadn't seen each other for a while.

I started to tell her I'd been drinking and writing some music.

"Leah," I asked, "do you remember that night in the bar when we were alone and you sang to me?"

Her eyes lit up like a child being given permission to do something they really wanted to do.

She replied with a subtle smile, "Yes."

"Leah, I want us to work on a song. One we write ourselves one that will help us get through all this. One that will help us both make it to the other side."

She was on board. I don't recall ever seeing her this excited and happy about something. It felt strange because with everything going on, Leah and I were finding something we both needed our own escape.

As wrong or careless as it might seem, we were going to be together.

So, we started writing words on paper, trying to capture our feelings. We wanted to feel better.

For me, alcohol played a part in that, but what I hadn't expected was Leah drinking and doing cocaine as well.

She pulled the coke out of her purse and asked if I wanted some.

At first, I hesitated, but reflecting on everything, I started doing some with her.

The drug took away any remaining self-control I had and she had.

So off we went on a drug-fueled, drinking binge.

After all, it was just the two of us in my house.

There was no threat to either of us; both our significant others were incarcerated.

No one was home. No one would be coming home.

Yes, it was irresponsible. We both knew that. We both felt it. But most of all, we both needed it.

The drinking and coke energized us, and we wrote words on paper diligently.

There was a drug-induced energy that engulfed us.

Not only did we write lyrics with depth and passion, but we also became more engaged with every moment we spent sharing creativity.

There was a sexual element to our experience a tension we both felt.

A sexual tension we somehow kept at bay, instead channeling our passion and energy into the words we wrote.

When we finished writing our lyrics, we worked on the music and started to see if we could create an actual melody. We both began to crash as we ran out of coke, and the alcohol brought us to a point of relaxation and eventual sleepiness. We decided to call it a night.

"Leah, would you like to sleep here?" I asked.

Leah paused for a moment before responding, "I better head home. It's late, and we both need to get up early tomorrow. If I stay, I have a feeling we won't sleep."

I listened to Leah's response, understood it, and knew she was right. Leah left to go home, and I set my alarm clock for 6:00 AM because I knew I had to be at the prison by 9:00 AM. Jessica, Pam's sister, and the boys were coming over at 8:30 AM as we all planned to meet Gabriel at the Riverhead facility to see Pam.

It had been one hell of an interesting day, to say the least.

So, I climbed into our bed, all alone, and for the first time in a long time, I felt very alone. Pam was not there next to me. The house was quiet. It was, after all, only me completely alone.

I went to bed but wasn't able to fall asleep. My ears kept ringing as my tinnitus dominated the silence. I kept thinking about all the events that had just transpired.

Eventually, I was able to fall asleep, and what sent me to that place was the experience of writing with Leah. With all that was going on, that creativity allowed me to get away. To escape.

This time, on this night, I did not do it alone. I did it with Leah.

You can judge me if you want, but life is short and happiness can be so fleeting. In my mind, rediscovering a moment of happiness was not a sin.

But then, my mind and perspective have evolved in ways I never would have imagined.

It was just such a very long and unbelievable day. It was time for this day to end.

CHAPTER 12

The next morning, Jessica called me and told me that she and the boys were running a little late but would be at the house around 8:45 AM. Jessica asked if we had opened her car last night because the car door was open. Jessica never leaves her car unlocked. I replied, "No, Jessica, we did not go into your car." When they left your house, I almost walked to your car but never tried to get into it. Jessica understood because we basically have the same model car. I said, "It can happen to anyone. There's a lot going on right now. I wouldn't worry about it just remember to lock it tonight when you get back home." Jessica reluctantly accepted that explanation, but I could tell it really bothered her. Understandably so.

After my conversation with Jessica, I woke up, got myself ready, grabbed a quick bite to eat, and waited. 8:45 AM came and went. Soon, it was 9:15 AM. I tried calling Jessica, but it went straight to voicemail. I tried Chris and Brian on their phones with the same result voicemail. Then my phone rang. It was Gabriel.

"Paul," he said, "where are you?"

I told him Jessica and the boys had not yet arrived and I was still waiting for them. Gabriel said, "I'll let everyone know to expect you at 10:00 AM, okay?"

I replied, "Yes, as soon as we're on our way, I'll call you." On that, we agreed.

Now it was approaching 9:45 AM. Still no sign of Jessica or my sons. I called Gabriel and let him know. I tried Jessica's cell phone again, but it went straight to voicemail. I called the boys' phones same thing, straight to voicemail.

"Gabriel," I said, "I'm starting to worry about them. I'm not sure what to do." I just waited.

I called Leah, but her phone also went straight to voicemail.

Doesn't anybody answer their freaking phone anymore? I wondered.

I was really worried at this point. What could have happened? Where were they? Right at that moment, my phone rang. I answered it. "Is this Paul?" the caller asked. "Yes," I replied, "who is this?" "Paul," the caller said, "this is Amanda with the New York State Police."

There was a long pause. Then I asked, "I do not understand. What is this about?"

She went on to say, "It's about your sons, Chris and Brian."

I paused and then said directly, "I need you to tell me what this is about, right now."

The officer paused again, then disclosed that Jessica, Chris, and Brian had been in an accident.

Immediately, I asked, "Is everyone okay?"

The officer did not reply right away. I repeated the question, louder this time: "Are they okay?"

Reluctantly, and sounding very uncomfortable, the officer said, "I'm so sorry, sir. They've been in an accident."

Again, I asked directly, "Are they alright?!"

Slowly, she responded, "They had an accident. Their car crashed on Sunrise Highway."

She paused once more and, with great reluctance, said, "I'm so sorry... they were killed in the crash."

The officer repeated, "No one survived. I'm sorry."

In a complete state of shock, I was unable to think or focus. I wanted to cry, but all I could think about was how to tell Pam that her children were dead.

I sat down for a moment to gather myself. But I just couldn't process it. How could I possibly tell Pam, with all she was already going through? Her sister... gone.

I put my hands over my eyes, dropped to my knees, and wept.

I heard the phone ringing multiple times, but I was paralyzed   unable to move.

As the reality of my sons' deaths slowly sank in, I felt numb, yet the emotional pain hit me like a ton of bricks   pounding my chest so hard I thought my heart would burst free.

Then the pounding subsided, only to be replaced by an even deeper ache.

Still emotionally paralyzed, I collapsed and begged God to take the pain away.

I kept asking why this happened. How could He do this to our family?

I can't remember ever feeling such intense pain in my life. The ache in my heart was so severe, I could barely breathe.

I had never known pain like this before. It crippled me.

Again, the phone rang, but I was still unable to move.

I remained curled up in the fetal position for hours.

I knew I had missed the meeting with Gabriel, and I knew I had to call him.

It was around noon now. Missing that meeting was something I shouldn't have done, but given the circumstances, there was no way I could have been there.

Struggling to function, I picked up the phone and dialed Gabriel.

I dialed the phone, and every moment felt like an eternity. Gabriel answered and immediately asked why we hadn't arrived yet. He was firm, and I had to stop him before he scolded me like a child. "Gabriel, the reason we didn't show up," I said, "is because Chris, Brian, and Jessica were killed in a car accident on the way to my house. I haven't had the strength to call until now. Besides overwhelming grief, I've been trying to figure out how and when to tell Pam her children are gone."

Gabriel paused, searching for words, then quietly said, "Paul, I'm so sorry." He promised to reschedule our meeting and asked if I was alright, and if I wanted him to tell Pam. I quickly replied, "No! I should be the one to tell her."

Though still in disbelief, I appreciated Gabriel's support and sense of friendship. He assured me he would do whatever I needed to help break the news to Pam. I told him I needed to hang up and process everything myself. After all, so much had happened in just a few hours, and I wasn't sure I fully understood it yet. It was almost impossible to accept that my children were dead.

Pam's sister Jessica and I had never been very close, but this was still incredibly hard to accept. I sat silently on the couch, tears coming and going as memories of the boys flooded my mind   their childhood, how much Pam and I had loved raising them. For a time, we had been a great family, loving Chris and Brian with all our hearts. I suppose this is what real heartache feels like. The pain in my chest refused to ease. I had never experienced loss like this before. This pain was something I would never forget or fully come to terms with.

The phone rang again, close to four o'clock. It was Gabriel, calling to check if I needed anything and to tell me he had arranged a time for me to visit Pam in the morning. I was grateful, though emotionally wrecked, and I knew I had to pull myself together if I was going to tell Pam the news. I promised I would be there.

After hanging up, I called Leah. Again, it went straight to voicemail. I was too numb to move, and I didn't want to go over to her place. All I wanted was to be alone.

As I lay there, I realized I had to get myself together. Arrangements had to be made; there was no time to be alone. Then the phone rang again, interrupting my thoughts. It was Amanda from the state police. This time, she had information about where I could go to identify the bodies of my children and Jessica. She was kind and asked if I

was okay and if I wanted to do this tonight. I
thanked her and told her I would be there.

So, I forced myself to get together whatever
strength I had left and made my way to the hospital.
Jessica and the boys had been taken to the medical
examiner's building that's where I was instructed to
go. Walking inside, I immediately saw Amanda
waiting. She was a short, thin, and attractive blonde
officer with long hair and a warm, welcoming
smile. That smile soft, compassionate was exactly
what I needed at that moment, like the polite, gentle
smile someone gives when the situation is painfully
uncomfortable but they want to offer kindness
anyway.

Amanda asked me to follow her. As I trailed behind
her, an older man who appeared to be the coroner
was walking ahead of us down the cold, sterile
hallway. A crushing sadness began to settle over
me, deep and overwhelming. We stopped before a
glass window, where Amanda told me to wait for a
moment. The seconds felt like hours as I stood
there, unable to move beyond the dread in my chest.
Soon enough, Amanda and the coroner reappeared
and motioned for me to come inside.

The room was cold and clinical, with three metal
tables arranged in a row. Thick blankets covered all
three bodies lying there. Amanda reached out,
placing a steady hand on my shoulder. Her voice
was gentle but firm as she asked if I was sure I was

ready to do this. I swallowed hard and nodded, managing to whisper, "Yes, I am."

The coroner began pulling the blankets down slowly, revealing the faces beneath. My two sons and my wife's sister. Seeing them like that so still and silent shattered any strength I had left. No matter how tough you think you are, no one can truly prepare for the unbearable weight of reality crashing down like that. I felt my knees buckle as weakness swept through me like a tidal wave. I could barely stand, my body trembling with grief. Amanda caught me before I hit the floor, holding me as I collapsed into sobs uncontrollable, deep, gut-wrenching sobs that shook me to my core.

Clinging to her, I finally found the words to speak, broken and raw: "Yes… that's Chris and Brian." Then, with a barely audible voice, "And that's Jessica." Amanda guided me gently out of the room, down the hallway to a quiet sitting area. She asked if I wanted water or anything else, but I shook my head, telling her I was okay for now.

"Paul," Amanda said softly, "Jessica was driving the car. It looks like the brakes failed. She did everything she could to keep control, but eventually, the car hit the guardrail and lost control." She expressed her sorrow again and explained that all three had died instantly from the impact. It was a tragic accident nothing intentional, no one else involved.

Amanda kindly offered to drive me home, but I declined. Despite everything, I could walk on my own. I thanked her sincerely   I hadn't had many dealings with state police before, but Amanda's compassion and professionalism made an unbearable moment just a bit more bearable.

I made it back to my car and started the drive home. During the trip, I tried calling Leah again. As before, it went straight to voicemail. No answer.

When I finally got home, I called Gabriel. He answered quickly. I told him I had just identified my children and Pam's sister, Jessica. His voice softened as he asked if I was alright. I managed, "I think so. As alright as anyone could be after this."

Then Gabriel said something I wasn't prepared to hear. "Paul, I have some other news." My heart sank. I immediately asked, "Is Pam okay?"

He replied, "Yes, she's alright, but Tony hanged himself in his cell early this morning."

I asked if he had told Pam yet. Gabriel said no.

"Gabriel, what the hell is happening?" I demanded.

"I don't know," he said, voice heavy with frustration and sorrow.

Then he asked me to keep trying to reach Leah and to arrange a meeting with him. "We really need to get together and talk about all of this   especially for Pam's sake. We must figure out the best way to break the news to her about her boys, her sister, and Tony."

I agreed without hesitation. Despite the crushing grief of losing our sons, I wanted more than anything to find a way to tell Pam that would spare her as much agony as possible   even though deep down I knew the truth would break her completely.

Gabriel and I agreed to meet soon to discuss everything, and he asked me to keep trying to reach Leah. I had to tell her about Tony and what had happened to my family. After trying Leah one last time, my phone suddenly rang. It was Leah. I quickly answered, my voice filled with concern: "Leah, are you alright? Where have you been?"

Leah's voice was tired but honest. "I had to take a break from it all."

I swallowed hard. "Leah, so much has happened. Did you talk to Gabriel?"

"No," she replied quietly. "I don't know why it happened... it just did."

The weight of the truth pushed me forward. I told her everything   about my sons being dead. As the words spilled out, tears overwhelmed me, and I broke down sobbing. Leah was silent for a moment, then gently asked, "Do you want me to come over?"

"Paul, I'm so sorry. My God, you must be hurting so much. I'll be right there."

Before I could respond, she hung up. I stood there, paralyzed. I just couldn't believe my sons were gone.

Minutes later, a soft knock came at the door. I opened it to find Leah standing there. Without a word, she pulled me into a tight embrace. I needed someone and Leah was there. She knew the depth of my pain.

She came inside, and after a long, quiet hug, we went to the bedroom and lay down. No words were spoken. Leah just held me, and in her arms, I finally drifted off to sleep. For the first time that night, there was no pain only an exhausted, fragile peace.

When I opened my eyes the next morning, Leah was still asleep beside me. She stirred and looked at me.

"I'm so sorry I collapsed like that last night," I murmured.

She looked at me kindly. "It's alright. You must be devastated."

"Leah, we have to meet with Gabriel today," I reminded her. "I forgot to tell you last night. He wants us both there. Pam has got to know. I have to find a way to break this to her."

I paused, remembering Gabriel's words about Tony.

"Leah, Gabriel told me last night before you came that Tony is dead."

Her face was blank for a moment, then calm.

"I visited him yesterday," she said quietly. "Alone."

I asked softly, "What did you talk about?"

Leah's voice grew sharper. "We didn't really talk much. I told Tony I was done with him that I didn't care about him or what happened to him. Then I just walked away."

I told her what Gabriel had said that Tony had hanged himself in his cell.

Leah looked me straight in the eye and said, "Paul, he was abusive. I hated him." Her voice cracked with emotion. "I used to love him, but over time, his abuse emotional, verbal, then physical turned that love into hatred. When he got arrested, I felt like a huge weight was lifted. Like I no longer had to figure out how to leave him. He made it easy for me. I'm glad he's dead."

Though Leah's coldness shocked me, it didn't raise red flags. Instead, I felt I understood her pain.

I thanked her for being there last night. She said she knew how much I loved Pam and the boys and promised she would help me through this.

The first thing I had to do was set a time to meet Pam. I called Gabriel and arranged for us to visit the prison in two hours.

Leah and I showered, ate a little, and then I drove us both to Riverhead.

My heart pounded as we neared the prison. Telling Pam about Jessica, Chris, and Brian was going to be the hardest thing I'd ever done. I feared how she'd survive it.

We parked, met Gabriel at the entrance, and entered.

There she was Pam, in an orange jumpsuit, handcuffed. I couldn't help but think: how did our lives come to this?

Gabriel began explaining the case, then said, "Paul, Leah and I will step out for a moment. You and Pam need to talk."

I looked at her the woman I'd loved, the mother of my children broken and confined.

"Paul, how are Chris and Brian?" she asked suddenly.

I froze.

Pam saw it. She knew something was wrong.

"Pam," I whispered, voice trembling, "Jessica, Chris, and Brian were coming to meet us."

Tears caught in my throat.

"This is so hard to say... they were in an accident. They didn't make it."

I was already crying, and then I watched Pam break down too. It was clear that after everything we had endured, the love we both had for our children was a shared, unbreakable bond. We loved our boys deeply   that was our common ground in the midst of all the chaos.

As expected, Pam was devastated. There was no point in continuing any conversation about legal plans or what came next. Pam was shattered, and so was I.

One thing overwhelmed me with sadness and compassion: Pam did not deserve this. Every struggle we had as a couple stemmed from her fierce desire to work hard and do right by her family. Suddenly, everything became so clear as I watched her break down.

Feeling helpless, the only thing I could do was tell Pam I loved her, then leave her to be alone.

Remembering how this news had crushed me emotionally, I could not begin to imagine what she was feeling now. I knew there was no place for me in her pain at that moment.

Leaving that room was the hardest thing I had ever done. Emotionally drained and spiritually broken, I walked away. I believed Pam felt the same.

I told Gabriel I had to leave and asked if we could reschedule the meeting. He looked me in the eyes and said, "Paul, I already did."

I thanked him and asked Leah to come with me. Leah and I left the complex and got in the car, heading home.

The drive back was quiet. Neither of us had much to say.

Once home, Leah went to the refrigerator and grabbed us both a few beers. We sat down and slowly began to come to terms with everything that had happened in such a short time.

Then Leah started to sing.

Just like that night at the bar, she sang "If I Close My Eyes Forever." I watched her, and with every lyric, my pain softened, turning to numbness.

One beer became two, and one shot of bourbon followed another.

In the silence of the house   broken only by our breathing   I asked Leah to stay the night.

She whispered softly in my ear, "Paul, I'm here for you."

Those five words brought a level of comfort I hadn't felt all day.

It had been a long day. We were both a little drunk. Together, we went into the bedroom and lay down. We talked about everything   for what felt like hours.

It was clear that what we had for one another was real. Even with all that had transpired, our feelings remained as strong as ever.

CHAPTER 13

We agreed to meet Gabriel at 10:00 AM with Pam. Upon entering the room, it was clear that Pam was emotionally drained. I, of course, understood this because I was also emotionally spent.

Gabriel began to explain the current status of the case. He broke things down in a straightforward way.

"Listen," Gabriel said, "something we should lay out on the table right now is this: since Tony and Pam were taken into custody, the murders have stopped. This doesn't help our case. It's not something I can just explain away."

He went on to inform Pam that Tony had killed himself. To my surprise, Pam showed no visible reaction to the news. That struck me as unusual, but after hearing about Jessica, Chris, and Brian, I supposed Pam was simply emotionally numb.

Gabriel then explained how the DNA evidence was obtained. The authorities were led to Pam and Tony because each victim had some connection to the rehab center   either as patients or through someone who drove them to appointments. Some victims had visited the facility once, others regularly, but that was the link.

Through this chain of information, investigators were led to consider Pam and Tony as people of interest. DNA matches were made based on evidence gathered both in the field and at the rehab center.

"Paul, Pam, Leah," Gabriel said, "I'm afraid the case against them is very strong. What we have to do is find holes in their case and present an alternative theory of the crimes."

He added that the victims' families were also filing civil suits for wrongful death.

Gabriel looked at me and said, "Paul, this will be a tremendous financial burden on both you and Pam. They'll be going after Tony's assets as well as yours and Pam's."

Then Gabriel continued, "Tomorrow, I'm filing a motion to suppress the DNA evidence collected from the rehab center on the grounds that it was obtained illegally   specifically, the DNA taken from the garbage there. It's a Hail Mary, but this is our first line of defense. This is how Pam and Tony's DNA were collected and then matched against DNA found at the various crime scenes."

Gabriel suggested we consider selling the house to prepare for the expenses of the civil suits that might come our way soon, regardless of what happens in the criminal case. I understood and assured Pam I would make it happen. The question then became: where would I live?

Leah offered me the opportunity to stay with her until I could find a place of my own. Gabriel objected, saying it wouldn't work because they would be going after Tony's property as well. Leah looked at Gabriel and said, "I own that house. Tony just lived in it. His name is not on the deed. It's mine, it's paid for, and it would be perfect for Paul to stay there while selling the house and using the money for the cases ahead."

Leah explained, "Tony and I were never married. Paul will live with me; I have the extra room, and it will help you both." Pam, Leah, and Gabriel seemed to agree with this plan, so it was decided: I would put the house up for sale and move in with Leah during the trial.

Pam appeared surprisingly calm during this conversation, which struck me as odd   as did Leah's offer in Pam's presence. But the plan made sense, and it was the most feasible path forward. I also knew Pam and Gabriel didn't know about Leah and me. If Pam did, she would never have agreed to this.

With that understanding, we forged ahead. Everything was set in motion, and we felt we had a strategy.

Over the next few months, I visited Pam frequently and consulted a real estate agent about listing the house. During our visits, Pam and I grew closer.

Our shared losses had created a new understanding between us.

The agent, Lisa Kreski one of the top producers in eastern Long Island kept me updated. Several potential buyers were already interested in the property. Pam and I were frightened about the murder case's outcome, but we knew selling the house was the only way to sustain ourselves financially.

I was unemployed due to the slow economy. No matter how hard I tried, I couldn't find a new job especially with Pam accused of murder and my association with the situation. We lived in a small town on eastern Long Island, where news traveled fast. No one wanted to hire someone involved in controversy. Thankfully, Pam and I had some savings, which I was living off of.

So, unemployed and spending most days packing up the house, I often found myself lost in memories. I kept coming across pictures of Chris and Brian, of Pam, of all of us together and it was too emotionally painful. Once again, I turned to drinking to quiet the pain.

Leah would sometimes walk in on me, finding me sobbing uncontrollably. But she always had a way to console me, to ease my pain. She didn't make me forget, but she provided relief, and she made me feel better.

At that point, all I could do was look back with pain and look forward with comfort in Leah's friendship. Packing was tough, and for the next several days, that was my routine: me, my emotions, and then Leah's steady support.

With each passing day, even as the pain grew, the bond between Leah and me grew stronger. Looking into her eyes, several times over those days, I felt a strong impulse to tell her I loved her.

It might seem crazy, given everything happening, but Leah and I were truly becoming closer with every day that passed.

We were starting to realize that the inevitable was on the horizon, and neither of us seemed to have any problem accepting it. You know, I never really understood much about love. I mean, I have been in love. I have loved, and I had the good fortune of being loved by my wife and my sons. But feeling love and claiming to understand love are two completely different things.

Like right now, for example. I know I have strong feelings for Leah, and I realize how wrong that is, how others will judge it but I have absolutely no control over my emotions. Sure, maybe my behavior is something I could try to control, but what I'm talking about is how I feel. That part of love is the one I don't understand.

Why do I feel this way toward Leah? I suppose being alone in this situation has a lot to do with it. Another thing that puzzles me is how Leah is finding comfort in caring for me. What does she have to gain from this? Looking at the situation, any fool can see what I'm getting out of it. Just look at Leah so attractive, so beautiful, and now so caring and loving toward me.

In my attempts to understand love, I only become more confused. No matter how I try to justify my feelings for Leah and her friendship toward me, I find myself at a loss. At the end of the day, I have to live with myself. It really is the classical dilemma between the head and the heart.

Right now, I know loving Leah is wrong, yet I still think that, over time, my love for her will be validated. It seems so odd to think this way.

CHAPTER 14

Another day, another meeting with Gabriel and Pam. It had almost become routine: I would get up, pick up Leah, and then drive to Riverhead. The house was finally under contract, and although I had almost packed everything, I was still living there, still moving our belongings into Leah's place.

We met again outside the facility and talked before seeing Pam. Gabriel told Leah and me that a trial date had been set. He was set to defend Pam and said he wanted to call both of us as witnesses to speak about Pam's hard work and dedication as a mother and a professional at the rehab center. Leah and I had no reservations about that.

So, we entered the facility and headed to the visitation room. Upon entering, we saw Pam not looking well. Her hair was matted, she appeared to have lost weight, and her eyes were bloodshot. She looked like someone who had surrendered, who had given up. I could tell she hadn't been sleeping. After all, Pam had just lost her sons, her sister, and even though she didn't acknowledge it, her friend and boss, Tony. All this loss in such a short time, along with being accused of murder, had taken its toll. She looked defeated.

As we sat and listened to Gabriel discuss trial strategy, Leah and I were engaged in the conversation, but Pam seemed miles away. During the visit, something about Pam's demeanor didn't sit right with me.

We wrapped up the meeting, and I told Pam that I loved her and would be back in the morning. She just looked at me lost, broken and said nothing. I wanted to say or do something, but no words came. We left the meeting, and I felt so sorry for Pam. In my heart, I knew she could never have done what they accused her of. There was no way. No doubt in my mind.

On the drive home, Leah and I talked extensively about Pam, Tony, everything that had happened, and about each other. We decided to pull over and stop at the beach. It was still fairly early, so we stopped at a convenience store, grabbed some food and a few beers, then found a quiet spot to settle down. The weather this time of year on Long Island can be unpredictable but often brings a peaceful beauty in early September. Leah and I found a place to sit and soak in the gentle breeze and serene surroundings. We listened to the sound of the water and the bay breeze while watching the ships slowly drift by. With every moment that passed, a sense of tranquility washed over me.

Leah rested her head on my shoulder, and we just talked. Then she asked if I remembered a night some time ago when she asked me a question about how I felt about her. The question was: if I wasn't with Pam, and she wasn't with Tony, would I find her attractive? I nodded, recalling it clearly. I told her I thought we could revisit the conversation later. Leah smiled and said, "I think this is that later." She looked into my eyes and said, "Paul, you're moving into my home with me. Pam's not here, Tony's dead. I want us to be together." She continued, "I know you still love Pam, but you and I have something special. I'm with you for the long haul, no matter what happens. I want us to be together right now. It's just you and me." Then she added, "I think you want the same thing."

I knew how this might look and sound, but Leah had held a hold on me from the moment I saw her. I simply looked at her, nodded, and whispered, "Yes. I want that too." It was a conversation that needed to happen, and part of me was grateful it did. We looked at each other and shared a deep, unforgettable kiss. Looking into Leah's eyes, I realized that no matter how wrong it might seem, it felt undeniably right. That moment marked a turning point in our lives. We were both ready to embrace one another and whatever consequences the future held.

We spent the next few hours at the beach, just being close and talking. Leah let me speak about Pam. She understood that I wasn't ready to jump into a new relationship, especially while still married to Pam and while Pam was going through so much. Leah was patient and reassuring, promising to stand by me through the trial with Pam. It was a side of Leah I hadn't seen before the compassion she showed me that day only deepened my feelings for her. I found myself growing even more attracted to Leah.

We ended up spending the entire afternoon there, and when it was time to leave, we quietly packed up and walked to the parking lot, holding hands. We left feeling emotionally closer than when we'd arrived. I drove us home and pulled up in front of Leah's house. As I said goodbye, she paused for a moment and said, "Paul, I think it's time for you to move in. Sleep here tonight." As much as I wanted to resist, I couldn't. Reluctantly though maybe not so reluctantly I agreed.

We went inside, and Leah asked, "Are you hungry?" I nodded; I was kind of hungry. She told me to take a seat in the living room and that she would prepare us some food. Sitting on the couch, I could see the kitchen from where I was. I watched Leah move about, making dinner. As I watched, I reflected on how we'd ended up here. Never in my wildest dreams did I imagine Leah and I together like this. My mind flashed back to when Leah and Tony first moved into this house the very moment I laid eyes on her. I felt something then, something that made me want to be with her, but also made me resist. She's that beautiful. And now, here we were.

I knew I needed to get my head straight. I had to be there for Pam. I doubted she could stand to lose me now, not when she was facing so much. I knew my choices hadn't made the path any easier for anyone.

Leah came into the living room, sat on my lap, and kissed me on the cheek. "Dinner's served," she said.

As we both stood and walked to the table, all I wanted was to forget everything going on around us and focus on this moment a moment for Leah and me to be alone, to catch a breath, and maybe just take a break from it all. After all, we still had to meet with Gabriel tomorrow.

Leah cooked us a great meal a rich, savory beef dish that was simply amazing. I asked her, "Leah, where did you learn to cook like this?" She smiled and said, "My mom." It really was incredible. Leah and I had sort of melted into one another, assuming the roles of significant others surprisingly quickly. But I have to say, in this transition, it felt very natural to both of us. After all, before Pam and Tony were arrested, the two of us had been great friends, growing closer with each passing day. Now, we both find ourselves really needing one another, with the strong foundation of that special friendship to build from.

I'm not sure what to make of all this. I don't really know how things will unfold moving forward. But one thing I am certain of is this: Leah and I have truly found something in one another. I don't want to look too far ahead because we both know what we're doing is wrong on many levels, yet we also both understand how we feel and that's something that can no longer be controlled.

After dinner, Leah and I cleaned up and decided to watch some TV. We had a few drinks and eventually fell asleep on the loveseat. It really feels like our relationship has grown into something else something we both seem ready to embrace. I carry a certain level of guilt, knowing Pam is locked up right now. But at the same time, having lost my wife to prison and my two sons in a car accident, my mind and heart have taken a serious beating. Leah and I just seemed to fall into one another when we really needed someone.

As I watch Leah sleeping on my shoulder, I feel love for this woman. Am I falling in love with her, or is this still just infatuation? We've connected on a deep emotional level as well as a physical one. I realize the path ahead is paved with confusion. As I watch Leah sleep, my thoughts drift to tomorrow and the meeting with Gabriel. Tomorrow, we're meeting the investigative team. Staring at Leah, still asleep, I begin to drift away myself. My dreams are the only place I want to be right now. As I fall asleep, a comfortable peace settles over me. As Joe Lynn Turner wrote, "Bring on the Night."

CHAPTER 15

I was up early this morning because I was really looking forward to my meeting with Gabriel, but also because I was going to visit Pam first. As I drove to Riverhead, I was silent, just remembering and reflecting on Pam and me and our lives together. She truly made me so happy, and our family made my life feel complete. I actually started to cry uncontrollably while driving, just thinking about the boys and Pam our lives together, where we were, and now where we are. It's so hard to believe that Chris and Brian are gone. In fact, it's quite sobering to reflect on where we stand right now. Even though I am an imperfect human who makes a lot of mistakes, I still consider myself blessed to have had a life with Pam. For both of us to have had a family together. I break down every time I think of what has happened over the past few weeks. The funeral for the boys is in a few days, and I was hoping Gabriel could arrange for Pam to be released for it. So much pain, so much suffering, and so much regret in some ways. I could have spent more time with the boys. Instead, I was too focused on other things trivial things now that I look back on it. I'm sure Pam feels the same way. She was working all the time. She hardly saw the boys these past few years. As a family, we hardly saw one another.

I arrived at the jail and went in to visit Pam. These rooms are so cold and impersonal. While I waited, the phone rang. It was Gabriel. He told me he had some information to share investigators had found new developments in the case, and he wanted to meet with me alone. I told him I would call him back after seeing Pam.

Pam entered the room looking tired and listless. I could tell she hadn't been sleeping, and the toll this was taking on her was clear at just one glance. Pam sat down and picked up the receiver; I did the same. Pam started: "Paul, I didn't do this." She continued, saying she didn't understand what had happened. Pam was crying. I wished I could hold her for just a moment, but that wasn't possible here. "Pam," I said, "I know you're innocent. We're going to do everything we can to prove it." Pam just stared at me with a stoic look in her eyes. I tried to reassure her, but she seemed indifferent, like she was in a trance. I repeated myself: "Pam, we will do all we can."

What happened next unfolded almost in slow motion. I saw Pam raise her hand from her side, holding something sharp. At first, I couldn't make out what it was, but then I saw it was a shank or blade of some kind. Without hesitation, Pam sliced her wrist right in front of me, looking directly into my eyes as she did it. It happened so fast, so seamlessly, that I barely had time to react. Then I saw Pam's blood everywhere, and I immediately called out for help. Within moments, guards arrived and dragged her out of the room by her legs. They took her away right before my eyes. I was in shock and couldn't believe what had just happened.

Guards and personnel escorted me out of the visiting area, and all I kept asking was if Pam was going to be okay. They took me to an office and told me to wait; I would be kept informed about Pam's condition. Everything happened so fast, and there was little I could do or say now. It was a waiting game.

I was still trying to process what I had witnessed. There was so much guilt inside me, and at the same time, so much confusion. I longed for information about Pam, answers, and some kind of understanding of why this was happening to us. My heart was broken, as was my spirit. I knew I had to meet with Gabriel soon, but he didn't know about what had just happened. God, please let Pam be alright. I prayed hard for hours as I waited for an update. Nothing in my life made sense anymore.

After being interviewed by the prison security team about what happened in the visiting room, I was left to sit alone in this cold, quiet room with nothing to do but wait. I was assured that medical professionals were working to treat Pam, and once she was stabilized, they would come back to update me on her condition. So, right now, it was just me alone, waiting. As I sat there, a whirlwind of feelings swept over me as my mind reflected on so many things, past and present. The look in Pam's eyes the desperate look of surrender and the moments that followed. I don't think I will ever forget that moment, and more than that, that look in her eyes. I had never seen Pam look like that before.

This whole thing is killing her. It's killing me too, but Pam is the one stuck in this prison.

While I waited, I thought I'd try to reach out to Gabriel. I managed to get him on the phone and told him where I was and what had happened. He basically said, "Paul, stay there, I'll come to you." It wasn't more than half an hour before Gabriel arrived with his paralegal, Patti, and two other people I didn't know. Junior was with him, as was Jayde. They asked if there was any news about Pam. Jayde looked particularly shaken. After all, she and Pam were pretty close. Junior hugged me and told me to hang in there the team was doing the best they could. Gabriel came up and asked how Pam was. I told him I didn't know. No one had updated me yet. "Are you alright?" Gabriel asked. "I'm as alright as I'm going to be," I said. Gabriel then asked if I had spoken with Leah today. "I really haven't, but I was with her last night," I replied. "Why do you ask?" I was intrigued by the question. Gabriel then introduced me to Patti, Scott, and Ray. Patti is Gabriel's assistant, and Ray and Scott are part of his team of investigators.

"Paul, we've been checking into things the best we can. We don't believe Pam was involved in this in any way. However, we do think Tony was. Unfortunately, Tony is no longer with us, so we can't question him." Gabriel went on to explain that the DNA they obtained was collected legally from discarded cups and materials gathered from the rehab center's trash. Unfortunately, that DNA will remain as evidence to be presented at trial. What Scott and Ray discovered was that each victim not only attended the rehab center, but all worked in hospitality, just like Leah and me. Without Tony's information, they are now trying to piece together what happened.

"Gabriel, I saw Pam she's so stressed and unstable right now. Why would she try to take her own life?" I asked. I realize we've both been through a tragedy the loss of our sons, Pam's sister, the murder charge against Pam, and Tony's suicide. It's a lot to handle, but I've known Pam my whole life. I never imagined she would try to take her own life. Gabriel said he wanted to ask Pam some questions once this was all over. He believes Pam knows more than she's letting on. He assured me that he, Patti, Ray, and Scott would keep chasing leads. He promised to update me in a few days and asked me to keep in touch with Pam's progress. I assured him I would.

Gabriel and his team left, and shortly after, a nurse came through the doors. "Paul," she said. I looked at her with anticipation. "Paul, she's going to be alright." "Thank God," I replied. "She's sedated right now. The doctor stitched up her wrist, and now we wait. She should be fine." "Can I see her?" I asked. The nurse said, "Wait here, I'll be right back."

Junior and Jayde were also anxious to see Pam. Jayde suddenly asked about my relationship with Leah. This caught me off guard. "Paul," she said, "I saw you and Leah at the sound yesterday, and I know you're now living with her." "Paul," Jayde continued, "do you have any idea how this looks to others? To Junior and me?" "Jayde," I replied, "I do know how this looks, but you don't know the whole story." Jayde just turned to Junior and said, "I'm done with him." Junior seemed calm after hearing that, like he expected it.

Then the nurse came in and took us to see Pam. At this point, there was no reason to discuss anything but Pam. As we entered the room, Pam lay in bed, bandaged with her eyes closed. The nurse reminded me she was heavily sedated. We all just stared at her, feeling so concerned and so sorry for all she has endured. I sat in the chair close to the bed, unwilling and unable to leave her side. I kept thinking how horrible this situation was. Junior and Jayde were ready to leave. They said goodbye to Pam, then to me. Jayde whispered in my ear, "Paul, she really needs you right now. She's your wife, for God's sake. We'll be praying for you both." With that, they left the room.

Everything going on right now was barely tolerable, hardly believable. The only thing keeping me somewhat engaged was Leah. I know how terrible that sounds. Here I am, with my wife going through so much, and I'm thinking about Leah. To be honest, I don't understand it either. Since Pam was arrested, it almost seems Leah has jumped into the role of my wife. Maybe I shouldn't have let that happen, but Leah, for whatever reason, has embraced taking care of me. As I kissed Pam on the cheek and started to leave, Pam grabbed my hand weakly. With a whisper, she said, "I love you." "I love you too," I replied. I told Pam to get some rest and that I'd be back tomorrow. I left the room and headed to my car, to go back to Leah's place. I guess I should call it my place now because I actually live there. I really have nowhere else to go. Our house has a contract, and the deal will close in about a week. Profits from the sale will go into a special account Gabriel set up to help pay for the court battles ahead. Gabriel told me people are coming forward to support the civil case. All this is unfolding so fast so fast I can't keep my head straight. I got in my car and headed home.

When I got to the house, Leah was there. She greeted me with a hug and looked into my eyes. "Paul," Leah asked, "how is Pam? How did it go?" Leah added, "Something happened to Pam." I went on to tell her what had happened during my visit with Pam. Leah hugged me tight and whispered in my ear, "Paul, I am here for you. I am so sorry." I explained that when I left, they had Pam stabilized. I was an emotional wreck at that point. Leah recognized this almost immediately and led me to the living room, onto the couch, where we sat down.

"Paul, let me get you something to drink," Leah said. She brought us both a beer, and we just sat there for a while and talked. Leah reminded me that Pam's sister Jennifer's funeral and services were tomorrow. What I don't understand is how the county could reject Gabriel's request to allow Pam to attend her sister's funeral. It seems so cruel. They also denied Pam's request to attend Chris and Brian's services in a few days. I was venting all this to Leah, who simply said she would go to both services with me for support.

"Unfortunately," Leah said, "we will have to deal with this the best we can." I felt so fortunate to have Leah there at that moment. She seems to be growing into the role of my friend and support system all rolled into one. We continued to drink and talk for hours. Sometimes Leah just held me, knowing the emotional pain and stress I was feeling. The interesting thing is that before all this, Leah and I were fighting back feelings of emotion and attraction, and now we were finding one another as soulmates while going through so much.

Sometimes I forget how close Pam and Leah were. They really were close and truly friends. As the afternoon turned into night, Leah and I just drank and talked. We talked until we both decided to go to bed. It is interesting that as we got ready for bed, almost without thought and seamlessly, we both retired to Leah's room the bed she and Tony used to sleep in. I didn't give it much thought as we went to bed, but as I lay there, it dawned on me that Leah and I were becoming something more. It was unintentional and very natural, and at the same time, emotionally gratifying and satisfying.

I did feel some guilt, but I also felt very fortunate to have Leah with me. As I watched her sleep, I drifted off myself. What a crazy day. Tomorrow is Pam's sister's funeral. I wasn't looking forward to it or the days ahead. I knew I would have to muster all my inner strength to get through it.

Pam's sister's services started at 11:00 AM. I had time to visit Pam before the service and told Leah early this morning that I'd be going to Riverhead. Leah said she wanted to go with me to visit Pam. I had no objection. My main reason was to ask Pam if she wanted me to say anything or had any requests. I still can't get over the fact that Pam wouldn't be allowed to attend her own sister's funeral.

Leah and I got ready, had a quick breakfast, and headed to Riverhead to see Pam. It was actually the first time Leah would visit Pam with me in some time. After Pam's attempt on her own life, we learned visits had to be supervised. Upon entering the building, Leah and I were both frisked and told we had only 15 minutes. In the room, Pam was there with a guard, and another guard stood on our side as Leah and I entered.

Looking at Pam, I could see she had been crying. Bags under her eyes, her face drawn. I picked up the receiver and asked if she was alright. Pam just glazed at me, speechless, then after several long moments, she yelled, "Paul, how the hell do you think I am?!! I'm alone. I'm scared. I'm a prisoner not to mention my sister is dead, my sons are dead, and my husband is here with my so-called friend, Leah."

Pam continued, "I suppose you two are a thing now, right? Right!?" I tried to respond, but Pam went on, "Oh, why not?! Why wouldn't you be with her, Paul? I've seen the way you looked at her when we were all out together. I wouldn't be surprised if you two were screwing each other before all this."

"Pam," I pleaded, but she wouldn't have any of it. She ranted, "You two couldn't care less what happens to me. You're made for one another. I hope you're very happy together." Finally, Pam slowed down. All this must have been bottled up inside her for a long time. She's been through so much.

Finally, silence. Just Pam, Leah, and me sitting there with only the glass between us.

"Pam," I said, "I love you very much, and we're all trying to find a way to get you through this. I promise Gabriel and his team are investigating, and we're trying to clear you of this."

Pam looked at me, then at Leah. She made strong, intentional eye contact and said, "Paul, I just don't care anymore. I don't care what the two of you do. Just leave me alone. I don't want to see you anymore."

Leah spoke for the first time during this visit. "Pam," Leah said, "I'm sorry, and I don't want you to worry. I'll take care of Paul until you get out." I looked at Leah as if to say, are you out of your mind saying that?!

With that statement, the visit was over not that we were done, but the guards told us we were finished.

That visit did not go the way I wanted it to. On the drive from Riverhead to Pam's sister's service, Leah and I argued. I asked her how she could say something like that. I told her I thought it was cruel. Leah just sat there, listened, and took it all in. When I had exhausted my verbal tirade, Leah asked me to pull the car over. I thought she was going to get out, and I was so mad at her that I just pulled over. When the car stopped, Leah leaned toward me. I thought she was going to yell or hit me or something, but instead, she kissed me. The kiss was one I reluctantly accepted and rather quickly surrendered to. We kissed for a while, and my heartbeat shifted from a high rate of anger to a high rate of passion.

Leah pulled slightly away and looked at me. She said, "I know you want to be with me as much as I want to be with you." I was silent but understood she was right. That was the truth. Leah returned to the passenger seat, and we both just sat there for a few moments. I then pulled the car back into traffic, and we continued on to Pam's sister's funeral service. All the things that had been building up to this moment had finally come together. I don't know how this relationship can be stopped. I am so attracted to Leah, and it really does feel like love.

We arrived at the church where Jessica's service was being held. Leah and I walked in, sat down, and watched as others entered the church. It was rather awkward because this was Pam's family, and there I was with Leah. Everyone knows what happened to Pam. I could already feel the eyes upon me and Leah passing judgment. This was going to be so awkward.

As we sat there, the first person who came over to me was Jessica's husband, Steve. I immediately stood and hugged him. After all, his wife had just died. Steve and I used to see a lot of each other when Pam and I first started dating seriously. Steve was the type of guy anyone would have a hard time disliking. I told Steve how sorry I was, and he really appeared to be handling this very well. Steve asked me how Pam was doing. I told him she was holding up, but not very well.

"Steve," I said, "this is Leah. Leah is a good friend of mine and she was with Tony before all this happened. Leah and I have been through a lot together with everything that's happened. She and I are supporting one another the best we can." Steve politely expressed to Leah that he was happy to meet her and sorry to hear about what happened with Tony. Leah, behaving impressively cordial, offered a softly spoken reply: "Thank you." Steve then asked me what happened to Tony, how it happened. I explained that he killed himself in his jail cell. I told Steve what I knew and that they really hadn't released much information regarding Tony's death.

Steve went on to express concern for Pam, and I assured him Leah and I were concerned for her as well. Steve and I talked about Jessica and Pam and how they used to have such a love-hate relationship. We both swore there were times they were going to kill each other. But we also agreed and were amazed at just how much they really loved one another.

As we talked with Steve, in the background I could see Pam's mom and dad. It had been so long since we'd seen them. Right now, they must be going through hell. I asked Steve if he knew how they were handling all of this, and he really didn't know. He has been disengaged since Jessica died. I let Steve know how sorry I was again, and he looked at me with immense compassion. He told me how sorry he was for what happened, the loss of my sons, and everything else. I was struggling with all my might not to cry. The empathy I felt for Steve and the absolute emotional void in my heart from losing my sons was enormous.

The service for Jessica was today, and the boys' service was in a few days. There was no way to overcome these feelings. Then, looking past Steve, I noticed Pam's parents heading toward Leah and me. The first thought I had was how hard this must be for them. Pam is in jail, their daughter Jessica has just died, and their two grandchildren have just died. I was so grateful Steve was there, as he served as a buffer because I really didn't know what to expect from Pam's parents.

As they headed toward us, I felt sorrow, fear for myself, and empathy for them. I thought they were going to speak to me, but they both just walked by, glaring at me and Leah with an ice-cold stare. Pam's parents didn't even speak to me; they just walked on by. I wasn't sure exactly why, but I could guess several reasons.

Junior and Jayde were seated, and I cannot even begin to describe the look Jayde gave Leah and me. It was obvious Jayde did not approve of Leah and me attending Pam's sister's service together. When Junior and I made eye contact, he just nodded his head in disappointment.

I was starting to feel the reality of where I was and what had happened as the pastor started his sermon. As I listened to every word, I began to come to terms with the fact that faith was nowhere in my wheelhouse. I heard every word the pastor was saying, but I failed to make any connection to what he was preaching or how I really felt about this about life.

I had never really thought about any of this in great detail before, but for some reason, today at Jessica's service, I was honestly engaged. I glanced over at

Leah; she appeared to have her eyes closed or was looking downward, just listening. She had no physical display that would indicate a reaction to the pastor's words.

Me? Well, I was listening, and I heard every word, but there was a reluctance on my part to let this man's words into my heart. In fact, the unexpected thing was that my mind and soul did not want to let this message in. It was a reflexive, rebellious emotional response to words I was not willing to accept. I continued to listen, wanting to let my guard down, but I just wasn't able to.

When the sermon ended, I felt no comfort from the words spoken. No healing or soothing of emotional pain. I felt nothing. In fact, I'm pretty sure I felt animosity. This God the pastor speaks of is this how He shows His love for us? By taking away the people we love and care about?

I'm not sure why, but it became clear I didn't trust faith, nor was I ready to let it in at least not yet. I have struggled with this for many years, but the recent series of events has created a much bigger separation between me and any possibility of faith. For whatever reason.

In this moment, I felt sadness for Steve and Pam's mom and dad. Steve and Jessica did not have children. It was just the two of them, so I'm sure the road ahead for Steve will be a hard one.

I also felt a sense of loss with Jessica's passing. We were never close, but Jessica did embrace me as Pam's boyfriend before anyone in the family. We may not have been close, but I felt appreciation and gratitude for Jessica and her willingness to guide me as I strove for a relationship with Pam. She was a really caring and giving person.

I felt anger knowing my boys were dead. All of this is just so hard to process. Yet through it all, as I glanced at Leah, I also felt a sense of comfort. Maybe comfort is not the right word, but I can't think of another word to explain how Leah makes me feel right now. I think it was just seeing her and how she is here for me. I realize she didn't have to be with me, be here, or give me a place to live while Pam and I try to work things out.

Leah is the one person I find I can really rely on right now. As the emotional storms ahead promise to challenge the fabric of my soul, it is comforting to have Leah with me.

We all paid our last respects to Jessica by placing a flower on her casket. It was a closed casket service because of the severity of Jessica's injuries. I choked up while paying my respects. I did love Pam's sister, and the reality of her no longer being with us was starting to sink in.

As I walked away from the casket, I fought back tears and did my best to remain strong.

After the service, Pam's mom and dad walked over to me and hugged me. I really believed they were angry with me, but it turned out they were feeling what I was feeling   incredible emotional pain and a sense of loss. We started talking, and I introduced them to Leah.

Once they understood who Leah was, there was a distinct change in their attitude. I explained that Leah and I were going through this together, and that I had not abandoned Pam. I also explained what Leah had gone through and what happened to Tony. I explained how close Leah and Pam were. I explained how close Pam and I, Leah and Tony were, and just how devastating all of this had been for us all.

We went on to discuss what was happening with Pam, and we all started to tear up when we talked about when we would next see one another. We all understood that it would be at Chris and Brian's funeral. Again, I completely broke down right in front of Pam's parents, Leah, Steve, and the remaining guests at the service. Leah was the first to hold me and comfort me. Everyone there kind of had an idea of just how much emotional pain our family had gone through in the past few weeks.

For the first time, my in-laws spoke with me since Pam's arrest and since the death of their daughter Jessica and their grandchildren, my sons, Chris and Brian. It was a very difficult emotional time for us all. I am glad, though. I am glad Pam's mom and dad were there and that we were able to talk again. I know that Pam and I are going through so much, but I also feel so much compassion for Pam's mom and dad, having lost their daughter and grandkids and having to deal with Pam's arrest. As a family, we are all going through so much.

As we walked out of the service together, we got into the car, and I immediately thanked Leah. I so appreciated her support. I asked Leah if she would come with me to the boys' services. Leah just looked at me, kissed me, and then replied, "Yes, of course." On that, we started to drive back home.

It is such an unusual situation. Leah and I are getting so close to one another. I can feel it in my heart and soul. I still love Pam. I do. I really do. But right now, the relationship Leah and I started before this madness all began has morphed into something neither one of us could have ever imagined.

I keep remembering the night at the bar when Leah asked me if I was not with Pam, and she was not with Tony, did I think we could be together? That question has been echoing in my mind for the last few weeks. In such a short period, that question seems to have answered itself just through the way things have played out recently. Not in the way I ever wanted or expected, but still in a way that is so miraculous, so unlikely, yet so necessary.

Leah and I have gone through something that really brought us closer together the kind of closeness only two people who truly care for one another can ever experience. We left the house tonight as two close friends with benefits, and we are returning home as two kindred spirits who have found one another in the most trying of circumstances.

We arrived at the house, went inside, and both agreed we would just sit and talk for a while. Leah wanted to talk about how she came to own the house outright. I told her I really didn't need to know about that, but Leah persisted.

"Paul," she said, "if we are going to be together, we have to discuss things like this." I just looked at Leah and replied, "You're right, I understand. So, on that note, please go on."

Leah told me that when she and Tony first got together, he told her he would buy her a house. Tony really believed Leah and he would be together forever. Leah explained that she did not want or really ask for anything, but Tony was very possessive and insisted.

Leah told me she was in love with Tony and wanted only to please him. She said she really didn't care about the house, but Tony insisted. When Leah and Tony bought the house, it was paid for in cash by Tony. Leah's name was the only name on the deed.

Leah went on to explain that then Tony started to become so possessive. It was like he thought he owned her. This caused most of the tension in their relationship and why Leah found comfort in me.

Leah told me she never intended to be unfaithful, but I treated and looked at her like a gentleman and respected the way she felt. Leah said she really liked how that felt. She felt appreciated, something she explained she never felt when she was with Tony.

Every night when she saw Tony, he became more demanding, obsessive, and verbally abusive. That led to the night when Tony actually hit Leah. Leah told me that running into me that night was the best thing that could have ever happened to her.

Leah explained she always felt she could trust me. And then, before we knew what hit us, Pam and Tony got arrested. Then Tony killed himself, and there was no contesting the house because only Leah's name was on the deed.

I somehow understood why she felt the need to explain this to me, but I looked her straight in the eyes and thanked her for telling me. I really feel the same trust in her that she said she feels in me.

We just hung around for a while longer, watched a little television, and then headed to bed. Once again, we went to the same bedroom and went to sleep together.

Can you see what I mean? Everything was just happening on its own, naturally, like it was something already written. Leah kissed me on the lips, passionately, and said goodnight. She went on to say, "Tomorrow is going to be a hard day for you, Paul. I will be with you all the way. Goodnight."

On that note, as sad as the day was and how hard the morning ahead would be, I was not able to fall asleep for a little while. While trying, I thought about Pam and how she could not be at her sister's funeral, how our sons will be buried tomorrow, and how Pam will not be there either. Something about all this seems so cruel, so wrong.

As I drifted to sleep, I had such mixed emotions about everything going on. This is something I will have to come to terms with. The guilt is killing me inside. Yet, still, I have not come to the realization of just what it all means right now. Right now, I am living moment by moment, with no real interest in looking too far ahead.

CHAPTER 16

I woke to the shrill, insistent cry of the alarm clock. The glowing red numbers read 6:00 AM. My body felt heavy, the kind of weight that comes from a night of restless turning rather than real rest. Pushing the blankets aside, I swung my feet onto the floor and noticed movement Leah was already up.

The faint, comforting aroma of fresh coffee drifted through the air, guiding me toward the kitchen. A pot was already brewing, the quiet drip filling the silence of the morning. But Leah wasn't there. I glanced around no sign of her.

"Leah?" I called, my voice echoing into the empty corners.

No answer.

I decided to pour myself a cup and wait for her to reappear. The mug warmed my hands as I powered on my cell phone. Outside, the sky had that early autumn grayness that promised an unpredictable day. Long Island weather in the fall was never quite sure what it wanted to be sun one minute, wind and chill the next.

A small notification caught my eye one new voicemail. I pressed play. Gabriel's voice came through the speaker, brisk yet warm.

"Good news, Paul! Pam will be allowed to attend today's services. I know this is a hard day for you both, but I wanted you to know she'll be there. I tried hard to get this for Jessica's services, but it didn't happen. This time, the judge signed off on Pam's temporary release into Riverhead Police custody to attend the services for Chris and Brian. Call me when you get this I have things to share."

I froze. A part of me felt deeply relieved Pam would get to say goodbye to our sons. But another part tightened with worry. How would she handle it? Not during the service itself, but afterward, when she would have to walk back into her cell and face the crushing silence again.

I wanted to tell Leah, but she was still nowhere in sight. So I dialed Gabriel back.

He picked up almost instantly. I thanked him, my voice tight, and asked how he had convinced the judge. Gabriel explained that his office had made serious headway in the investigation. There were developments things his team had discovered that he was deeply concerned about.

"Paul," he said, "I want to bring you up to speed on where we are, and where we may be headed over the next few weeks."

I told him again how much I appreciated his efforts. We set a meeting for tomorrow morning at his law offices in Riverhead. Before hanging up, he paused, his tone softening.

"I can't imagine how you and Pam must feel today. Please accept my deepest sympathies for your loss."

I sat in silence for a few seconds, letting the words land.

"Thank you, Gabriel," I said simply, and ended the call.

The side door creaked open. Leah stepped inside, cheeks pink from the cold, hair slightly wind-tossed she'd been out walking or jogging. She crossed the kitchen in a few strides, pressed a kiss to my lips, and asked, "So, Paul, how did you sleep?"

"Not well, Leah," I admitted. "I can't get over all this. It's so sad, and my mind still hasn't caught up to any of it. But I'm glad you're here. Gabriel called with some news Pam will be at the services today."

Leah stilled, her eyes searching mine. "That's… good," she said finally. "It's good she can say goodbye to her sons."

Then she tilted her head. "Will you be able to handle this?"

I took a breath. "It won't be easy, but I have to stand strong for me and for Pam."

She stepped closer and wrapped her arms around me. "I'm going to take a shower," she murmured. "I won't be long."

As she disappeared down the hall, the soft sound of running water filled the space. I refilled my cup, watching the coffee swirl into the dark liquid already there.

All I could think about was how unbearable this has been. How unbearable it still is.

When Pam and I had Chris and Brian, it was the greatest day of our lives. We were overwhelmed with joy. As I drifted into memories, I pictured Jessica with the boys and how much she adored them. She had been a wonderful aunt playful, caring, and always ready to spoil them. I thought about the times Pam and I took the boys to the Long Island Sound, spending entire days at the beach, letting the sun and the sea wash our worries away. Original: "When Pam and I had Chris and Brian, it was like the greatest day of our lives. We were so excited."

I suppose today will be a day of remembering. I just don't know how well I'll handle it, especially once the day is over and the reality sets in again. While I was lost in thought, the phone rang it was Pam's parents. Gabriel had already called them to share the news that Pam would be at the services today. They asked if I needed anything, and I told them I was fine. I promised that if I did, I'd call before the service began.

Still, the uncertainty of how everything would unfold weighed heavily on me. As I ended the call with my in-laws, Leah came out of the bathroom wrapped in a towel and asked if I could help her choose an outfit for the services. At that moment, any distraction was welcome. She led me into the bedroom and tried on a few options. My heart was too heavy for any romantic thoughts, but one outfit stood out simple, black, conservative, and dignified.

Leah wanted to be sure I felt comfortable with her choice, mindful that my in-laws would be there. "I don't want to offend anyone," she said softly. I met her gaze, and we kissed not out of romance or desire, but as an expression of mutual care and understanding. Our situation was far from ordinary, and with each passing day we seemed to grow closer. I wasn't proud of that, but I couldn't deny that having Leah's presence had been a lifeline for me, just as I suspected I had been for her.

After she settled on her outfit, I went to take my shower. In the steam and solitude, the weight of the day crushed me. At first, it was just a few tears, but as the truth sank in that we were about to bury our boys I collapsed to my knees, sobbing uncontrollably. The grief was unbearable. Slowly, I pulled myself together, reminding myself that I had to stay strong for Pam, her parents, and even for myself. That thought gave me just enough strength to stand again.

The boys had been our whole lives, and now they were gone. Leah and I dressed in silence and drove to the church. As we pulled into the parking lot, the sight of police cars confirmed that Pam was already inside. We sat quietly until Leah spoke.

"Paul," she began, "you never talk about your family your mom and dad. Why is that?" She reminded me that even when we all used to go out, Pam and I with Leah and Tony, I never mentioned them.

It wasn't an easy topic, but in that moment, I decided to answer. "Leah, there's not much to tell. My parents and I were never very close. When they found out the boys were born, they tried to connect, but it was too late. My mom died before their first birthday, and after that, my dad and I drifted apart again. He passed away a few years later."

"I'm sorry, Paul," Leah said gently. "Do you have any brothers or sisters?"

"I had a sister," I replied, "but I couldn't tell you where she is or what she's doing. I'm basically alone now just Pam, and you." My voice cracked. "I don't know how I'm going to get through today."

Leah looked at me with steady, sincere eyes. "No matter what, I'll be here for you." She took my hand, and together, we stepped out of the car and walked toward the church.

As we walked up the stairs, I honestly didn't know what to expect once we got inside. All I knew was that I wasn't looking forward to seeing Pam. Don't misunderstand me   it wasn't that I didn't want to see her; it was the reality of what was about to happen settling in. As I approached the church doors, anxiety and sadness weighed heavily on me. If I was feeling this way, I couldn't imagine how Pam was coping.

Leah and I pushed open the church doors and stepped into the lobby, then moved to the pews. In just a few moments, Pam and I would be burying our sons.

A kind man escorted Leah and me to our seats in the front row, close to the altar. Pam wasn't there yet. Junior and Jayde sat nearby but didn't even look our way. I think Jayde was still really upset with me, and being there with Leah certainly didn't help. Both Junior and Jayde clearly disapproved of me being with Leah   and I think they knew it was more than just friendship. Considering how close Jayde was to Pam, I guess I could understand her feelings.

Scanning the room, I saw my brother-in-law Steve and Pam's parents sitting nearby. I recognized many of Pam's relatives   people I hadn't seen in years, some who probably attended our wedding. I fought to hold back my tears. Looking at the altar, I saw the coffins and summoned every ounce of strength to stay strong. Chris and Brian were so young, so full of life and now they were gone, their lives cut tragically short.

My thoughts turned to God and faith, and I asked myself: what kind of God would do this? What kind of God would take my children from me? My faith felt like it was slipping away as my questions multiplied and answers remained absent.

Then, in the right corner of the room, I saw Pam. She was dressed up, not handcuffed, but closely watched and escorted by two armed guards. Watching her walk toward her seat, I noticed her stoic, emotionless expression. She looked thin, her face drawn.

I stood up. Pam and I shared a moment that felt endless as we locked eyes. Emotions boiled inside me, and I knew I was ready to break. Then I noticed tears in her eyes one, then another, and another. As Pam broke down, so did I.

We embraced, holding each other tighter than we had in a long time. I felt her pain, and she felt mine. In that moment of raw emotion, Pam and I became who we once were filled with love and compassion that had been buried beneath years of turmoil.

As we separated, Leah stood and hugged Pam. To my surprise, they held each other tightly, both crying a lot. I had forgotten just how close Pam and Leah had become over the years. They really were good friends.

How things turned out the way they have is something I cannot explain. I realize that men who love their wives do not cheat on them, and good friends aren't supposed to be interested in their friend's husbands yet here we all are. One thing that cannot be denied in all of this is that the real feelings we all have cannot be discarded. In such tragedy, self-reflection and faith are our ways of getting through it all.

As I watched Pam and Leah, I thought about how things used to be. I wish we could somehow go back in time, but we cannot. When Pam and Leah finished, we all sat down, and the preacher was about to speak.

Jayde and Junior walked over to us. Jayde hugged Pam first, then Junior did the same. They both looked at me and whispered, "We are so sorry for your loss." Then they returned to their seats.

The service was about to begin. We sat in silence for a moment, but my mind drifted into a cold place as anger welled up inside me. This anger came out of nowhere but stemmed from what was happening now.

The services started, and we listened to a man of faith try to spiritually explain the death of two young men   my boys.

The preacher spoke about how God has a plan and how we are all part of it. We may never understand why these things happen because we don't get to see the plan. We must have faith in God's plan.

As I listened, anger, resentment, sadness, and confusion built inside me. I still couldn't see the light. I couldn't understand how God could take these two boys away from Pam and me. No matter what the preacher said or the words he chose, nothing could make me accept what he was trying to convey.

Of course, I listened like everyone else. I stood when they stood, sat when they sat, but inside, I reveled in my own silent form of emotional torture and went through the motions.

Then it was time to pay our last respects. The service was closed-casket because the car accident that took Chris and Brian was so devastating there was no way the boys could be made presentable.

Pam and I were the first to rise and walk toward the caskets. We were given flowers to place on them.

It was the hardest thing we had ever done, both as individuals and as a couple. They say burying a child is the hardest thing a parent can do. I had heard that before but never gave it much thought until now, living through it with Pam.

There really are no words to describe what I am feeling right now.

As we placed our flowers on the caskets, we broke down again and held each other. The grief was unbearable. No matter how much we comforted one another, it was clear this pain wouldn't subside anytime soon.

As we walked away from the caskets and reached the floor, the guards came for Pam. It was clear she had to leave.

As they took her, I let her hand go and started walking back toward our seats. Leah joined me and walked beside me for a moment.

We stopped, standing with everyone else, still in disbelief. Leah held my arm, pulled me close, and hugged me. Her gesture was sincere; she genuinely tried to comfort me.

I think Leah understood that nothing could make this better for me. Still, just like she has been doing since Pam's arrest, Leah is assuming the role of my wife.

I know that's a harsh thing to say, but the truth is Leah and I have become for one another what we

both once had   like Pam and I once were, and like
Tony and Leah once were.

When two people share an experience like what
Leah and I are sharing right now, there is bound to
be some commonality a sense of companionship in
an otherwise impossible emotional situation.

Leah and I said goodbye to everyone at the service
and headed back home. In the car, we remained
mostly quiet. There was little to say because, after
all, what could possibly be said after something like
this?

As we pulled away from our parking spot, we saw
the police cars leaving with Pam back to Riverhead.
All of this had really taken a toll on me, and I could
see Leah starting to become emotionally affected as
well.

For a while, I thought Leah was unemotional and
disengaged, but slowly, surely, the more we went
through this together, the more Leah opened up.

I was so emotionally drained. As Leah and I pulled
into our driveway, Leah asked, "Paul, would you
mind if we just went inside and did nothing?" She
continued, "I think you could use some quiet time to
think and be alone. I could go to my room and leave
you be for a while if you need time."

I replied, "Leah, I would like to be alone, but at the
same time, I want us to spend this time together.

Alone, together. I appreciate you so much and want you to be with me   to get me through this. Nothing more than two people supporting one another. I really do need someone right now, and I could think of no one else but you, Leah, to get me through this time."

Leah turned to me and kissed me gently on the lips. She said, "Anything you need, I am here for you."

With that, we went inside and did just that. We did nothing. We sat alone, together, reflecting on the last few months as we both had so much to process.

After all, next on the list of unpleasant events was Pam's murder trial. Everything was happening so rapidly. Leah was right to recommend that we take some time today to be alone. Maybe it was just what we needed before the firestorm of Pam's trial began.

Leah and I started to talk as we unwound from the stress of the day. We discussed our families and how we ended up here.

One thing that intrigued me was that Leah has a sister named Lydia. Lydia and Leah are identical twins.

Leah talked about Lydia, her mom Leanne, and her life. She told me how her father and brother died in a car crash, and how traumatizing that was for her mom, Lydia, and herself.

Leah asked about my family, and I didn't have much to add to the conversation.

We drifted into other subjects and then began to reminisce about how we met and how we both felt when we first saw each other.

I was surprised to learn Leah felt the same way I did initially   the day Tony and I met and talked in front of my house. I had no idea Leah felt the same attraction toward me as I felt toward her.

Leah and I both had drinking problems, so when we talked like this, the more we dove into our feelings, the more we drank. We were both buzzed when we finally called it a night.

Hours passed, and we were both tired.

In my mind, I struggled with my feelings for Leah and my feelings for Pam. I was emotionally struggling with the loss of Chris and Brian.

Those emotions came and went. They overwhelmed me at times and then receded, allowing me to recover for a while.

This emotional wave rolled in and rolled back out. It just hurt so much.

The unpredictable turn my life had taken left me unprepared to deal with reality.

In this moment, my life felt like I was living in some kind of dream   maybe, at times, some kind of nightmare.

Little by little, glimpses of sanity were visible through the cracks in my psyche.

As a man who feels broken and lost, Leah seemed to be the only light.

CHAPTER 17

Yesterday feels like a blur. Waking up this morning feels strange. When I opened my eyes, sunlight was peeking through the window blinds. Leah was still asleep next to me.

Glancing at the alarm clock, I realized I hadn't set it last night. It was already 8:45 AM.

As I tried to get out of bed, I looked again at Leah. She was still sleeping so peaceful, so tranquil. She looked beautiful. She had become so special to me amid life's maze of confusion.

When things between Leah and me started, I never planned for anything beyond a fantasy that lived only in my head. But as time went by and all the craziness unfolded, Leah became so much more. She became real.

Don't get me wrong I still love my wife. But my wife is in prison, and the one constant in my life amid everything has been Leah.

I lay there watching her, both in admiration of her beauty and with the growing realization that my feelings for her were deepening. It was no longer just attraction. I felt myself falling in love with Leah.

As Leah began to open her eyes and stretch, the first thing I did was kiss her. She smiled as she woke and kissed me back.

We had both been through a rough stretch.

As we got out of bed, Leah asked if I wanted some breakfast.

"Sure," I said. "If you're in the mood to make it, I'm definitely in the mood to have some with you."

Starting the morning, I turned on my phone. Within moments, there was a message from Gabriel.

I played the voicemail.

"Paul, when you get this message, please call me. My team and I have new information and want to bring you up to speed. We want to get you prepped early because you and Leah will be taking the stand as character witnesses for Pam."

I immediately called Gabriel back. He answered after two rings.

"Hey, Gabriel," I said. "I'm just calling you back. What's the plan?"

Gabriel responded, "Paul, can you and Leah meet me at the law office today? We have some information to share and want to discuss the trial."

"Sure," I replied. "I'll ask Leah, but I'll definitely be there. What time?"

"How about 11:00 AM?" Gabriel asked.

"That's fine. I'll be there," I said.

After hanging up, I asked Leah if she could come with me, but she told me she was supposed to meet the new owner of "The Rock n Roll Bourbon Cafe."

Leah and I were both between jobs right now, and she wanted to see if she could meet the new owner. Leah hoped to get back to bartending. After everything that had happened, Eastern Long Island was a mess. The murders and the economy had really taken a toll on the local nightlife in this part of Long Island.

Leah told me she would meet the new owner and encouraged me to meet with Gabriel by myself. Of course, I was fine with that. It was really an informal meeting to update me on where we stood in this legal situation.

I wasn't sure what to expect, but I had gotten to know Gabriel over the last few months, and I felt like he was genuinely trying to do the best for Pam.

With that in mind, the plan was set: Leah would meet the new owner of the Rock n Roll Bourbon Café, and I would head over to meet Gabriel to get an update on the investigation and the courtroom strategy he had been working on.

I finished my eggs and coffee, then headed over to Gabriel's office. Leah and I only had one car, so I was ready to drive to the law office, and Leah planned to walk to the bar since it was just a few blocks away.

Gabriel met me in the lobby of the law offices. We exchanged some cordial conversation before agreeing to sit down in his office to discuss where we were in the investigation.

"Paul," Gabriel began, "I want you to brace yourself for this because my team hasn't been able to figure it out, but this is where we are. The trial starts in a few days, and the prosecution has overwhelming evidence against Pam and Tony. With Tony being dead, there is only Pam, and this is the impossible situation we find ourselves in. You're aware of the DNA found at the crime scenes, correct?"

I just nodded. This was not the start I was hoping for. I asked Gabriel to continue.

"Paul," he said, "we came across email exchanges between Tony and Pam. Some are very incriminating, and others might make you angry."

Gabriel continued, "Paul, take a look at this series of emails and text exchanges. There are many of them, but the most concerning for this trial are the emails and texts that spell out how Tony and Pam chose their victims. Everything is right there in the exchanges."

"The prosecution released this evidence to our team yesterday. With the DNA evidence and these emails and texts, we have very little hope of clearing Pam."

While Gabriel talked, I kept reading the emails and texts. As I scrolled through them, I came across several exchanges where Pam and Tony were intimate in their conversations. These messages were written by two people who were more than colleagues or friends.

As I read more, I realized just how close Pam and Tony really were.

"Gabriel," I asked, "is it possible these emails and texts are fake?"

"We're still trying to authenticate them," he replied, "but they appear to be real."

I paused for a moment, and all I could think was that my wife was not only unfaithful but also a complete stranger I thought I knew but obviously didn't.

"Paul," Gabriel said, placing his hand on my shoulder, "listen, this is all the evidence we have. We can't be certain these emails and texts are real. In fact, my plan is to create reasonable doubt for the jury that they're not real or at least that there's a possibility they're not."

I replied, "That's all well and good, but after seeing this, how can I ever trust Pam again? I know she's in a prison cell until we prove her innocence, but at this stage, I'm really worried. I'm worried for a few reasons, but mainly because after seeing this, I don't believe Pam. I honestly think she did this."

Gabriel paused for a moment and gathered his thoughts before responding. "Paul," he said, "I understand how you're feeling, but we are not going to stop investigating. We're going to see this through."

After this meeting with Gabriel, I really lost any confidence in the possibility that Pam was innocent. After reading the emails and text messages, I concluded that when I thought I was losing my wife and feeling all alone, there was a legitimate reason for that feeling. I really was losing my wife, and I really was all alone.

"Paul," I said, "I really have to go. I want to go. I really need to process this information."

Gabriel responded, "Paul, I really need you and Leah to be prepared for this trial. The two of you may be our best chance at creating reasonable doubt."

I replied, "I'm not so sure if I personally can get on the stand and be a character witness after what I've just learned. Don't get me wrong I love Pam, but by the same token, my love for her and faith in her innocence was before I learned that maybe Pam wasn't so innocent. It's going to take me a little while to come to terms with this."

Gabriel responded rather directly, "Don't take too much time because your wife's life may hang in the balance."

I stood up and yelled at Gabriel, "Did you read this stuff?" Then I read aloud, "'Tony, after this kill, I want you to make love to me. I want to feel this excitement with you.'"

I asked, "How do you expect me to just move forward after reading that?"

Gabriel was silent and understandably so because what I just read would cause anyone to pause. No other words were exchanged between Gabriel and me. On that note, we parted ways.

I was going to head back home. Letting all of this sink in would take some time.

As I headed back to the house, I happened to catch Leah walking toward the front door on the walkway. Leah saw me and waited. I walked up to her and asked if we could talk for a moment.

We both went inside, and I told Leah what Gabriel had revealed to me. I told her that Pam and Tony may have been cheating on both of us for some time.

Leah firmly replied, "I know that, and I know that you must have known that too."

I responded, "I did not know that."

"Well then, Paul," Leah said, "you're not all that bright."

Leah spoke those words with a firmness and harshness that cut right through me. I felt like Leah had just stabbed me with a dagger through my chest.

"You knew?" I asked.

"Yes, Paul, I knew," Leah replied. She went on, "Tony was a major fraud, and he was an emotional manipulator as well. He emotionally abused me for a few years and manipulated me to stay with him."

Leah continued, "I knew he was seducing Pam. The night you picked me up was the night I found out Tony was sleeping with Pam. I confronted Tony, and that's when he hit me. I ran out the door, and fortunately, I found you."

"That's why when we were alone together in the car, I made love to you," Leah said. "I made love to you because you and I were trying so hard to keep our attraction at bay. All the while, your wife Pam and my boyfriend Tony were already not only sleeping together, but obviously much, much more intimate in other ways."

"I'm so sorry," Leah said.

"Paul, I want us to be together. Remember that night in the bar, you told me that maybe someday we could revisit the thought of the two of us being together. Paul, I think that time is now. You need me."

"I do need you," I replied. "I appreciate all you have done to help me through this. Through it all, you have been my guardrail."

Leah and I went inside and the first thing we did was have a few drinks. Then we talked for a while.

Leah told me she had met the new owner of the Rock n Roll Bourbon Café and that they were planning a grand opening in 30 days. Leah said the new owner, Jonie Miller, had hired her for a bartending position.

"That's great, Leah," I replied.

What had happened during all of this madness was that the café had closed down, and Leah was out of a job. At the same time, I was out of work as well.

Leah seemed very excited to be going back to bartending.

As far as I was concerned, I had sent out several resumes but really had nothing yet. The economy was still rough, and in my line of work sales it's hard to sell stuff when people just don't have money to buy.

But it did appear that things were improving, so maybe, just maybe, I would find something soon.

Until now, Leah hadn't asked me for rent, and I had the cash from the sale of Pam and my house in the bank. That cash was for whatever the trial sent our way.

But I have to share this with you: after what I learned today, I was this close to just letting Pam go. I mean, why should I be there for her after all that I learned?

Leah could see I was really struggling with the whole thing. She asked me to grab my guitar and play for her. I know she knew that music would clear my mind, if only for a little while.

So, I did. I played for a little while, and then Leah asked if I wanted her to sing to me. Of course, I couldn't deny that.

She really has such an amazing voice.

I asked her to sing whatever her heart desired.

Leah started singing "Goodbye to You" by Scandal. I knew the chords, so we did an acoustic version of the song.

The ironic thing was that Leah resembled a young Patty Smyth. She had it all going on the dark hair, the right clothes, the seductive movements. Even her raspy singing voice was spot on.

After this heartbreaking day, Leah and I spent the afternoon and evening at home. We drank and flirted playfully with one another well into the early evening. Then Leah got up from the couch and told me to wait there that she would be right back. Of course, I waited, feeling sedated and relaxed.

When Leah returned, she came into the room wearing a very sexy outfit. Her hair was pulled back into a ponytail just like she used to wear it when she bartended. She had on sheer stockings, a garter belt, and a see-through top. I was in awe, and I just melted into her.

We were together, and this time it was with a feeling of tranquility, as we both could not deny we had been waiting for this moment for some time possibly from the very moment we first met.

When we were together the first time, we were well aware of the dangers, and we knew we were doing something forbidden. That was then before the emails and text messages between Tony and Pam were made available to me. That time felt like a mistake. I personally felt guilty because I knew I was being unfaithful to Pam.

Tonight, with Tony dead and Pam seemingly having given up on our marriage long ago, Leah and I finally felt a level of approval and comfort in letting ourselves go and being together. No guilt, no regrets just us. It was the most amazing feeling I have had in a long time.

I once thought Pam was the love of my life, but I have had such strong feelings for Leah for so long, and now it just feels like the time is right.

After Leah and I were done, we embraced for a while and talked. I told Leah I was thinking of asking Pam for a divorce.

Leah asked, "Do you think that's a good idea? Won't that just complicate things?"

I thought about what Leah said and replied, "Leah, it's the right thing to do. If you and I are going to take our relationship further, I have to divorce Pam."

We talked about it for a while, and eventually, she agreed that this would be best.

It's so unusual to feel this way about Leah. I really believed I would spend the rest of my life with Pam yet here I am with Leah. Honestly, when I look at her, I feel so much love for this girl.

As our conversation ended and we found warmth in each other's embrace, we eventually fell asleep in one another's arms.

It was a crazy day, but as I lay there falling asleep, I finally felt a sense of calm. It feels like Leah and I are really meant to be together.

CHAPTER 18

We woke up to the sound of the doorbell this morning. As I got out of bed and headed to the door, the doorbell rang again. Leah was still asleep. I opened the door, and there was Gabriel.

"Paul," he said, "sorry to bother you so early, but we need to discuss some things about the case."

I replied, "Gabriel, I'm having second thoughts about taking the stand for Pam as a character witness. In fact, I want to ask her for a divorce."

Gabriel paused for a moment and said, "Paul, I get that, but without you and Leah, our case gets even weaker. It's already weak enough."

I asked, "Do you believe the emails and text messages are real?"

Gabriel responded, "I don't know. Our team is diving deep into these emails and text messages to find anything that could exonerate Pam."

I said, "At this point, my desire to help Pam is next to nothing."

Gabriel asked, "Paul, can you give us a few days? At least to authenticate the evidence, the source?"

I reluctantly agreed, and we ended the conversation on that note.

Leah must have heard us because shortly after the conversation with Gabriel, she walked through the bedroom door into the living room.

"What was that all about?" Leah asked.

I told her that despite the emails, texts, and DNA evidence, Gabriel believes Pam is innocent or at least that there's a way to create reasonable doubt.

"Leah," I said, "I have to tell you that after seeing all this information, my desire to help Pam has significantly diminished. Gabriel has asked for a few days to gather more information and investigate further."

Leah said, "Gabriel said that without our testimony, their case may not have a chance."

She looked at me for what felt like quite a while, then asked, "Paul, what should we do? Even with what we've learned, Pam is still your wife. Pam is still my close friend."

Leah continued, "I know how messed up things have gotten with you and me and everything that's happened. We both have to pause and think about this. None of us are immune from sin here, Paul. We've all made mistakes, myself included. Pam is as human as you or I. No one really knows what happened except Pam."

She went on to say that she doesn't believe what happened between her and me was a mistake. In fact, she insisted it was meant to be our destiny.

"Paul," Leah said, "we are meant to be together."

As I listened to Leah, as crazy as it sounds, I realized I really feel the same way.

Leah and I spent the rest of the day focused on getting prepared for work. Leah is set to start bartending at the bar in just a few days, while I've been filling out resumes and sending them to companies, hoping to land some interviews. We shared lunch together and afterward took a long walk along the Long Island Sound.

Most of the time we spent walking hand in hand, simply talking. Mostly, we talked about us. Leah asked me if I had thought about our future together. Given everything that has happened, I found it a bit odd, but at the same time, I felt a flicker of excitement and curiosity. I hadn't expected Leah to feel this way, and discussing our relationship seemed somewhat out of bounds. But then I thought to myself haven't Leah and I already crossed so many boundaries during all of this?

So, I warmed to the conversation. Leah and I spoke not just as lovers, not just as friends, but like two people in love, openly discussing how we saw our lives moving forward. The conversation was surprisingly refreshing and stimulating. For a little while, Leah this beautiful woman managed to take my mind off Pam and all that has happened over these difficult months.

After leaving the beach, we stopped for dinner at a cozy little place called "The Elbow Room" in Jamesport. Leah and I enjoyed each other's company it truly felt like a date. It's hard to explain, given everything going on, but here's how I see it: Leah and I have come to terms with the reality that what we've wanted for so long has suddenly become not only possible, but permissible in our minds.

After everything we learned about Pam and Tony, Leah and I felt validated. I'm not even sure if that's the perfect word, but it's the only one that fits right now. We now see a path forward an opportunity for us to be together. The way we connected tonight felt like turning a page, and I was genuinely excited about the next chapter of our lives.

Even though we've been through so much, we've faced it all together. Maybe that's why we feel so close.

After dinner, we returned to Leah's place. I suppose I should start calling it our place it's becoming just that with each passing day that I live with her. We decided to turn in early because the first day of Pam's trial starts in the morning. As I lay in bed next to Leah, a sense of peace washed over me something I hadn't felt in a very long time. And with that, I slowly drifted off to sleep. Tomorrow is a big day, and we want to be ready.

CHAPTER 19

Leah and I woke up, had breakfast, and then drove to the courthouse in Riverhead. We didn't talk much along the way both of us were apprehensive, unsure of what to expect. After parking, we walked up the stairs to the lobby, where Gabriel and his team were waiting. Gabriel quickly updated Leah and me on the status of the case and what we should anticipate on this first day of trial.

He explained that the prosecution would open by presenting their case this is how the trial begins. Gabriel advised us to simply listen and pay close attention to the prosecution's arguments. He also reminded us that, even though the trial had started, his team was still working hard behind the scenes to uncover anything that could create reasonable doubt in the jury's mind.

Now that Leah and I were up to speed on the process, we all entered the courtroom and took our seats, waiting silently. We remained seated until the judge entered the room. Then, just like on television, a voice called out, "All rise. The Honorable Judge Justine Conte…"

Hearing those words felt surreal like I was trapped in some kind of dream. I knew it wasn't, but it still felt that way. Then came the instruction: "Please be seated."

The judge then asked, "Are the people ready to proceed?"
"We are, Your Honor," responded Donna Rose, the prosecutor.

Leah and I sat quietly in the gallery, glancing toward Pam seated with her legal team.
Gabriel held her hand firmly, while Pam remained expressionless.
She was clean, dressed neatly, and appeared calm.

Pam's eyes briefly met mine and Leah's, though her face gave away no emotion.
Looking around, I noticed a few familiar faces from our neighborhood in the courtroom.
The media frenzy surrounding this case never ceases to amaze me.

Junior and Jayde were present as well. The cold looks Jayde gave me spoke volumes.
If looks could kill, I would have been dead multiple times over by now.
I won't pretend I don't understand her feelings   I do, completely.

I know how this all looks from the outside.
Leah and I aren't trying to justify anything; we're just trying to move forward and survive this ordeal.
Are we wrong? Bad people? Only someone in our shoes could truly answer that.

The courtroom fell silent as the prosecutor began her opening statement:

"Ladies and gentlemen of the jury, we stand here today to bring justice for fourteen victims.
We will prove beyond a reasonable doubt that Tony Santos and Pam Turner conspired to commit murder.
DNA evidence places both Tony Santos and Pam Turner at each of the fourteen crime scenes.
We have emails and text messages exchanged between the two, revealing their chilling plans.
We will show the timeline of each murder, aligning perfectly with the evidence presented.

At the conclusion of this case, we believe you will have no choice but to find Pam Turner guilty of fourteen counts of first-degree murder."

With that, the prosecutor returned to her seat.

Gabriel, Pam's attorney, stood and approached the jury.
Leaning against the petition wall, he began his opening statement:
"The prosecution will present DNA evidence they claim links my client to these crimes.
They will show emails and texts alleging conspiracy.
They intend to tarnish Pam Turner's character and make you dislike her.
But what they cannot do is prove her guilt beyond a reasonable doubt.

Pam Turner is innocent of these charges.
When the prosecution's smoke clears, you will see

there is more than one reasonable doubt.
And you must find Pam Turner not guilty."

Leah and I were paying close attention, and the seriousness of this trial began to sink in. We both understood the gravity of what had happened but had been too wrapped up in our own little world to truly grasp just how serious it all was. Now, sitting here in the courtroom, witnessing everything firsthand, the weight of it all was very sobering.

The prosecuting attorney then called her first witness. "Your Honor, I call Brian Evans to the stand."

Leah and I watched as Brian Evans took the stand. He stood about 5'11" tall with brown hair. He walked with a limp and spoke softly. Brian Evans did not appear very confident but seemed likable.

The court clerk swore him in. "Do you swear or affirm that you will tell the truth, the whole truth, and nothing but the truth, so help you God?"

"I do," Mr. Evans replied.

The prosecutor began, "Mr. Evans, how did you know Tony Santos?"

"I had known Tony for many years. We went to high school together and stayed friends for a time afterward," he answered.

"Where did you attend high school?" the prosecutor asked.

"Trenton High School," Mr. Evans replied.

"Is that here on Long Island?" she continued.

"No," Mr. Evans chuckled, "it's in New Jersey."

"If I were to ask you what kind of person Tony Santos was, how would you describe him?"

"He was a very nice person, but unstable at times," Mr. Evans answered.

Gabriel immediately objected, "Objection! Is Mr. Evans qualified as a psychiatrist?"

Judge Conte responded promptly, "Sustained."

The prosecutor quickly rephrased, "Let me rephrase, Your Honor. Mr. Evans, how would you describe Tony Santos based on your personal experience as a friend in high school and later?"

"I would have to say Tony was somewhat unstable. He was very unpredictable," Mr. Evans repeated.

"Was Tony ever violent? Did he get into a lot of trouble in high school? Fights, arguments?"

"Yes, he was always fighting someone or arguing about something," Mr. Evans replied.

"Last question," the prosecutor said, "Do you believe Tony Santos was the kind of man who could kill someone? Just your opinion as a friend, not as an expert."

Mr. Evans answered, "Tony had a temper and a mean streak, so I wouldn't be surprised if he hurt or killed someone. When I found out, I wasn't surprised."

"I have no further questions for this witness," the prosecutor concluded.

Gabriel stood and began his cross-examination. "Mr. Evans, you claim it wouldn't be out of the realm of possibility for Tony Santos to kill someone. Am I correct?"

Mr. Evans answered very confidently, "Yes." Gabriel continued, "And how well do you know Pam Turner?" The witness quickly responded, "I have never met Pam Turner." Then Gabriel said something that caused the entire courtroom to pause. "So, you think Tony is capable of these crimes. Is it possible that Tony is responsible and that my client, Pam, had nothing to do with these killings?" Mr. Evans paused, then replied, "Yes, I suppose that is possible."

The prosecution immediately objected. Donna Rose said, "Calls for speculation! Your Honor, Mr. Evans is not a psychic and cannot be allowed to speculate on such an absurd question."

A very confident Gabriel looked at the judge and said, "Withdrawn. No more questions." He then walked back to his seat.

Leah and I both felt a little different after that cross-examination. Maybe there is a path forward for Pam. Gabriel appeared solid.

Then the prosecution called their next witness. "Your Honor, we call forensic examiner James Kelly to the stand." Leah and I watched as Mr. Kelly took the stand and was sworn in. Mr. Kelly was a short man, standing about 5'4" tall. He had straight, dark black hair and wore glasses.

The prosecuting attorney, Donna Rose, stood and approached the witness stand. "Mr. Kelly," she said, "what can you tell us about the DNA gathered from these 14 crime scenes?"

Mr. Kelly explained, "We tested DNA from all 14 crime scenes collected during the investigations. We found that the DNA matches are all within 5 percent, or the margin of error, as matches for both the defendant Pam Turner and the recently deceased Tony Santos."

He continued, "The margin of error with DNA evidence can vary depending on several factors, including the quality of the sample, the methods used for analysis, and the laboratory conducting the test. Generally, DNA evidence is highly reliable."

The prosecuting attorney then asked, "What is the probability that Pam Turner and Tony Santos committed these crimes?"

Mr. Kelly answered, "I cannot answer that, but I would say the probability that they were physically present at each crime scene is extremely high."

"Thank you, Mr. Kelly. We have no further questions," the prosecuting attorney said.

Gabriel then stood and approached the witness stand. "Mr. Kelly, you just testified that the margin of error with DNA evidence can vary depending on several factors, including the quality of the sample, the methods used for analysis, and the laboratory conducting the test. Generally, DNA evidence is highly reliable. Is that correct?"

"Yes sir, that is what I said," Mr. Kelly responded.

Gabriel asked, "Would you say that DNA evidence is a perfect science and is not infallible?"

Mr. Kelly paused, preparing his answer, but Gabriel pressed him, repeating firmly, "I asked if DNA evidence is infallible."

"No, it is not infallible," Mr. Kelly replied.

"So, what you are saying is that this evidence really is not a perfect science. You are saying that we should have reasonable doubt as to the reliability of the DNA evidence presented here today. Is that what you are saying, Mr. Kelly?" Gabriel asked.

Mr. Kelly reluctantly replied, "Yes sir, no sir, well, not exactly." He appeared shaken, as if taken off guard.

Gabriel said, "I have no more questions for this witness," and confidently returned to his seat. To me and I'm certain to everyone in the courtroom, he won that first round of questioning.

Judge Justine Conte then said, "This court is in recess until 9:00 AM tomorrow morning." She rose and left the courtroom, and everyone else stood as well.

Leah and I walked up to Pam and Gabriel. Pam was silent; I simply hugged her and asked Gabriel how he thought the first day went.

Paul, he said, "I think we just treaded water today." He continued, "I still have my investigators diligently working to find any evidence that could discredit the emails and text messages the prosecution will introduce to the jury tomorrow."

Leah looked at Pam, then walked up and hugged her. They held each other tightly for some time. Both had tears in their eyes when they finally let go.

Then Pam spoke very quietly to Leah, "Please take care of my husband." She repeated, "Leah, please be sure to take care of Paul for me." Gabriel and I exchanged looks it was the first time Pam had spoken in quite a while. Leah simply met Pam's gaze and replied, "I will, Pam. Believe me, I will."

At that moment, I hugged Pam. Although she said nothing more to me, I understood how much she had been through, and how much she was still enduring. Soon after, the officers escorted Pam away.

I asked Gabriel, "Is there anything you need from us right now?" He shook my hand and said, "No, just pray for your wife."

It was then that I realized, despite how well Gabriel performed in court today, he understood the mountain of evidence against Pam. I sensed in his gut that he doubted he could win this case. Still, he did an impressive job, and I felt a glimmer of hope I hadn't expected. Maybe I was jumping the gun being so angry about those emails and texts. Could it be possible Pam didn't write them? I don't know. Though I want to believe it, I am still reeling from what I read. I cannot unread those words they have affected me deeply, emotionally and psychologically.

Leah and I left the courthouse and headed home. Leah asked if we could stop at the Rock n Roll Bourbon Café. It was close to happy hour, and she wanted to see what changes had been made. Leah was excited to go back to work there, and honestly,

I looked forward to seeing the place and having a drink. After today, I think we both needed one.

Walking into the bar felt special to me because it was here that I really fell for Leah. This was the place where we opened up to one another as friends, sharing conversations that helped us through difficult times. Not much had changed except for some new decorations and pictures on the walls.

Leah and I walked up to the bar. It was empty no bartender, no one but us. Music played softly. As we stood there talking, a woman emerged from the back room. She stood about 5'6", dressed in jeans and a tight T-shirt. Her light brown hair was cut to shoulder length. She walked with the confident strut of someone who owned the place.

Leah immediately went over and hugged her. Leah called to me, "Paul, I want you to meet Jonie Frazer, the new owner of this place." I walked over and introduced myself. Jonie and I started talking.

Jonie said she used to own a bar in Brentwood, Long Island, but sold it and moved on because the neighborhood declined. "As good as the bar was to me over the years, the community went downhill," she explained. She wanted to give eastern Long Island a chance, which seemed like a much better place.

Jonie talked about her plans for the bar and how excited she was to have Leah involved. Turning to me, she said, "Leah told me this is the place where you two got together." I instinctively replied, "Yes, it is." At the same time, part of me worried Leah might share something so personal with a relative stranger. But that feeling quickly faded. What Leah told Jonie was true.

Sometimes I feel bad about everything about Pam being locked up while Leah and I started our relationship. Deep down, I want to divorce Pam, but with all she's going through, it doesn't feel right to throw that on her now. Even with all the evidence of her unfaithfulness and deceit, it just doesn't feel right.

I'm so wrapped up in these emotions that I don't want to share them with Leah or anyone else.

Jonie then asked, "Can I get the two of you something to drink?" Leah and I looked at each other and simultaneously asked for a shot of Jim Beam with a beer chaser. We smiled at one another like teenagers on a first date.

When I look at Leah, I feel like the luckiest man alive. She's stunningly beautiful with such a soft, emotional, and creative side. We've grown so close I can't imagine life without her.

Jonie served our drinks and had one herself. We toasted to whatever lies ahead. One drink turned into two, then three. It was just Leah, Jonie, and me at the bar. There was a pool table, so we shot pool for a while. Leah and Jonie really hit it off.

After a few hours, Leah and I had to go. We thanked Jonie; she seemed like a genuinely nice person.

Back at Leah's place, she wanted to keep the party going. We broke out more drinks and, to my surprise, Leah had some cocaine. She laid it out on a glass cutting board in the kitchen, and we each did a few lines.

We drank more and then started talking really talking. We were high, but we needed that to face the guilt we both felt for what we were doing behind Pam's back.

Eventually, the talking stopped. Leah and I began kissing, then made love in the living room. If there was any doubt about our attraction or love, it was gone that night. It was one of the most passionate nights we had shared.

When it was over, we went to bed. I held Leah close, but neither of us could sleep, still wired from the cocaine. We talked on and off until we finally drifted off. We both knew we had to get rest tomorrow was another big day at trial, and we had to be ready.

CHAPTER 20

Leah and I got up, both feeling a little beat up after the events of last night. We barely spoke, grabbed a quick breakfast, and then headed to Riverhead. We arrived right on time and made our way into the courtroom, taking our seats in the gallery. We both looked exhausted. Gabriel and Pam were already seated at the defendant's table.

Then came the announcement: "All rise." The honorable Judge Justine Conte presided. "Court is now in session." Judge Conte walked to the bench and sat down. "Please be seated," she said.

The prosecution began their case. Donna Rose, the prosecutor, started speaking: "Your Honor, I call Detective Rick Simmons to the stand." Rick Simmons, standing about six feet tall with dark hair and a commanding presence, walked deliberately to the witness stand. After being sworn in, Donna Rose began her line of questioning.

"Mr. Simmons, you were one of the investigators present when Pam Turner and Tony Santos were apprehended, is that correct?"

"Yes, I was," Mr. Simmons replied.

"During your investigation, you focused on Tony and Pam after examining the crime scenes. Why?"

"We were contacted by an anonymous employee of the rehab center who provided concerning details about the murders in our area. The employee wished to remain anonymous but informed us they believed there was a connection between the rehab center and the victims. They reported observing several arguments between clients and both Pam and Tony, mostly regarding billing issues."

"Clients discovered their insurance companies were being charged for services not rendered. This employee gave us records and names, which helped us piece together what happened and why."

"We launched an investigation into the rehab center. After executing a subpoena, we obtained the client list and matched several victims to that list. We also found questionable billing practices in the victims' files. We believe these victims were killed to keep them quiet."

"We collected DNA samples from garbage and kitchens at the rehab center and found two matches to DNA collected at some of the crime scenes. Pam and Tony's DNA was obtained from discarded coffee cups in their offices."

"We obtained lab results tying both Pam Turner and Tony Santos to each crime scene. We arrested them because we had enough evidence to get a search warrant for their residences."

Donna Rose then asked, "What is the current status of the rehab center?"

Mr. Simmons replied, "It is still a crime scene and is no longer open for business."

Donna Rose thanked Mr. Simmons and indicated she had no further questions. Gabriel stood up to ask one question.

"Other than the DNA evidence, is there any other proof tying Pam Turner to these crimes?"

Mr. Simmons asked, "Do you mean emails or text messages?"

"Yes, but I mean real physical evidence such as surveillance footage or eyewitnesses."

"No, not at this time," Mr. Simmons answered.

Gabriel concluded his questions. Donna Rose quickly rose again.

"Redirect, Your Honor," she said.

"In your professional opinion as a crime scene expert, Detective, would you say that DNA evidence, text messages, and emails constitute strong evidence?"

"Yes, I would."

"Since Pam and Tony's apprehension, how many murders resembling their method have been committed?"

"None that I am aware of."

"To be clear, no murders like these have occurred since law enforcement apprehended Pam Turner and Tony Santos?"

"Yes, that is correct."

As Gabriel stood and approached the witness stand for redirect, he paused and stared at Mr. Simmons. For a few moments, no words were spoken. Gabriel looked directly into Mr. Simmons's eyes before asking his question.

"Mr. Simmons, how long have you been in law enforcement?"

"About twenty years," Mr. Simmons replied.

Gabriel continued, "And in that time, how many cases would you say go unsolved?"

"I do not know, but quite a few," Mr. Simmons answered.

"Why would you say that is?"

"I guess because there is not enough evidence to convict, or a case gets too cold."

Gabriel paused, then added, "Is that because there has to be a preponderance of evidence? Or is it because to find someone guilty, it has to be beyond a reasonable doubt?"

"I suppose so," Mr. Simmons replied.

Gabriel pressed on, "Mr. Simmons, is it possible that Pam, my client, was innocent and just in the wrong place at the wrong time? Could these crimes have been committed by Tony Santos alone? Is it possible Pam was manipulated by Mr. Santos and was an unwilling participant?"

"I do not think so," Mr. Simmons said firmly. "Pam's DNA was at each crime scene."

"Yes, I am aware of that," Gabriel responded, "but is it possible that Tony killed these people and Pam was merely present?"

"Yes, I suppose that is possible," Mr. Simmons admitted.

As Mr. Simmons began to elaborate, Gabriel cut him off. "No further questions, Your Honor."

Mr. Simmons was then asked to step down. Once again, Gabriel had performed as well as anyone could have hoped.

Gabriel returned to the defendant's table. Donna Rose spoke up, "Your Honor, I call tech specialist

Kimberly Lee to the stand." Kimberly Lee stood and walked toward the witness stand. She was about 5'6", with blond hair and rimmed glasses. Her nervousness was evident as she approached.

Donna Rose asked, "Kimberly, I understand you were the technician who collected the emails and text messages revealing communications between Tony Santos and Pam Turner, is that correct?"

"Yes, that is correct," Kimberly confirmed.

Donna Rose continued, "Is there any way these emails and texts could have been altered or tampered with?"

"No, they are authentic," Kimberly answered.

Donna Rose then addressed the jury. "Ladies and gentlemen, we are about to display the emails and text messages between Tony Santos and Pam Turner that we found most revealing and incriminating. Please prepare yourselves; the content is difficult and may be offensive."

Her assistants projected the emails and texts on the screen. The court dimmed the lights, and the prosecution scrolled through the messages. Leah and I read them, as did the jury.

I understood, then, how wrong what Leah and I had done was what we were doing was wrong, even ill-advised. But our actions had developed over time.

We both knew our relationships with our partners were nearing an end. We became friends and eventually fell in love.

Yet, as Leah and I read the messages displayed that day in the courtroom, we were shocked. Our suspicions were confirmed. Pam and Tony expressed how much they loved being together. Their emails and texts contained very intense, often explicit sexual conversations some even resembling phone or text sex.

As the prosecution presented the messages, some were disturbingly detailed about how Pam was turned on by killing and wanted to do it again. This was deeply disturbing to Leah and me, and it was clear the jury was shocked as well. We all were.

For Leah and me, our feelings about our own relationship were validated. Even worse, as we read those messages, it became clear that Tony and Pam were guilty not only of betraying us, but also of killing these people and deriving pleasure from it.

What hurt me the most was one text that read, "Tony, I have never loved a man as much as I love you, and I have never been as turned on by a man as you have turned me on tonight." After reading that, I felt completely deflated.

I could not believe it. What made it worse was that the message was sent on the day of Pam and my anniversary the last anniversary when we postponed dinner because Pam said she was working late. At that moment, I was out of breath, out of hope, and done with it all.

After Donna Rose finished presenting the emails and text messages, the courtroom lights came back on. I glanced at Pam, whose face was once again expressionless.

Donna Rose then said to the judge, "The prosecution rests, Your Honor."

Then it was Gabriel's turn to present his case. "Your Honor, I would like to call Paul Turner to the stand."

I looked at Leah, got up, and walked to the witness stand. I was sworn in, and Gabriel began asking questions about Pam's character how we met, how long we had been married, and what kind of mother she was to our kids.

As Gabriel asked his questions, I was so devastated by the testimony about the emails and texts that I struggled to present Pam in a positive light. After all, I now knew what my wife was doing behind my back. And as if that wasn't enough to cause me great emotional anguish, now I had to be a character witness in Pam's defense? I didn't know how I would come across to the jury, feeling the way I did.

As agitation grew inside me, I glanced at the one woman I knew I loved in that moment Leah. My God, how did I get to this place? Yet I looked at Leah, and she looked back. I wanted so badly to help Pam, but for that, I needed to harness some hidden or buried strength.

When Gabriel asked his first question, I took a deep breath and looked at Leah. Somehow, I gathered my composure and felt ready to answer.

Gabriel asked, "Paul, when did you meet Pam?"

I have to admit, I didn't expect that question. Even though Gabriel had prepped Leah and me, this wasn't one he mentioned. After a brief pause, I answered.

Gabriel's questions allowed me to revisit who Pam was and what we once had. He asked about Pam as a mother, her work ethic, and how she managed to work while carrying the twins. He asked about her professional life and the hard work she put into earning her degree. Gabriel did a great job humanizing Pam through my testimony.

When Gabriel concluded, Donna Rose stood and approached the witness stand for cross-examination.

"So, Paul, I really enjoyed hearing about Pam and what she was like when you first met, and the life you built together," Donna Rose began. "But what I'm really interested in is how you feel about your wife's infidelity. How do you feel after reading those emails and text messages we just all viewed?"

I sat silently for a few moments and said, "I don't really know that she was unfaithful. I have doubts about whether those emails and texts are real."

"Okay," Donna Rose replied. "Then why not tell the jury about your and your wife's friend Leah? I'm sure they'd love to know whether you're an honest and trustworthy guy."

Once again, I felt cornered and trapped. I knew how I answered this mattered deeply, so I paused before responding.

"Leah and I befriended each other when Pam and I would go out to dinner with Tony and Leah. Pam and Tony discussed work most of the time, often leaving Leah and me to talk. Over time, we formed a close friendship, and only after Pam and Tony were arrested did Leah and I become closer."

"Isn't it true you're living with Leah now? Yes or no?"

"Yes," I answered.

"Would you like to explain this?"

"No, I really wouldn't," I said.

"Were you aware of what Pam was doing all those nights she claimed to be working late?"

"She was working late. Pam would call me and check in frequently."

"Did Pam call you from her own cell phone?"

"Yes."

"How could you be sure where she was calling from? She could have been calling from any number of the murder scenes."

Gabriel stood and objected. His objection was overruled.

Judge Conte looked at me and said, "Mr. Turner, please answer the question."

I replied, "No, I guess I couldn't be certain where Pam was calling from."

Donna Rose returned to the emails and texts. "Paul, you don't believe the emails and texts are real, correct?"

"Yes."

"During this trial, has anyone presented evidence that the messages are fake?"

"No."

"I know my wife, and although they were hard to read, I just can't believe they're from Pam and Tony."

Donna Rose concluded, "Paul, what you believe and what has been proven are two different things."

The judge said, "I have no more questions for this witness."

Donna Rose ended her cross-examination.

Gabriel stood and said, "Redirect, Your Honor. Paul, I want to ask you more about your wife, your children, and your relationship with Leah." Donna Rose quickly objected. The judge took a moment and then responded, "Overruled."

Gabriel continued, "Paul, earlier you explained how you and Leah became friends and why, but what I want to ask is how important was having Leah there for you when Pam was arrested?"

I looked at Gabriel, feeling him open an emotional scar I hadn't yet come to terms with. Still, I answered honestly, "Leah was everything to me during that time. I knew Pam and I were having problems, but I never thought in a million years that she would just be taken away from me. When she was, I was lost and hurting. Leah helped me pick up the pieces."

Gabriel then asked a question that immediately brought me to tears. "Paul, when your children died in that car accident with Pam's sister, Jessica, was Leah also there for you?"

I struggled to contain my emotions, searching for strength to answer. "Yes," I responded. "When my boys were killed, Leah was there to help me through the emotional devastation and pain."

Gabriel followed, "And wasn't it also Leah who visited Pam every day to help her through everything she was going through?"

"Yes," I replied. "Leah has been there for both Pam and me."

Gabriel pressed on, "Paul, when did you realize you had feelings for Leah?"

Again, Donna Rose objected. Gabriel addressed Judge Conte: "Your Honor, the prosecution opened this door when they used Leah and Paul's relationship to attack Paul's character."

Judge Conte replied, "I'll allow it. Please answer the question, Paul."

After losing Pam to incarceration and then my two sons to the car crash, I was spiraling downward. Leah was there to help me. When we were told we had to sell the house to prepare for civil suits, Leah let me move in with her. Leah is the reason I can function now. Leah is why I'm still standing here in Pam's defense.

I am a man who lost his wife, two sons, job, and home all within a short time. So you may stand in judgment of me if you wish, but I believe Pam did not do this. No matter how many text messages or emails you show me, I have reasonable doubt about her guilt.

I turned to Pam. "Pam, I am so sorry. I know you've been through so much. I never meant to hurt you. Please forgive me."

Gabriel cut me off, saying, "No more questions."

I stepped down from the witness stand. Judge Conte then said, "Court is in recess until tomorrow morning at 9:00 AM."

After recess, Gabriel sat down with Pam, Leah, and me. He looked unsure if he could win the case. "I think it's time we consider putting Pam on the stand. The evidence presented to the jury is overwhelming, and I don't see how we can overcome it."

Gabriel added, "My investigative team is still working to find something to exonerate Pam, but I'm afraid time is running out."

As Gabriel spoke, Pam burst into tears. It was understandable it didn't look good. Although unsure what to think, my heart still ached for Pam.

Throughout all this, Leah has been a good friend to Pam, visiting her frequently. Leah hugged Pam, and that seemed to help a little.

As for where we stand, this is how I see it: If Gabriel can't get Pam off, I believe it will kill her. What she needs is a miracle.

Later that afternoon, Gabriel called me. His team found new evidence that we might introduce tomorrow morning at trial. Several additional DNA samples were found both at the rehab center and crime scenes. Gabriel said this new evidence doesn't prove anything, but it may create doubt about Pam's involvement because it shows others were present.

"Paul," Gabriel said, "make sure you're there tomorrow, ready to go. I want Leah to testify, and I'll be recalling DNA specialist James Kelly to the stand. I will also be calling Pam to testify. If all goes well, this trial will wrap up tomorrow with closing arguments."

He added, "I'm going to give it my best shot. I need you and Leah ready for anything, but most of all, I need you there for Pam."

"Well, Gabriel," I replied, "we'll be there, and we'll be ready."

When Gabriel hung up, I started to understand how bad this looked for Pam. I also found it hard to believe Pam was truly innocent.

With these feelings inside of me, I just do not see how the jury could ever find Pam not guilty. If I feel this way, I can only imagine how the jury is seeing this. Gabriel has assured both Leah and me that he is going to do his best, but personally, I just do not see a path where the jury does not convict Pam.

Aside from that, after all that I have learned, I have developed a combination of disdain and resentment for Pam. The woman that I once loved so much is now a vision in the rearview mirror, and unfortunately a vision that I want so badly to fade into my past.

Leah and I cooked dinner and talked a little bit while we worked on dinner. When we sat down to eat, we continued talking about all of the things that we have been living through recently. We then retired to the living room and watched a movie.

Leah wanted to watch a movie because she felt that we really needed to get our minds off of everything, even if only for just a few hours. It was one of those romantic flicks that Leah enjoys watching. These movies always put me to sleep for some reason. I was led into just what I needed, relaxation and sleepiness.

With the feeling of uncertainty and anxiousness subsiding, we both drifted into our own little world for a little while, Leah with her movie, and me with my drifting off into a nap. When the movie was over, Leah woke me and we both headed to bed. Neither one of us was in the mood to stay up, and we both were really both emotionally and physically tired. We kissed goodnight, and we both went to bed.

CHAPTER 21

Leah and I were up and ready to go, knowing that the trial was set for 9:00 AM in Riverhead. We arrived a few minutes early and took our seats. Next to us were Junior and Jayde. We greeted them both and exchanged brief words. Jayde did not respond when I said hello. Both Leah and I felt the resentment Jayde harbored toward our relationship. I understood why Pam and Jayde were very close. Junior had been cordial to both Leah and me. Privately, he made it clear he strongly disapproved of Leah and me being together, especially openly. I understood that, but what Junior didn't realize was that what Leah and I have isn't something I can hide or conceal.

We all sat, waiting for the court session to begin. Gabriel and Pam were already seated. We watched as the jury entered the courtroom, and then the trial commenced.

"The honorable Judge Justine Conte presiding, court is now in session," the bailiff announced. Judge Conte walked to the bench and sat down. Then came the words, "Please be seated."

As the trial started, Gabriel asked permission to approach the bench. He was about to introduce new evidence. Donna Rose had no objection, and the judge allowed it to be entered.

Gabriel then called forensic expert James Kelly to the stand. James had testified earlier. Gabriel asked, "Mr. Kelly, earlier you testified on the reliability of forensic evidence, such as fingerprints and DNA, correct?"

Mr. Kelly replied, "Yes, I did."

Gabriel then asked Mr. Kelly to review the new evidence just entered moments ago. "How do you explain this?"

Gabriel continued, "It appears there is another DNA sample and a set of partial fingerprints collected alongside Pam and Tony's at the crime scenes. To me, this looks like it could be the DNA or prints of someone else at the scene maybe someone who actually participated in the killings."

Mr. Kelly examined the evidence. Gabriel asked, "Is there anything about this forensic report that you would consider unusual or inaccurate?"

Mr. Kelly responded, "No, sir."

Gabriel then asked, "Are these results from the same lab as the earlier ones we viewed?"

Mr. Kelly answered, "Yes, sir, they are."

Gabriel continued, "At each crime scene, there has been one unexplained fingerprint a partial print. One that cannot identify the third person but suggests there may have been a third individual at each of the 14 crime scenes. There is also additional DNA. Would you say that is true?"

Mr. Kelly paused, then replied, "I would have to say that is true, yes."

"Thank you, Mr. Kelly," Gabriel said. "I have no further questions for this witness."

Donna Rose stood and approached the witness stand. She asked, "Mr. Kelly, is the presence of a possible third person enough to create reasonable doubt as to Pam Turner's guilt, or does it just mean that Pam and Tony may have conspired with a third person in committing these crimes?"

Mr. Kelly replied, "I cannot answer that, Ms. Rose. In my opinion, that evidence only does one thing: it suggests the presence of a third person no more, no less."

Donna Rose thanked Mr. Kelly and said, "I have no more questions for this witness."

Gabriel then called Pam to the witness stand to testify. Pam was sworn in and promised to tell the truth, the whole truth, and nothing but the truth. She sat down, and Gabriel asked, "Pam, did you kill anyone?" Pam responded, "No, I did not."

Gabriel continued, "Were you having an affair with Tony Santos?" Pam answered, "Yes, I was."

Gabriel then asked, "How did you meet Tony, and how did this affair happen?"

Pam began to tell her story how she met Tony, how long she had worked at the rehab center, how she was promoted to manager, and how she essentially ran the place while Tony took off most nights. After several minutes of testimony, hoping to sway the jury, Gabriel concluded his questioning and sat down. He then said, "The defense rests, Your Honor."

Donna Rose stood and said, "The prosecution has no questions for this witness."

Judge Conte announced, "Court will take a two-hour recess and resume at 1:00 PM, where we will hear closing arguments."

The morning flew by quickly. Gabriel did not call Leah to the stand, and I wanted to ask why, so I stopped him in the hallway. "Gabriel, why didn't you call Leah to testify?"

Gabriel replied, "Pam did not want her to, and I agreed Leah didn't have anything positive we could present. We also felt it could open the door to more prosecution questions. Look, Paul," he said, "we were already behind the eight ball. We did our best, and now we wait to see how the jury responds after closing arguments."

Leah, Gabriel, and I walked together to grab a bite for lunch. Junior and Jayde joined us. Over lunch, we discussed "what ifs" and possible next steps while considering the different outcomes. Gabriel thought that if the jury returned a guilty verdict, we would appeal but reminded Leah and me of the lengthy process and financial burden that an appeal would bring. Considering all the financial obligations from the civil suits, we knew no matter the verdict, things would be unsettled and messy.

We ate, and soon it was time to head back to the courthouse. Just before standing, Jayde said sharply, "Paul, I want to know how you can live with yourself. How can you be with someone else right in plain sight, right in front of Pam? It's cruel. Pam doesn't deserve this."

Then Jayde looked directly at Leah. "And you, Leah, you should be ashamed of yourself. The two of you are made for one another."

As Jayde spoke firmly and sternly, Junior took her hand and said, "Jayde, come on, let's go." As they walked away, Junior glanced back at Leah and me with a disappointed look. I knew he agreed with everything Jayde said.

If they expected us to feel guilty, it didn't work. Leah and I had fully accepted our decision to be together, and no one else would ever understand what we were going through except the two of us. Despite everything, we both felt that something good could come from all this. As hard as it was for others to see or understand, it was true. That didn't mean Leah and I lacked compassion we both had felt as much pain and heartache as anyone, including Pam.

We stood and headed back to the courthouse, not knowing exactly what to expect but reluctantly forging ahead, fully aware the jury would render a verdict soon. In situations like this, no one can truly be prepared. It's not like we've been here before because we haven't and there's no template for how to deal with this process.

When we arrived, we hurried into the courtroom and sat down just barely on time. The trial resumed almost immediately.

"The honorable Judge Justine Conte presiding, court is now in session," the bailiff announced. Judge Conte walked to the bench and sat. Then came the words, "Please be seated."

Judge Conte asked, "Is the prosecution ready to present their closing argument?"

Donna Rose stood and said, "Yes, Your Honor," before addressing the jury. "Ladies and gentlemen of the jury, we hope all twelve of you have carefully weighed the evidence presented during this trial." Donna Rose continued, "I am confident that after reviewing the forensic evidence, emails, text messages, and all testimony, you can see there is no doubt Pam Turner had a part in these crimes. We expect you, members of the jury, to find the defendant guilty on 14 counts of first-degree felony murder as an accomplice to Tony Santos. The prosecution believes we have presented a solid case and you must find Pam Turner guilty."

Donna Rose returned to her table and sat down.

Gabriel then stood and addressed the jury. "Ladies and gentlemen, Ms. Rose claims the prosecution has proven beyond a reasonable doubt that my client, Pam Turner, is guilty of 14 counts of first-degree felony murder as an accomplice to Tony Santos. I disagree. We were never able to authenticate the emails and text messages with enough certainty to convict Pam Turner to 25 years to life. The unexplained partial fingerprints, not belonging to Pam or Tony, must create doubt about who else was involved and what role they played."

Gabriel continued, "If you're like me and not convinced beyond reasonable doubt of Pam's guilt, you must find her not guilty. We thank you for your service and simply ask you to see past the smoke and mirrors and find the defendant not guilty."

Gabriel returned to his table and sat down.

Judge Conte instructed the jury on deliberations, and the jury left the room as the judge declared court in recess. Now, it was a waiting game we didn't know how long the jury would deliberate.

Leah and I sat together in the hallway, talking nervously for a while, not quite sure why. At this point, both of us wanted to move on with our lives. Though we had compassion for Pam, we were still wounded by everything that happened and what we learned in court.

During our conversation, I told Leah, "Once the trial's over, I'm going to ask Pam for a divorce." Leah looked at me, and I wasn't sure what her expression meant. I asked, "Hey, do you still want us to be together?"

Before I could say more, Leah kissed me. She told me she'd love for us to stay together. Leah looked genuinely happy, and I felt a measure of peace too.

We waited, unsure what the jury would decide.

Love only goes so far when you feel taken advantage of and lied to. In my heart, I no longer felt anything for Pam except sorrow and anger. After this trial, I couldn't wait to get on with my life. I was convinced Leah and I were in love and that good things lay ahead.

Suddenly, Gabriel yelled, "The jury has returned!"

We were called back into the courtroom. The jury's deliberation had lasted only about an hour. Gabriel told us this wasn't a good sign. A quick decision often indicates a unanimous verdict usually not in our favor.

The courtroom quieted as the trial resumed.

"The honorable Judge Justine Conte presiding, court is now in session," the bailiff announced. Judge Conte took her seat on the bench and said, "Please be seated."

Judge Conte then asked, "Madam foreperson, have you reached a verdict?"

The foreperson replied, "Yes, Your Honor."

Judge Conte asked, "On the first count of first-degree felony murder, how do you find?"

The foreperson answered, "We find the defendant, Pam Turner, guilty."

This verdict repeated for all thirteen remaining counts Pam was found guilty on all 14.

Judge Conte said, "Will the defendant please stand?"

She sentenced Pam, "Pam Turner, this court has found you guilty on all 14 counts of first-degree felony murder. You are hereby sentenced to life in prison, to begin immediately at Suffolk County Maximum Security Prison in Riverhead, New York."

I saw Junior and Jayde quickly walk out, clearly disappointed by the verdict.

Pam, who had been mostly silent during the trial, suddenly erupted screaming and crying loudly. "I did not do this! I did not do this!" she shouted repeatedly.

Court officers struggled to restrain her as she went off the rails. It felt like everything was happening in slow motion like a scene from a movie.

In the chaos, Pam reached for a court officer's gun and grabbed it. She fired a shot, causing everyone to take cover.

Her second shot struck Judge Conte's arm. The judge fell and took cover behind her bench.

Pam broke free momentarily and aimed at me. She fired, but I dove to the ground, avoiding the shot.

Then she aimed at Leah and fired again. I saw Leah hit the floor, but I wasn't sure if she was struck the gunshots were deafening, and my ears rang.

Pam was tackled from behind by an officer, but as she fell, she fired again striking Gabriel in the right shoulder.

The officers struggled to control Pam and disarm her. She managed one more shot before going down, hitting Gabriel in the side of the head.

Blood splattered everywhere as Pam was finally subdued. It soon became clear several others had been hit as well.

There was smoke everywhere and the smell of gunpowder thick in the air. When I managed to get up, I looked around for Leah and saw her lying on the ground, motionless. Blood stained the top of her back, and I was sure she had been shot. I rushed to her side and, to my relief, found she was unharmed. The blood on her clothes was someone else's. I hugged Leah tightly, overwhelmed with gratitude that she was okay. I kissed her and held her like she was my lifeline. Tears welled in my eyes, and Leah was crying too.

After the insanity subsided, everyone in the courtroom was left in disbelief and shock. A calm settled over the chaos, but none of us could fully grasp what had just happened. By then, Pam had been subdued and taken into custody, while EMTs rushed in to tend to the wounded. I watched as one EMT approached Gabriel, and it was quickly clear Gabriel was dead. Others who had been shot were badly injured.

Leah grabbed me again, holding on tightly. I could tell she was shaken, as were we all still in shock.

The police arrived, and everyone was asked to give a statement. This was something no one expected a moment no one could have foreseen in a million years.

Leah and I gave our statements and slowly walked out of the courtroom, into the hallway, then out the front doors to the parking lot where our car was waiting. No words were exchanged. We were both stunned as we got into the car and headed home.

Leah finally looked at me and asked, "Are you alright?"

I replied, "Yes. Are you?"

Leah said, "Yes, I'm okay."

We both knew the ordeal was over, but what we couldn't come to terms with was the side of Pam we had just witnessed not just how it affected us, but how we had never seen that darkness in her before. How could we have missed it?

We had spent so much time with Pam and Tony. How had this eluded us? Neither Leah nor I ever imagined Pam or Tony capable of such horrors. I couldn't believe Pam was capable of all those murders and especially what had just unfolded moments ago.

How do you recover from something like this?

All I know is I'm so grateful Leah and I made it out alive. I wasn't going to let another moment pass in the chaos we'd just survived.

Once in the car, I turned to Leah and asked, "Leah, will you marry me?"

Without hesitation, Leah said, "Yes, I will marry you!"

I know if you're an outsider hearing this story, you might think the timing is wrong, or the proposal is in poor taste. But to Leah and me, after such an insane day, it was the perfect ending. On this day, Leah and I looked forward, not back.

Our love had grown through every twist and turn in this crazy journey. Having just barely escaped death, I knew there was no better time than now.

In my heart, marrying Leah was the only sensible thing I'd thought of in what felt like forever like a lifetime. After today, a new chapter begins.

The way I feel about her, I know one thing: I'm never looking back. Holding Leah tightly, I looked up to the sky and whispered, "Thank you, God."

I don't know why, but I was just reacting to everything that had happened. I am truly grateful to God, for Leah, and for sparing both our lives in that courtroom.

CHAPTER 22

Leah and I both slept well last night. It was hard to believe after everything we went through, but I think we were both just exhausted and passed out at the end of the day. Stress can do that to you. Lately, we've been under tremendous pressure.

This morning, we woke to something somewhat unexpected though in hindsight, we should have seen it coming. As soon as we opened our eyes, we heard people outside the house. It was strange because it was barely 9:00 AM. Looking out the bedroom window, I saw news trucks, vans, and reporters standing around, waiting for us to step outside. Neither Leah nor I wanted to be interviewed by the media.

We went into the kitchen, and thankfully, the blinds were still down from the night before, so no one could see inside. I made us a pot of coffee, and we looked at each other for a few moments before Leah asked, "Paul, how long do you think they'll wait out there? Is this going to be a thing?"

I told her it probably wouldn't last long but might take a few days to subside. We really shouldn't be surprised. Pam was just convicted of murdering all those people, and after yesterday's ordeal in court, this was a big story. I didn't think the media cared about what we had been through they just wanted their story.

Leah asked, "What should we do?"

I said, "I think we just sit here, have our coffee, I'll make us some breakfast, and then we'll see where things stand after that." I also told her I planned to contact a divorce attorney to have Pam served with papers. Earlier, when I discussed this with Gabriel, he offered to help. Since he's no longer with us, I'll reach out to someone else for assistance.

Leah looked at me silently for a moment, then said, "Paul, you have no idea how happy that makes me. I want you to know I love you, and once your divorce from Pam is finalized, we can start planning our wedding." She went on to say how hard sneaking around had been for so long and that after everything we've been through, she'd never felt this way about any man before. Leah told me she loved me, and we should begin planning our new life together. Of course, I agreed completely.

We had our coffee and breakfast, and just as I expected, the media crews eventually left. Leah was scheduled to work at 4:00 PM that afternoon, while I was still looking for a job. My plan was to keep job hunting today, but after last night, Leah and I got off to a slow start.

A few minutes after cleaning up breakfast, there was a knock on the front door. Peeking out the window, I saw a police car. The media circus had dwindled. Two officers were at the door, so I opened it and asked how we could help.

Apparently, Leah and I had left the courthouse too quickly the day before and hadn't given the police our full statements. I explained that we'd given a statement, but in the chaos, we might have thought we had given the complete version. The officers were there to get an official statement.

We invited them inside and all sat down in the living room. Leah gave her statement first, then I gave mine. Our accounts were very similar understandably so, since we witnessed much of the same, though I saw Gabriel get shot while Leah was already on the ground. There was little difference between our statements, so the officers thanked us and left.

Then the phone rang reporters calling for a story again. Leah and I decided it was best to get out of the house for a while, so we did.

As we drove out of the driveway, we headed to the beach and parked for a while. It was the same beach where Leah and I had first been intimate in that parking lot. It was quiet today, since it was off-season, which worked in our favor as we were looking for privacy and a break from the house.

Leah and I went for a walk along the sound, something we both really enjoy. We talked at length about everything that's happened over the past year. It's been crazy, but what amazes me is how Leah and I connected through all the chaos.

The next few days were much calmer than life had been before a welcome change of pace. Leah did her first bartending shift since the Rock n Roll Bourbon Café reopened.

Of course, I stopped by each afternoon and was happy to see a good happy hour crowd. This was great for our town and even better for Leah and me financially. The hardest thing so far had been finding a job, but I still had a few prospects to explore. Leah's house was paid for, and although I didn't fully understand how she acquired the money, I hadn't given it much thought. Right now, all that mattered was that we had each other and her place to start our new life together.

I did feel stressed because everything I owned had to be sold to pay for Pam's legal fees. The civil trials were starting soon, and I was confident that whatever money we got from the house sale would be spent on that. That money was in a special account Gabriel had set up for Pam and me. Beyond that, the reality of being broke and living with my girlfriend was beginning to sink in.

I supposed I could try to claim some money in the divorce, but to do that, I'd have to spend money first. Leah and I discussed it, and she felt I should just let it all go and start over with her. Something told me she was right. Still, not having a job or any money of my own was weighing on me a bit.

Walking out of the bar and getting into the car, my phone rang. When I answered and heard the voice on the other end, I was thrilled! It was my old boss from the seafood company. He called to offer me my job back. Things had picked up, and they wanted to expand their territory. When he asked if I wanted to come back, there was no pause just an emphatic yes!

I got out of the car and ran inside to tell Leah. She came out from behind the bar, hugged me, and congratulated me. Just when things had looked so grim a few days ago, today felt so much better. Realizing Leah and I were embarking on a brand new life a second chance if you will my anxiety started to fade, and the future seemed a whole lot brighter.

I decided to stay at the bar and have a drink. Hard to do with no money, but not when your girlfriend is the bartender!

CHAPTER 23

Well, today is the day I say goodbye to Pam. It's been a few weeks since everything happened in the courtroom when Pam was convicted of murder. A few days ago, I contacted a local divorce attorney, Vince Dolan, who helped me with the divorce papers and the process. I sort of found Vince through Gabriel's office. Today is the day the papers get signed.

As I drive to Suffolk County Maximum Security Prison in Riverhead, I keep thinking about how much I once really loved Pam. It's hard to believe where we once were and where we are now. There was a time I would have done anything for Pam, but now I just want to get this over with so I never have to see her again.

When I arrive at the facility, I meet Vince Dolan at the entry, and we enter together. We talk a little as we head to the visitation area. This is a maximum security prison, so armed guards accompany us the whole time. Once inside, we are asked to be seated as we wait for Pam to be escorted in.

Through the small glass in the solid door, I see Pam's face as she is brought into the room. The door opens, and Pam enters handcuffed and in chains. She is escorted to the table and sits down. Vince and I take seats across from her.

Pam shows no emotion expressionless, offering only an ice-cold stare. Vince begins and says, "Pam, do you understand why Paul and I are here?" Pam nods yes. Vince asks if she has read the divorce papers, and Pam replies affirmatively.

Vince hands Pam his pen and asks her to sign the papers. Pam nods again. Then, in a quick motion, she attempts to stab Vince in the arm with the pen. Fortunately, the chains prevent her from succeeding. She lets out a loud scream.

"I hate you, Paul! I hate you! I hope she kills you! I hope she kills you like she killed the others! You deserve each other! You should die together! I hope she makes you pay! You will pay, Paul. She will kill you, and I'll be here to read all about it when she does."

Then, almost shockingly, Pam composes herself as if transforming into another person before our eyes. Calmly, she asks for the pen back. The guards give it to her but stand right next to her.

Pam signs the papers, then looks directly at me and says calmly, "Paul, she will kill you, and I will enjoy the day I read about that in the newspaper. You really have no idea what you're in for, do you?"

I don't respond. At this point, I consider Pam's behavior what I expected she has clearly lost her mind. Her words pass right by me, and I pay them no attention. All I know is the divorce papers are signed, and she agreed to the terms. That's all that matters.

Her words seem meaningless now. I see Pam as a broken person, and I expected some level of insanity after everything that transpired. It was obvious the meeting was over.

Then Pam asked the guards to take her back to her cell. Vince just looked at me and said, "You really know how to pick them!" Vince and I headed out of the room, down the corridor, and to the parking lot where we parted ways. Before we did, I thanked him thanked him because I was finally a free man, free to be with Leah and start a new life. I really wanted to put all of this behind me, and this felt like the one thing I had to do to start moving forward.

I decided to take it easy the rest of the day, so I stopped by the office at Braun Seafood in Cutchogue. I got to talk to my old boss, Jerry. He wanted me to come in and get reestablished, as I would be starting work in just a few days. Jerry gave me my old office back and even most of my original route. Jerry and I talked for a while, and I have to say it was the most normal I had felt in what seemed like a century! It felt good to be back.

Leaving Braun's, I felt like a million bucks and couldn't wait to get back to see Leah. I wanted to share the news that Pam and I were finally divorced and that Leah was now spending time with an employed man! Something finally clicked, and it just felt right. Driving home, I cranked up the music and listened to "Screaming in the Night" by Krokus. I've always loved that song; it's perfect for driving. I had about a half-hour drive, so I buckled in and let the music carry me. I felt like I was on top of the world.

Still, I couldn't stop thinking about what Pam said that Leah would kill me like she killed the others. Was I supposed to take that seriously? Or was it just the rantings of someone who had completely lost their mind? After everything I learned about Pam during the trial, and all I witnessed since, I could only conclude that Pam had lost her mind and maybe, just maybe, that explained so much of what had happened. Perhaps it was better this way. After all, God only knows what would have happened if Pam had been released and none of this had come out.

When I got home, Leah was in the kitchen, standing in front of the open refrigerator, looking inside. "Hey, girl," I said. "What are you up to?"

"I'm trying to figure out what to make us for dinner," Leah replied.

Leah had really embraced being the woman of the house. She had been amazing she just naturally assumed the role of taking care of both of us. It had happened gradually, and looking back, I wasn't sure when exactly, but Leah had been more of a wife to

me in a short time than Pam ever had. I wasn't sure
what to attribute it to maybe Leah's yearning for a
relationship with a man who didn't take her for
granted. I guess we both were yearning for
something we thought we'd never find. And then,
through all of this, we found each other.

I said, "Leah, why don't we just go out to dinner?"

"No," Leah replied. "We have a wedding to save
for!"

I wasn't expecting that response, but I understood
we finally had a goal. I was actually excited that
Leah and I were going to be together. It all just felt
so right.

Leah and I ended up grilling some burgers and
having a few beers. After dinner and cleaning up,
we decided to take a walk on the beach. We jumped
in the car and drove to the beach just a few minutes
from the house. We chose the same beach parking
lot where we were first together. We loved that
place it served as a reminder of our story.

We parked for a while and talked about the
wedding. Leah wanted a small, quaint, romantic
ceremony. After listening to her wishes, I couldn't
help but agree. All I could think about was how
amazing Leah would look in a wedding dress.

When we finished discussing the wedding, we
walked along the Long Island Sound. It was

beautiful this time of year the gentle sound of water kissing the sand, the stars above, and the lights from ships passing through the sound. It was a breathtaking scene. Looking at Leah, I couldn't control the emotion I felt for her. Kissing her was just as exciting now as it had been the first time. I really loved this girl. I truly knew in my heart that Leah loved me.

We talked about our families for a while. I told Leah my parents had passed away some time ago and that I was an only child, so since then I'd pretty much been on my own. Leah told me about her family her mother, Leanne, and her sister, Lydia. Leah and Lydia are identical twins, which always intrigued me. I couldn't imagine another Leah.

Leah shared how much she wanted her mom and sister to meet me. She insisted I'd love them, and after the way she described them, I didn't doubt it. What shocked me was when Leah told me her father and older brother had died in a car accident a few years back. It was so tragic her dad had an affair with her mother's best friend, leading to her parents separating. One night, Leah's dad took her brother Tom out for his birthday. On that night, he ran a red light and crashed, killing both of them.

"That's so terrible, Leah," I said. "I'm so sorry."

Leah composed herself and repeated how much she wanted her mom and sister to meet me. Of course, I had no objection.

After the conversation, Leah and I felt elated to have each other to be planning our life together. I looked at Leah and knew there was no way I could ever be without her.

That night was special, and we looked forward to whatever life had to offer next. We returned home, watched a movie, and went to bed. I wasn't sure when it happened, but Leah and I already felt like a married couple. We kissed goodnight, and as I settled in, I noticed a text on my phone. Leah had already fallen asleep.

The message was from Rick Simmons the investigator from the trial. It read: "Paul, can you call me tomorrow? I have some things to tell you that you might find interesting." I replied, "I'll reach out tomorrow, thanks."

I wondered what it could be about. I'd find out tomorrow. It was late, and I was tired, so I plugged in my phone, turned it off, and went to sleep.

CHAPTER 24

You know that feeling when you're supposed to remember doing something but fail miserably? That's what this morning felt like. Leah didn't have to be at work until 3:00 PM, and I had to head over to the office to meet with Jerry and start working on our new marketing plan. My day was set to begin at 10:00 AM.

Leah made us both breakfast, and we talked for a little while before I had to shower and get to work. On my way in, I texted Rick Simmons to let him know I was available to talk for a few minutes if he wanted.

Not long after, my phone rang. "Paul, this is Rick. I want to talk to you about a few things. Is this a good time?"

"Sure," I replied. "What is this all about?"

Rick continued, "Paul, we investigated your sister-in-law's car accident, and we have proof the brake system was tampered with. It's beginning to look like that accident wasn't really an accident. Paul, we think Pam's sister and your sons were intentionally killed."

I paused for a moment, stunned by what Rick had just said. "Are you sure?" I asked.

"Yes, I'm afraid so," Rick replied.

"Who could have done such a thing?" I asked.

"We're not sure yet, but there's more I'd like to discuss with you," Rick said.

At that moment, Leah's phone beeped. "Rick," I said, "I have to take this call. Can I call you later?"

"Yeah, call me back but don't forget," Rick replied.

Turning to Leah, I asked, "Is everything okay?"

She smiled and said she just wanted to tell me she loved me and that she'd packed a lunch for me, which I had forgotten to take. I thanked her and assured her I'd bring it tomorrow.

After the call, I couldn't stop thinking: why would anyone want to kill Jessica and my sons? I started to wonder if Rick was reaching too far trying too hard to find something that could justify his shortcomings in the case.

But I didn't have much time to dwell on it. Soon enough, I arrived at work, and honestly, I was so happy to be back. I was ready to start a new chapter one where Leah and I were a couple, and one where I had the opportunity to make a living. It felt really good to be back.

As troubling as Rick's words were, right now, I just wanted to put the past behind me. I wasn't sure I wanted to dive back into the events of the past year with him. Can you blame me? It's been way too crazy for way too long.

After stopping by the office, organizing things, and completing our new marketing strategy, I headed to the Rock n Roll Bourbon Café. Leah was tending bar, and there were a few people at the counter. It was slow early in the day, just before happy hour. Leah immediately came over to me with a beer and started talking.

"How was work?" she asked.

I told her it felt really good to be back. Leah said she felt the same way.

Then she asked if I would mind if her mother came over and stayed for a few weeks. Of course, I didn't mind.

"Does your mother even know about us?" I asked.

Leah smiled. "Yes, I told her we're engaged, and she really wants to meet you, Paul. She's very excited."

"Leah, can I get a shot, please?"

"Bourbon?" she asked.

"Yes, a shot of Woodford."

Leah poured me the bourbon, and I told her how excited I was and how glad I was that things were finally starting to come together.

While Leah took care of the other customers, we talked intermittently. One thing I remember most about falling for Leah is how she looked the very first time I came to this bar to visit her. Pam was working late that night, and Leah was here. It was a slow evening, but I couldn't get her out of my mind, not then and not to this day. It's hard to believe she's mine now.

When we first started getting close, Leah seemed like an unattainable fantasy. Honestly, I thought she was out of my league and obviously someone else's girl, off limits. I was married to Pam then, and I loved her. The fact that Leah and I are together now feels nothing short of a miracle.

As I sat at the bar looking at her, I was reminded again how stunning Leah is. I could watch her all night. Sometimes when she talks to me, I just drift away. She still does that to me.

Leah and I talked some more before I decided to head home. Her shift was supposed to end around 11:00 PM. Before I left, I kissed her goodbye.

"Paul," she reminded me, "when you get home, my mother may be there, so please introduce yourself and do your best to be a gracious host until I get home."

"You never mentioned your mother was coming tonight," I said.

Leah smiled and blew me a kiss. "That's because you never listen when I talk!"

I couldn't argue with that, so I headed home, knowing Leah's mother someone I hadn't met yet might be there. Well then, I thought, I can't wait to meet her. This should be interesting.

It was still early. I left the café around 9:00 PM and headed home. The drive was short, but I used every minute to wonder what Leah's mother would be like. Leah and I had never really discussed much about our families. This visit was a mystery, but I was intrigued.

Pulling into the driveway, I saw the lights on in the living room and kitchen. There was a car parked curbside a Mercedes. Leah's mom had done alright for herself, it seemed.

I pulled into the garage, turned off the car, and walked toward the side door. As I climbed the steps, I thought I heard Leah's voice. That couldn't be she was at the bar.

I opened the door and announced, "I'm home."

Within moments, Leah's mother appeared, walking in from the living room. "You must be Paul," she said. "I'm Leanne. It's so nice to meet you."

I took a moment to absorb her presence. Leanne was beautiful just like Leah. Absolutely stunning.

"And you must be Leah's mother," I said calmly.

"That's what they tell me," she replied with a smile.

We both laughed cordially.

"Would you like to sit and get to know each other?" I asked.

"Yes, that would be nice," Leanne replied.

I asked if she wanted something to drink, but she said she was fine for now. I poured myself a bourbon, and we settled into the living room.

I asked what Leah was like as a little girl. Leanne shared stories enthusiastically; it was clear she loved talking about her daughter.

As we talked, Leah came into the room from the kitchen. I stood, went to kiss her, and told her how much I was enjoying her mother's stories.

Before I knew it, Leanne stood up and grabbed me.

"Paul, no!" she said, almost tackling me. I was confused.

"This is Leah's twin sister, Lydia," Leanne explained.

I was stunned. Lydia looked exactly like Leah. I mean exactly.

Leanne chuckled. "Don't feel bad, Paul I've confused them both countless times growing up."

I had no response other than being thoroughly confused.

The moment was awkward but quickly passed, replaced by easy conversation.

Leanne, Lydia, and I spent the rest of the evening talking about Leah. They asked about Pam and all that had happened. It was strange to discuss, but Leah had already filled them in.

The conversation shifted to Tony neither Leanne nor Lydia liked him. They'd met him once after Leah reconnected with them and were clear about their disapproval.

We talked about how Leah and I met and marveled at how amazing it was that we ended up together.

Throughout, I kept focusing on Lydia. She was a dead ringer for Leah, and I couldn't shake that thought.

Eventually, the topic turned to Leah's father and brother, who had died in a tragic car accident years ago.

I wasn't prepared for this. Leah had barely mentioned it before.

Leanne and Lydia explained what happened and when.

I had no idea it was shocking.

Leah's father and brother were pronounced dead at the scene. After their deaths, Leah disappeared for a long time. No one knew where she was or what she was doing. It wasn't until Leah called from New Jersey that the family reconnected.

It was clear both Leanne and Lydia loved Leah deeply and were happy to have her back.

They repeated their dislike of Tony and weren't shy about sharing it.

When Leah walked in, seeing her and Lydia together was overwhelming. The two sisters were identical in every way.

Leah kissed me hello and sat next to me, looking happy to be with her mom and sister.

The four of us talked for hours before going to bed. Leanne and Lydia stayed in the hallway bedrooms, each with its own bathroom. The house was set up well.

After saying goodnight, Leah and I went to our room.

She asked what I thought of her mom and sister. I told her that her mom was very cool and that I'd enjoyed talking with her.

Then I admitted, "Leah, I have to be honest. Your sister looks so much like you, I actually stood up to kiss her when she walked in I thought it was you! Thank God your mom stopped me."

Leah laughed, clearly unbothered.

We stayed up talking about her night. She told me how well things were going at the bar.

I was so happy for Leah and honestly for myself. We were finally starting to piece our lives together.

Eventually, Leah fell asleep. It was late, and I was tired too. I kissed her on the cheek and went to get a glass of water before turning in.

As I walked out of our bedroom, through the living room, and toward the kitchen, I saw the light on in the den.

I grabbed a glass of water and peeked inside.

Lydia was there, wearing headphones, eyes closed, relaxing and listening to music.

For some reason, I was intrigued. She really did look exactly like Leah.

Lydia wore pajamas shorts and a long t-shirt.

What Lydia was wearing was very similar to what Leah wore to bed. I have to admit, I was both curious and mesmerized. I couldn't stop watching her. She was just lying on the recliner, listening to music. Why was she so hard to resist? Why couldn't I stop looking at her? Leah is my fiancée, and Lydia only looks like her. She's not Leah. Yet, something about Lydia made me want to keep watching. I suppose it's because she looks exactly like Leah that I seem to fall into a trance whenever I look at her.

After a while, I decided it was time to go to bed. As I started to turn toward the kitchen, Lydia opened her eyes and caught me watching her. We made eye contact. In that moment, it felt like forever. I was both embarrassed and worried. Lydia stood up from the recliner and asked, "Paul, were you watching me?"

I responded, "No, Lydia. I just walked in and saw you there. It's late I was wondering why you were still up."

Lydia smiled. No words were spoken, but that smile seemed to say a lot. Of course, I couldn't quite translate what it meant, but it meant something.

A few moments later, Lydia said, "Goodnight." She turned and walked toward the hallway where her bedroom was.

I replied, "Have a good night, Lydia," then went back to the bedroom and climbed into bed with Leah. She was sound asleep.

Lying there, waiting to fall asleep, I thought about why I had watched Lydia so long. There's so much mystery with twins. Not necessarily anything sexual more mysterious. Yes, there's a sexual element, but it's extraordinary how much Leah and Lydia look alike.

What's even more fascinating is how they both captivate me, holding my interest. Maybe it's because they appear so much alike. Maybe it's something else. All I know is I hope Leah's mother and sister won't be staying long. Leah missed them and wants them here, but I'm going to have to learn to adjust.

Not because of temptation or any thought of cheating on Leah with her sister not at all. It's just curiosity. A fascination. Imagine seeing two of the most beautiful women in the same room at the same time and they're identical.

I have to stay away from crossing that line the line between reality and fantasy.

I'm somewhat familiar with twins because my sons
were twins too. When twins are born, and you
watch them grow, you learn so much that the "twin"
aspect becomes something you get used to.

In this case, seeing Leah and Lydia together in the
same house having never met Lydia before is
overwhelming. It will take time to absorb and
adjust.

Hopefully, I can get some sleep.

As I start to drift off, I glance over at Leah and feel
grateful to have her next to me.

CHAPTER 25

In the morning, I was the first one up, so I decided to make breakfast. Leah works late afternoons into the night, so I'm used to her sleeping in a little. Our guests didn't seem like they were getting up anytime soon, so I thought the smell of food might wake them eventually. I was right.

About half an hour into cooking, they all started to rise. First came Leah, slowly walking into the kitchen, kissing me good morning before taking a seat at the breakfast nook table. Then Leanne appeared, moving with the same calm posture as Leah, walking past me to say good morning, and sitting down next to her. Leah and her mom clearly had a great relationship they hugged and immediately started chatting.

Their conversation was about their nights, but it quickly shifted to wedding plans. Shortly after, Lydia came down the hall into the kitchen, offered a brief good morning, and sat at the table next to Leah and Leanne. The three of them dove right into discussing the wedding. It felt like I wasn't even there, like my input had no place in the conversation.

I stayed focused on cooking breakfast, though I noticed another text from Rick Simmons. I know I need to call him back, but right now, I'm focused on making a good impression on Leah's mother and Lydia.

The girls had been talking for a while when I served up breakfast. I made scrambled eggs, bacon, sausage, and toast. I mostly just listened to them plan the wedding. They shared every thought and idea, and I took it all in quietly.

After breakfast, I cleaned up while Lydia helped, and Leah and Leanne stayed engaged in conversation. Lydia did the dishes, then she and I went into the living room and sat down. We started talking about Leah, and Lydia really wanted to know more about how we met and how everything came together.

So, I explained my relationship with Pam, my sons, and what happened over the past year. Lydia was very compassionate and sympathetic; I don't think Leah had told her everything. I could see her eyes water, especially after hearing about what happened to Chris and Brian.

During our conversation, I felt Lydia and I had grown somewhat closer. I think she began to understand why I loved Leah so much. It was something I was glad to share and happy she understood why I cared for Leah deeply. Lydia saw me as the lost soul I was and Leah as the anchor of our relationship. It was a good moment for us.

Lydia now knows my heart belongs to her sister. I think she was looking for something to convince her I wasn't just another guy in Leah's life. The dynamic became abundantly clear, and I was grateful for the time we shared.

It still felt unreal talking to Lydia it was like looking at Leah. It was early, but I wanted to get a start on the day. I asked the girls if they would mind cleaning up, and of course, they agreed. One of the perks of cooking breakfast is that someone else does the dishes.

While getting ready to shower, my phone chimed again. It was Rick Simmons. I let it go to voicemail and hopped in the shower. My mind raced as I thought about how much I want to put the past behind me. Rick's endless investigation only keeps the wounds open.

I decided that after my shower, on my way to work, I would tell Rick I didn't want to be contacted about this anymore. Leah and I just want to move on.

After dressing, I walked into the living room and said goodbye to Leah, Lydia, and Leanne. They were deep into wedding planning, so what's a man supposed to do? Naturally, the only thing expected of me is to show up on the wedding day and I plan to do just that.

I kissed Leah goodbye, said goodbye to her mom and sister, and walked out the front door. As I headed to the car, my phone rang again Rick Simmons. I was starting to get angry that he kept calling.

In the car, I listened to Rick's voicemail: "Paul, Rick Simmons here. I know you're busy, but I really need to talk about what our team found regarding the case. Please call me as soon as you get this voicemail."

Suddenly, I was in no mood to talk. Leah and I have traveled a long road through this experience. We deserve happiness and to move on.

I paused, thought hard about calling Rick back, but decided it would only prolong the negativity. I don't want to go back I want to move forward.

So, I blocked Rick Simmons' number right then and there. I felt that to move past this horrible year, Leah and I need to stop looking back. We must focus on our relationship, our wedding, and starting a life together.

With that decision made, I chose not to tell Leah about Rick's attempts to reach me.

I arrived at the office, picked up some files, and headed out to start my day. I've always loved sales because much of the day is spent on the road, mostly alone with time to think.

I took advantage of the silence during my drive, which was unusual because I usually listen to music to relax. But today, silence was as good as any rock song on the radio.

I started to feel like I was being offered a second chance at life all because the most beautiful girl in the world wants to be my wife.

I honestly never thought I could fall in love again. I thought Leah and I were mostly a physical thing until we got to know each other.

Falling in love with Leah was easy. It happened so fast. Now, we're going to be married.

All this was sinking in as I pulled up to my first meeting with Mike Prescott, owner of Café 112 in Patchogue, Long Island. It's a nice place near Sunrise Highway.

I arrived a little early, so I worked on my laptop in the parking lot until it was time. This was a big opportunity to land a solid account.

Feeling enthusiastic, I prepared myself for the meeting. I was determined to get this account it was the first real big chance I'd had in a long time.

It felt good to be back in the saddle. Well… here goes.

Mike Prescott and I had a productive conversation, and by the end of the meeting, I was able to close the deal! It was official Café 112 would be exclusively supplied with seafood from our company.

The drive home was amazing. This time, I listened to the entire *Back in Black* album. What a rush to land a new account and to be forging ahead with a new life. I felt like my life had been reset, like I had been given a second chance. I hadn't felt this good or alive in quite some time. It was just what the doctor ordered, and I had the feeling things were finally starting to go our way.

When I arrived back at the house, no one was home, so I decided to grab a quick lunch and relax. It always feels good to kick back and enjoy the moment after making a sale and that's exactly what I did.

After lunch, I settled into my recliner with a beer. While chilling out, I had some words rattling around in my head, along with a melody that fit them perfectly. It had been a while since I wrote music, but for some reason, on this day, I really wanted to capture it.

I picked up my acoustic guitar and started playing. Within moments, the song began to take shape. I frantically wrote lyrics, not wanting to lose a single word that came to mind. When I finished, I had written a song. I named it "We Still Had Something."

Interestingly enough, the song was about Pam and me. Despite everything that happened, and the fact I no longer have feelings for her, I still remembered and reflected positively on what we had before things fell apart. I decided I wanted to record it.

Writing the song felt really good. The chord progressions came as naturally as the lyrics. In no time, I was playing the song on my acoustic guitar and singing it.

Here are the lyrics:

The sound of the ocean and the glow in your eyes
Watching the ships and the moments go by
The feel of the sand under our feet and your smile
The magical passion we're feeling right now
The heat of the moment we're wondering how
How much longer that we have together

Life is a gamble; we knew that all along
We had one shot and we took it

So, tell me
What do you do when it all goes away?
What do you do when there's nothing left to say?
What do you do when it all falls down to nothing?
Girl, we still had something

The stars in the sky and the ocean breeze
If we live for the moment then would you please
Remind me that my feet are still on the ground
If I blow you a kiss, do you think you'd catch it?
If I sent it directly, would you accept it?
What if I just wanted to hold you tight?

Life is a gamble; we knew that all along
We had one shot and we took it

So, tell me
What do you do when it all goes away?
What do you do when there's nothing left to say?
What do you do when it all falls down to nothing?
Girl, we still had something

The clouds roll in and the thunder roars as lightning
strikes the ground
The wind picks up and the sand blinds my eyes
The tide rolls in and it starts to rain, we feel so
washed away
We try so hard but we just can't hold on

And now we both look back after all this time
We were yearning for something we could never
find
There was something in our moment we couldn't
deny
These memories we'll take to our grave
The feelings that we had will be saved
We were living in the moment and it all seemed
right

Life is a gamble; we knew that all along
We had one shot and we took it

So, tell me
What do you do when it all goes away?
What do you do when there's nothing left to say?

What do you do when it all falls down to nothing? Girl, we still had something

After playing the song, I realized it was really good it just kind of came right out of me. Hours had passed without me noticing. I played it one more time to record it so I wouldn't forget what I had written.

I can't wait to play this for Leah. I'd love for us to sing it as a duet.

For now, though, I had to get back to the office to input the new account information from this morning's sale. As I was leaving, I called Leah's cell to let her know where I was and when I'd be back.

It was close to three o'clock, and I knew I probably wouldn't make it back before Leah left for work. Her phone kept ringing but didn't go to voicemail, so I hung up and texted her.

I hopped in the car and drove to the office. No response from Leah. That was strange maybe the girls were out shopping or something.

By the time I got to the office, it was nearly four o'clock. My phone rang as I walked up the walkway. Hoping it was Leah, I looked no, it was Jonie, Leah's boss.

"Hey Jonie, what can I do for you?" I asked.

"Paul," Jonie said, "can you let Leah know some people came by from New Jersey looking for her? They already left but didn't say what they wanted. I couldn't get her on the phone, so I thought you should know."

"Sure, Jonie. I haven't been able to reach her either. Her shift starts soon, and I'm sure you'll see her before I do. After I leave the office, I'll swing by to see both of you."

"Okay, Paul, but if she calls you, please tell her. I don't want these people to come back and Leah be surprised."

"No problem, Jonie," I said, then hung up and headed inside.

I quickly processed the sale and picked up my appointments for tomorrow. No one was in the office, so as I left, I locked up something we all do when we're the last to leave.

Back on the road, I couldn't get that new song out of my head. Feeling great about writing it and having a successful day, I couldn't wait to see Leah.

Then I thought about Jonie and what she said about some people from New Jersey stopping by looking for Leah. I really wondered what that was all about. About half an hour later, I pulled into the Rock n Roll Bourbon Café and walked in the front door. Leah was behind the bar, and Leanne and Lydia were talking with Jonie. The girls were all laughing, so I knew things must be okay. As I approached, Lydia and Leanne both stood and hugged me hello. I greeted Jonie and then went behind the bar to kiss Leah hello. Leah told me that some friends from New Jersey were in town and that we were all going out to dinner. Leah seemed very excited, and her mom and sister were too. I knew I had no say in this decision; obviously, I was going to meet her friends. We hung around for a bit and had a few drinks. Jonie had to get to the office for some work. The bar was crowded for happy hour, so Lydia, Leanne, and I grabbed a table. We talked about the wedding plans they had made earlier. Leah wants to get married in two weeks! That was much sooner than I expected, but again, not my place to ask questions. Lydia and Leanne were so excited, raving about how much they liked me and how perfect Leah and I were for each other. It was a great conversation, and I felt privileged it seemed like our lives were finally looking up. With this news, I asked to be excused so I could call a few friends about the wedding. Lydia and Leanne told me Leah wanted a small wedding, only about 25 people. Jonie agreed to have the reception at the Rock n Roll Bourbon Café. It was exciting but also sad. What hit me was that the friends I had when Pam and I were together no longer spoke to me. After Pam's arrest and seeing me with Leah, many just disowned me Junior and Jayde included. For the last year, I'd mostly been a loner when it came to friends. Funny how this happy occasion suddenly brought me down for a moment. I left the café and headed home. On the way, I felt strange upset and tired at the same time. I didn't understand why. I drove in silence, wondering what I was feeling. I should be happy after today. What was going on? Suddenly, the happiness and excitement vanished, replaced by anxiousness and unease. Then, out of nowhere, I started crying. Alone in the car, I sobbed uncontrollably like a child. In my head, I heard Pam's voice calling to me for help while she cared for Chris and Brian, as memories of when the twins were born flooded in. Those memories, as vivid as they were, brought an overwhelming feeling of loss. The reality was harsh my ex-wife Pam in prison, my two boys dead. I tried to pull myself together, but the sadness was crushing. I needed a moment to pause. Driving, I passed our block and a few miles later, a church caught my eye. I felt compelled to pull into its small parking lot. I parked, turned off the car and lights, and just sat. I wasn't sure what I was looking for or if I understood it yet. As minutes passed, I thought about the song I'd written today, "We Still had Something," and the conversation with Lydia and Leanne about the wedding. Wiping tears, I started to pray something I hadn't done in a long time. My faith had been shattered when God took my sons. At that moment, I reached out to God in anger, asking how He could do this to my family. So much time had passed since then, and I paused, reflecting in silence, parked at a church I honestly didn't remember seeing before on state road 25A. After a while, I got out and walked toward the church, only to find it boarded up. Maybe that's why I never noticed it. As I calmed, I realized writing "We Still had Something" must have taken me back emotionally to a time when feelings overwhelmed me. Here I was, finally settling down after what I'd consider a massive emotional breakdown. Then, I saw it a wooden cross in the middle of the property behind the church. I stood staring at it for minutes. It felt like I needed God then, and somehow, there He was. After some self-reflection, I felt a renewed spiritual strength and began to regain control of my emotions. I'm not sure if I heard a voice in my mind or out loud, but the message was clear: "In time. In time." The words were brief, direct, and nothing more. I left the property feeling a peaceful calm that had eluded me earlier. I think it wasn't a mistake that I ended up at this abandoned church that night. It had to be a sign. Now composed enough, I headed back to the car and home, deciding maybe to walk a bit before going in. This experience wasn't something I'd share people might think I'd lost my mind. The breakdown frightened me it came out of nowhere and I had little control over my feelings. I used the night's quiet and surroundings to regain composure. The weather was perfect; the crisp air helped me gather myself. I walked around the boarded-up church. No one was around. It was the quiet I needed. As I walked, I heard crickets chirping, the distant hum of passing boats, the clinking of sailboat rigging, and the steady ding of navigational buoys. At night, these sounds on Long Island Sound are so pronounced. All of it helped me think about everything I'd experienced today. Maybe, finally, all the pent-up emotion from losing so much in such a short time had caught up to me. I started thinking maybe I should open myself to faith again.

I truly want to look to God for strength, but I find it so difficult to reconcile that so much bad has happened. Losing my kids is the deepest wound I've ever carried, and recovering from it emotionally has been nearly impossible. I want to let God back into my life, yet I just don't feel ready. I don't know how to overcome the negativity. I know how harsh that might sound, but it's simply the reality of how hurt I am, and how hard this has been to face.

Part of the problem is that I've kept all my feelings bottled up. The other part, I realized only tonight. I truly believed I was ready to marry Leah at least I thought I was. But then I had to ask myself: if I were really prepared for this wedding, why would I have such an emotional breakdown?

I walked back to the car and decided to head home. It was getting late, and I wanted to get back before everyone went to bed. When I arrived, Leah wasn't home yet, but Lydia was in the recliner, headphones on, wearing her pajamas. I don't think she heard me come in. Leanne's bedroom door was closed she must have already gone to bed. They'd both been drinking when I left the bar, so maybe Leanne had had a little too much. She's older, and I can understand that.

I went into the kitchen for something to drink and settled on a beer. I didn't need to turn on the kitchen lights; the lamp in the living room was enough. Once again, I found myself watching Lydia. She lay there so peacefully, so relaxed. I still couldn't get over how much she looked like Leah. It had been a few days since I met her, yet she continued to intrigue me.

Just like before, I turned to walk toward my bedroom. As I did, Lydia opened her eyes and caught me looking at her. This time, there was no awkwardness just a knowing smile, as though she fully understood my curiosity. No words were spoken. After a moment, she got up and walked into the kitchen.

We sat down and talked. She asked if I was alright, if I was nervous about the wedding. For some reason, I felt comfortable with her, answering without hesitation. I opened up about how I was still struggling emotionally after everything that had happened. I told her about a song I had written earlier that day. She asked me to play it for her, but I reminded her it was still rough. She didn't mind.

I asked if her mom was asleep, worried we might wake her. Lydia replied that her mom was still out at the bar with Leah, so it was just the two of us. I explained the song's meaning and the emotions it stirred in me, then I played it.

When I finished, Lydia said, "Paul, that's a beautiful song. I love it." I told her I wanted to play it for Leah and ask her to sing it with me as a duet. Lydia's expression shifted. "Paul, I wouldn't do that," she warned. "Leah will probably think you still have feelings for Pam. Is that what you want her to think?"

Obviously, it wasn't. "Thank you, Lydia," I said.

Our conversation drifted, and we discovered we had a few things in common. We talked for about an hour before deciding to turn in. "Goodnight, Lydia. I should get to bed," I said. She asked what time Leah usually came home. I told her it varied, but at least her mom was with her.

"I'm going to take a shower before bed," Lydia said. "If you go to bed, please lock the front door." I told her I'd wait until she was finished, just watching television in the meantime. That's exactly what I did until I fell asleep in the recliner.

The sound of the front door opening woke me. Leah and her mom had returned. I stood, kissed Leah, hugged her mom, and asked about their night. Leanne said she was tired and went to bed. Leah told me she'd had a great night, full of tips, and that her boss was happy with how things were going. She wanted to shower and then sleep. I told her I'd wait in the living room.

I watched the news for a while politics and weather, nothing interesting then went to the kitchen for a glass of milk. As I drank, Leah came in fresh from the shower, wearing only a towel. I kissed her, told her how attractive she was, and said I was happy we were getting married. I held her close and kissed her again, this time more passionately. She smiled at me, and I told her I'd meet her in the bedroom.

When I walked into the bedroom, I heard water running in the shower. Confused, I went into the master bathroom and saw Leah finishing her shower. My stomach dropped. I realized I had just kissed Lydia in the kitchen, mistaking her for Leah.

I went back out. Lydia was in her pajamas again. She looked at me and said, "Paul, now you don't have to wonder what it's like to be with me. Sweet dreams." Then she walked past me into her bedroom. I was speechless.

I didn't tell anyone what had happened. Still processing, I went to bed, where Leah was waiting. "How tired are you?" I asked. She smiled, and we embraced. We made love, ending the night in passion.

I know how this sounds. But it was one wild turn of events, and with that thought, I drifted off to sleep after a very eventful day.

CHAPTER 26

Lydia and I were the first ones up this morning, and we discussed what happened last night. I told her I didn't appreciate the little trick she played. Lydia snapped back, "Paul, maybe if you stopped staring at me the way you do, I wouldn't have to resort to such drastic measures."

I paused, then explained that my staring was more fascination than infatuation. I still can't get over how identical the two of you are. "Lydia, promise me you won't do that again, please."

Lydia flashed that smile again and replied, "I do, I promise." Her smile bordered on laughter, and to me, it came across as a devious little girl being told what to do recognizing it but already advertising her intention not to listen.

Right after our brief conversation, Leanne came into the room and offered to make breakfast. Shortly after, Leah woke up and joined us in the kitchen. Once again, the girls were discussing the wedding, and I quietly left the room to be alone. I was still struggling with what had happened to me yesterday the complete breakdown I had.

I have a light schedule today, so I plan to take it slow. My idea was to visit Chris and Brian's graves. For some reason, I felt I needed to face my emotional instability head-on by visiting the boys.

The cemetery is located off Ocean Avenue, near Patchogue.

I went back to the kitchen and interrupted the girls, asking to speak with Leah privately for a moment. Taking her aside, I told her my plans and explained what had happened to me yesterday. Leah appeared very concerned but also very understanding. She hugged me, kissed me on the cheek, and told me she understood whatever I needed to do.

Leah added that if I wanted her to come with me, she would. I told her I'd let her know after breakfast.

Leanne had finished making pancakes, and we all sat at the table. Our conversation shifted to wedding arrangements. Leanne and Lydia planned to remain with Leah and me in our house until the wedding. They would stay for a week while Leah and I were on our honeymoon.

I have to say, getting to know them in such a short time has been good. I like them both. Even though Lydia is a bit promiscuous, she has a way about her that I trust and like. Despite the controversy, we get along well.

She knows that I love her sister, and I can clearly see that Leah is loved by Leanne and Lydia. As the wedding plans started coming together, the reality of it all sank in more and more with each passing day.

When breakfast was over, we all went our separate ways because everyone had things to do this morning. I was headed to the office to pick up some paperwork, then to a sales appointment before lunch. As I left the house, I prayed that today would be a better day no more emotional breakdowns.

Since I had only one appointment scheduled, I called my boss to let him know I would be late. He was fine with it. I knew he would be, but I always feel it's good to keep management informed. So, I headed to Patchogue.

While driving, I rode in silence. This was unusual for me I love listening to music in the car, but lately, whenever I'm driving alone, I've come to prefer the tranquility of silence and the time to think. So much has happened; so many thoughts swirling through my mind.

Take today, for example. This was my first visit to Chris and Brian's graves. The boys are buried next to each other. Pam and I wanted them to rest together in the same place. It was an emotional decision, but I think it was the right one. This was my first time visiting the cemetery I just couldn't bring myself to come sooner. Honestly, I couldn't stand the emotional pain. Still, not knowing how it would affect me, I knew I had to visit the boys. It just felt like it was time.

Often, I reflect on what happened and still feel anger and resentment that my sons were taken from me so young. It's so hard to come to terms with.

When I pulled into the cemetery parking lot, I parked, got out, and walked to the graves. As I approached, I saw the tombstones. At that moment, I knew nothing in this world could ever make me feel as I did right then. The feelings were overwhelming.

I calmly sat on the grass and started talking to the boys, as if they were still alive. I stayed there for quite some time. This felt like the only way I could deal with realizing that my only way to ever communicate with my sons again would be like this. At first, it felt awkward, but after a while, there was something very gratifying about talking with them.

I never thought I'd understand why people do this, yet here I was, rationalizing that human beings can find ways to spiritually connect with loved ones who have passed. I felt like they heard me when I spoke. With that confidence, coping with the moment became a little easier.

I guess just feeling close to the boys even if only in spirit was what I needed. It seemed to make all the difference in the world. At least it did, at that moment.

Then someone came up behind me and put a hand on my shoulder. Looking back, I saw Rick Simmons. At first, I was very upset. I wanted to tell him off, but as soon as he said, "Paul, I am so sorry for your loss," I gathered and corralled my anger. Instead, I thanked him.

Rick asked if I could give him a few minutes. I agreed I wasn't in a rush.

"Paul," Rick said, "I want you to understand something. Gabriel was very fond of Pam. He truly believed in her innocence honestly, we all did. He put his heart and soul into the investigation. His team and I wanted to continue it to see it through, in honor of Gabriel. Everyone investigating felt your wife Pam was innocent. We all saw the evidence, and yes, Pam looked guilty, but many things didn't add up. After months of digging and researching, we've put together a solid case a reconstruction of what we believe really happened. I know Pam's trial is over, but we wanted to do this for Gabriel, for Pam, and also for you. Having said that, there are some things we should discuss."

I replied, "Rick, I appreciate how much you've put into this, but Leah and I are getting married in less than a week. Right now, all I'm focused on is our wedding. Putting the past behind us is important to both of us."

Rick immediately interjected, "Paul, I think you should at least look at what we've learned before you marry this girl. I respect what you're saying, but if you'd just take one hour to discuss it, I believe it'd be in your best interest."

"Look, Rick," I said, "let me finish my visit with my sons and think about it, okay?"

"That's all I'm asking, Paul. Please give it some thought." Rick then walked away.

At that moment, I don't know why, but I took out my phone, went into my contacts, and unblocked Rick Simmons. I had to ask myself why this man would go out of his way to persuade me to look at what they uncovered if it wasn't important.

So now, the choice before me was between putting all this behind me and living forward or turning back to revisit the most painful time of my life. The question was: what do they know? The next question: do I really want to know?

While these thoughts rattled in my brain, my phone rang. It was Leah.

"Hey Leah, how are you?" I asked.

With genuine concern, Leah replied, "How are you? Are you alright?"

She knew I was visiting the boys' graves for the first time, and I think she was truly worried about how I was holding up.

"I'm really okay. Please don't worry," I told her.

"I love you, Paul," Leah said.

"I love you too," I answered.

"Okay, I have to go. I'll see you later tonight. I'll stop by the café."

"Okay," Leah said. "I love you. Goodbye."

Well, I certainly had a lot to think about.

Before walking away from the boys' graves, I told them I loved them, missed them, and would never forget them. Fighting back tears, I turned and walked toward the parking lot.

I had to meet a client this morning, so I really had to go.

Visiting my sons felt good. It felt like something I really needed to do.

As I headed to my appointment, I tried to gather myself so I could land another account. I was heading to Brian's Steak House in Sayville, Long Island. This could be a great opportunity.

I knew Brian before everything happened with Pam and Tony. We used to talk all the time.

I arrived at Brian's during lunch hour, on time for my appointment. But as I walked through the dining area, people stared at me. It felt like a scene from a strange movie.

Then it dawned on me the murders and Pam's conviction were all over the news, along with my picture as Pam's husband. I guess I'd forgotten that this was bound to happen.

As I made my way to Brian's office, he greeted me with open arms. He gave me a big, friendly hug and immediately asked how I was doing.

"Honestly, Brian," I replied, "I'm not doing well. Losing my sons has been so hard to accept."

I guess because of our past relationship, I didn't hesitate to be candid with him. There was already a level of trust between us.

Brian and I talked for what felt like hours. When it was over, he gave me his business. It was a great appointment finally, at least one part of my life was starting to resemble what I once had.

After we concluded, I felt a little better.

Driving home, I thought about what Rick Simmons said. The question: did I want to know what they found? Would learning the truth hurt me or the people I love?

Remember, Leah has been my fantasy since I met her. After everything, being so close to marrying this amazing woman, do I really want to risk it all?

Truthfully, I want to live. I want to marry Leah. I want to forget the past. Everything recent has caused me so much pain.

I want to marry the girl I love and have another chance at romance a chance at life.

These desires cause me to ignore what Rick wants to tell me. Maybe it's ignorance. Maybe fear. Whatever it is, I don't want to ruin what I have now.

I don't want to ruin my future with Leah.

You could say I'm a man in conflict with himself, a man with self-inflicted problems. But in this moment, all I see is myself and a brand-new life ahead.

Isn't it strange how everything changes? How things feel different now?

Somehow, I feel like I'm living on borrowed time. I want to make the most of it. I want to marry Leah.

I feel Rick's information can wait. I want Leah and me to bring this home this love we've found.

Somehow, I've convinced myself that ignorance is my best option.

With the wedding just days away, I've convinced myself that forging ahead is right.

I do love Leah. I want a new life moving forward. I don't want any more pain or heartbreak.

So once again, I went into my contacts and blocked Rick Simmons.

CHAPTER 27

Before I knew it, it was just a few days before our wedding day. Honestly, I feel like a man who has traveled down a long journey and finally arrived at the place I've been seeking my whole life. Waking up this morning, I feel energized and excited, and as I glance at Leah still asleep next to me, I feel so ready to marry this beautiful woman.

So, as I lie here in bed, drifting in and out of sleep, I can't deny the reality of what I'm feeling right now. I start flashing back to when I first saw Leah how I was in awe of how incredibly beautiful she was. How my desire was to be with her, even though at the time I was with Pam, and she was with Tony. Something inside me wanted to be with her.

Fast forwarding to today, just a few days away from marrying this woman, I can't help but feel both grateful and excited. Leah is someone I wanted from the moment I laid eyes on her. Back then, I was a married man and still in love with Pam, but everything has changed dramatically.

Now, making Leah my wife is just days away from becoming my reality. Still, I think back and feel so torn when I remember how much I loved Pam. Torn because no other words could describe how one goes from loving someone so much to feeling so deceived that the love disappears in an instant.

I asked God why all this happened why I lost Pam, why I lost my sons, and why I deserve this second chance, to have found Leah. After all, wasn't I being punished for something? Somehow, I decided I was guilty of sin, and God was punishing me by taking from me the people I loved. But then I wondered why God would bless me with Leah. Why should I end up with this person I'm so in love with?

Honestly, sometimes I overthink things too much.

As Leah stretched, yawned, and woke up right before my eyes, I just stood still and stared at her. To think, soon I will be marrying this amazing girl. Still conflicted, a large part of me wanted to forge ahead. Nothing would stop me from marrying Leah. I love this woman with all my heart and soul.

This would be yet another morning waking up and having breakfast with Leah, her sister, and her mother. The girls really enjoy the planning part of everything, and now they seem to be savoring the moment and the lead-up to the wedding.

With each day they've been here, Lydia and I have become pretty close. After the unusual thing she did to me last week, we now have an understanding. I promise not to stare at her with such curiosity, and in return, she doesn't mess with me. Very fair arrangement.

Today, I have some appointments scheduled and have to hit the road early. Leah is also working later this afternoon. I showered and got ready. On my way out, I kissed Leah goodbye and said goodbye to Lydia and Leanne.

It's an interesting day today. One of my appointments is at Junior's Tavern in Jamesport that's not until after 4:00 PM. It's been some time since I saw Junior. The last time I spoke with him was during Pam's trial. Junior was in law enforcement and is friends with Rick Simmons.

I've been avoiding Rick because I really don't want to hear what he has to say. I thought that once all this bad stuff was behind me, I could just get on with life.

It'll be interesting to see Junior though. I should ask him and his wife to come to my wedding. The thing is, Junior was really friends with Pam and me, and I don't know if they will be able to get used to my relationship with Leah. What I've decided is to play this meeting by ear and feel things out.

It's been a very long time since I saw Junior's wife, Jayde. It was at the trial, and that didn't go well. If I invite them to the wedding, will that cause a problem? Will they be uncomfortable with Leah and me being together? Well, I guess I'll find out this afternoon. Until then, I have a few sales appointments to tend to.

The day is turning out to be very productive. Two appointments in the books and two renewed contracts! I'm on a roll with sales this month.

It was coming up on 3:30 PM when I started heading to Jamesport. On the ride there, my phone rang. I picked up to find Rick Simmons on the other end.

"Paul," he said, "I need you to meet me at the rehab center. There are some things you need to see."

I responded, "I have a 4:00 PM meeting in Jamesport. I really can't be there."

"Paul," Rick said, "I can meet you after your meeting."

"Rick, this better be worth it. I can be there around 6:00 PM."

"Fine," Rick replied. "I'll meet you on the fifth floor. Remember to use the stairs there's no power in the building. Bring a flashlight so you can see where you're going."

"Alright, Rick. I'll see you there."

After hanging up, I called Leah to let her know what I was doing. Leah had some questions, but I assured her I'd fill her in when I saw her later at the Rock n Roll Bourbon Café. Leah was fine with that.

As I hung up, I pulled into Junior's Tavern. Junior was waiting outside at the front door. We hugged, said hello, and went inside. Jayde was there too. We immediately hugged and greeted one another.

"Jayde, it's been so long. You look amazing."

"Thank you," she said. "You look good too. Paul, how are you holding up?"

"Actually, Jayde, I'm doing much better now. It's been a while since we talked, but during Pam's trial, Pam's friend Leah and I started becoming close. You remember, right? Leah's boyfriend killed himself in his cell, and we were there for one another throughout that whole experience. Leah helped me get through the death of my sons, and when Pam was convicted, she helped me a great deal. We became friends and then started seeing one another. I'm engaged to Leah now, and we're getting married in a few days."

Jayde looked at me and after a long pause said, "Great. So happy for you."

I could see she wasn't really happy for me. She seemed a little disappointed that's how it felt anyway.

Then she said, "Let me go and leave you and Junior to talk business." Jayde went into the back room.

"Hey Junior, what's with her?" I asked.

"Paul, you know Pam and Jayde were close. She was so upset about Pam's conviction, and seeing you with Leah is just really unbelievable. It's like just yesterday that Pam was convicted, and you and Leah were already a thing. It's hard for Jayde to see, and honestly, for me too, bro."

I stopped and thought for a moment, then replied, "Junior, Leah and I have gone through so much together. It was hard for both of us when all this happened. We just found comfort in one another at a time when the world stopped making sense. Listen, you and Jayde are invited to our wedding. I'd love for you to be there only if it's something you feel you can do. I'd understand if you can't. Anyway, here's the invitation. Leah knows I was going to ask, and she knows that because Pam and I were close with you guys, you may opt not to attend."

"Junior, about business, do you want to renew your order with us?"

"Of course," Junior said. "Just write it up and I'll sign it. Just make sure you lock in my price."

"Sure thing," I replied. "Consider it done."

"Hey Junior, I have something to ask you. Do you remember Rick Simmons?"

Junior paused for a moment and replied, "Yes, I do. Why?"

"Well, Rick and his investigative team have contacted me several times because they think they have important information regarding Pam's conviction, but I'm reluctant to meet with him. I just want to put this all behind me."

Junior replied, "How could you not want to at least look at what they have? It could help Pam on appeal."

"I don't get it," I said. "I read the texts and emails between Tony and Pam. Her DNA was found at the crime scenes. She shot and killed her attorney in front of dozens of witnesses. We've gone way beyond the point of no return. I don't want to feel the pain any longer. Prolonging this seems unnecessary so much evidence was presented at trial."

Junior looked at me, put his hand on my shoulder, and said simply, "Paul, you must find the strength to face what they have head-on. What if it's important?"

"Junior, I'm actually meeting Rick at the rehab center after this. I'm going to see what he has to show me."

"That's good to hear," Junior said. "Isn't that place still closed up?"

"Yes," I replied. "I'm meeting Rick there basically in the dark."

Junior asked if I wanted company. I thanked him but decided to go alone.

"Hey Junior, do you think Jayde will ever forgive me? After Leah and I are married, I'd like the chance to get reacquainted, maybe be friends again. Will you please talk to her?"

Junior nodded and said, "Sure, Paul. I can't make any promises, but… yes, okay, I'll try. Maybe I'll see you at the wedding on Saturday."

Junior smiled and said, "Yeah, maybe."

So, it ended up being a great day for sales and potential friendships, which really lifted my spirits a bit. Now, I was heading off to the rehab center to meet Rick Simmons.

As I left the parking lot at Junior's Tavern, I called Leah.

"Hey, Leah, I'm heading over to meet the investigator, Rick, at the rehab center. I'll head over to the Rock n Roll Bourbon Café after the meeting."

Leah sounded very concerned. "What do you think he wants?"

"I don't know," I replied, "but as soon as I see you tonight, I'll share what he tells me. I'll see you at the bar, okay?"

"See you then," Leah said, and we ended the call.

As I headed out to the rehab center, I couldn't help but think of everything we'd gone through this past year. The reflections were inescapable, and the recollections made me feel very depressed once again. I think that's why I was initially avoiding Rick Simmons. To dredge up those awful feelings again was the last thing I wanted.

After about a 15-minute drive, I pulled into a dark parking lot. I parked the car and started walking to the building. I had brought a flashlight and took the stairs to the fifth floor. Surprisingly, none of the doors were locked.

I entered the office where the rehab center was located. Sitting behind the reception desk was Rick Simmons. I could only make out his silhouette in the darkness, but he immediately said, "Hi Paul, so glad you decided to come. I have some things to tell you. But first, I want you to take this thumb drive and review it later tonight or tomorrow when you have time. It will help explain everything after I share the information I have. Please, Paul, have a seat, and let's talk."

"The first thing you need to understand is that our investigation ran very deep, well before the trial even started. We were looking for a serial killer, and based on everything we knew then, we felt confident we were on the right path."

"Rick, what changed?" I asked. "What do you mean? Are you saying this was about something else?"

Rick stopped me and replied, "Paul, for you to understand, I need you to put everything you know or think you know about the whole thing aside for me. Please just listen to what I have to share, okay?"

"Alright."

"So, in the beginning, you thought you were dealing with a serial killer, but then you learned it was something else?" I asked.

"Yes," Rick replied.

"When Gabriel was defending Pam, he always maintained she was innocent. Many of the investigators, including myself, had our doubts, so we just followed the evidence. Unfortunately, the evidence we found only reinforced Tony and Pam's guilt. There was DNA found at the scenes, text messages and emails between Tony and Pam, and what we found when we visited the rehab center."

"Like any investigation, time is necessary to get to the truth. So, Paul, what I'm about to tell you will be somewhat unbelievable, but we can back it up with actual evidence. This is what I put on the thumb drive for you to see for yourself. Tonight, I wanted to offer you an overview an alternative theory specifically regarding Pam's guilt."

"Paul, are you ready for this?" Rick asked.

"Honestly, Rick, I don't think so, but I'm here. You have my attention," I responded.

"Paul, the start of it all actually began in New Jersey. Tony owned a rehabilitation facility in Newark, and Leah was with him there. Leah managed the facility. Both had ownership in the business. In New Jersey, they were known as Thomas and Sarah Perci husband and wife. They ran the business for four years before it was dissolved."

"When we dove into investigating that facility, we uncovered a settlement with the state of New Jersey. Tony and Leah were accused of stealing hundreds of thousands of dollars through insurance fraud. They were submitting claims for additional sessions and treatments that were never performed. Some patients caught on and filed complaints with the New Jersey Office of the State Comptroller."

"The Insurance Fraud Prevention Act empowers the state to investigate insurance fraud, which is what happened. As part of a plea deal, the business had to close. A settlement was reached because the state couldn't prove all charges, and Tony and Leah wanted to avoid court. The rehab center closed, and they paid a $750,000 fine, along with agreeing never to practice in New Jersey under any business name."

"Tony and Leah then relocated to Long Island, where they started the rehab center again this time under their real names. No one made the New Jersey connection until we did now."

"Paul, did you ever ask Leah where all her money came from?"

"No, I didn't," I admitted.

Rick said, "Well, this is plausible, don't you think?"

I just nodded, still in disbelief but letting Rick continue.

"When Tony and Leah came here and got the business running, everyone knew them as Tony and Leah boyfriend and girlfriend. They started the insurance fraud again. We only learned this because of our investigation. They might not have been caught if it weren't for Gabriel's insistence that we keep digging."

"What happened here was like New Jersey. A few patients caught on, but this time they didn't get a chance to file complaints because Tony and Leah killed each one of them. They realized this was the way to keep the fraud concealed."

"The news called it the work of a serial killer, but now we know it was two criminals trying to keep their scam going."

I asked, "Still, with all this, how did Pam's DNA end up at the crime scenes? How did the emails and texts between Pam and Tony happen?"

Rick explained, "Those emails and texts were really between Leah and Tony. Leah planted Pam's DNA at the scenes. She did it all on her own. Leah was a computer tech major and knew how to do what she did, fooling everyone. She changed sender and recipient information and altered writing styles to mimic Pam. Pam was never involved. She didn't send a single message presented in court. Her DNA was planted. We strongly believe this is true."

"That's what's on the thumb drive. We have copies of everything. Review it, and if you want, you can get rid of it. This isn't definitive proof, but it raises enough concern for a prosecutor to investigate."

I asked, "What is Leah's real name?"

Rick replied, "It's really Leah. She used Sarah in New Jersey and reverted to Leah in Long Island. Thomas was fake, but Tony is his real name."

"This is all too much for me to process," I said.

Rick responded, "I wanted to tell you as a courtesy. I'm very sorry. Authorities will arrest Leah tomorrow on suspicion of fraud and murder. I thought you should be the first to know."

"Thank you, but what am I supposed to do now? I'm supposed to marry Leah. We have a wedding scheduled."

Rick said, "There's more. Leah's father and brother died in a car accident. We have strong evidence she tampered with the car. We think she did the same to Pam's sister and your sons, Chris and Brian. We can't prove it beyond reasonable doubt, but this will be used to show what kind of person she is."

"We also believe Leah had something to do with Tony's suicide. We found a letter Tony wrote on a notepad from prison a confession implicating both himself and Leah. We believe he told Leah he would expose her, and although we can't prove it, we think she arranged for someone to make his death look like suicide."

"We're still investigating, but we believe we have enough for a case against Leah and enough to petition a judge to allow this new evidence to possibly overturn Pam's conviction, at least for the crimes she didn't commit."

"Paul, this is why it was so urgent to talk to you alone."

I just sat there, staring at Rick. How do I deal with all this? I feel like I've been kicked in the stomach, struggling to breathe.

Rick, I asked, can you please let me handle what I need to handle tonight, without getting involved? Please. I really don't know what to do, and I need some time to think. Rick just looked at me and said, sure Paul, I can do that. He stood up, shook my hand, and thanked me for taking the time to meet with him. "Remember," Rick repeated, "Leah will be arrested tomorrow." I thanked him, and as he left, I sat there in darkness. I looked up and started to pray to God. At that moment, I felt like I truly needed to turn to Him for direction. After all the resentment I'd held against God, I felt myself surrendering now. Feeling like I'd reached the end, I knew I had to ask for help. So, I prayed, hoping God would forgive me for my bitterness   for losing my sons, for losing Pam to prison. All I needed was a shoulder to keep me afloat. I asked God to be that shoulder.

I finally found the strength to stand up. I was still holding the thumb drive Rick had given me. I needed time to study the information, but I also needed a friend   someone to help me process all this and decide what to do next. Honestly, I had no real ideas other than to hit the road and meet up with Leah. But was that even a good idea? While I pondered, my cell phone rang. It was Junior from the tavern. "Paul," he said, "I just spoke with Rick Simmons. I think you should come back to the tavern. Meet me here   I want to talk." Of course, I was going to take Junior up on his offer because I didn't know what else to do. So, I headed to the tavern. It was only about a 15-minute drive.

It turned out Rick had already called Junior after our meeting. I should've guessed   Junior's background in law enforcement meant Rick probably gave him a heads-up that authorities would arrest Leah tomorrow. This whole situation was weighing heavily on me as I drove toward the tavern. First Pam gets arrested and kills Gabriel, and now Leah will be arrested tomorrow, leaving me with no one. My sons are dead. What a fool I've been. My first real love   my true love   was taken from me. Then I fell in love again, only to discover Leah was not who I thought she was, and now she was being taken away too. As I drove, my thoughts flashed back to my boys   how they were taken from me, the way they died alone, without their mother or me. At the top of my lungs, I screamed toward the heavens, asking God how He could be so cruel. This anger toward God has grown louder in me over the years, magnified by all He's asked me to accept and bear.

When I pulled into Junior's parking lot, I sat there for what felt like half an hour, reluctant to move. Finally, Junior came out to get me. He helped me walk into the tavern, through the crowd, and into his office where we began talking. Junior put the thumb drive into his laptop, and together we looked over what Rick had compiled. Needless to say, the evidence was overwhelming   and shocking.

Then my phone rang. It was Rick. "Hey Rick," I said, "I'm here with Junior looking at the stuff on the drive." "Paul," Rick replied, "hang in there a little longer. There's a hang-up with the arrest warrant   it may take a few days to clear up." "What do I do?" I asked. "Business as usual. No one knows you know anything. I want you to pretend you know nothing. Understand?" "Yes," I said, "but you realize the wedding is in two days, right?" "I get it," Rick said. "You'll have to live each day like you never learned this. Junior will help you   he and I have already talked." "What I need you to do," Rick continued, "is stop by Leah's place where she's tending bar, like you always do. Talk about the things you usually talk about. Just let this unfold." Rick sounded confident, and so did Junior. Me? I was rattled but understood what I had to do. I just needed time to absorb it all.

Junior and I talked for a while after Rick and I got off the phone. Jayde came in and knew everything too. She apologized for being so harsh earlier. Junior explained all that had happened, and Jayde finally understood Leah had played just about everybody   including me. The three of us talked for about half an hour before I headed out to the Rock n Roll Bourbon Café to see Leah.

On the drive, I listened to music to gather strength for the role I had to play until Leah's arrest. When I arrived at the bar, I walked through the crowd and stood at the bar, waiting for Leah. Watching her serve drinks reminded me of all those nights we shared intimate conversations right here. Leah finally walked over and kissed me hello. "So glad to see you," she said. "Thanks for coming." "So, what did that guy Rick want?" Leah asked. "He wanted to show me something and set a time to meet after the wedding," I said. "He didn't show tonight, but he called and wants to meet in a few weeks." "How's your night going?" I asked. Leah smiled. "Busy all night, but it's finally slowing down." We talked for a bit, then Lydia and Leanne joined me. We all started chatting, and I offered to buy a round of drinks. We decided to hang out until Leah's shift ended.

Staying engaged with Leah's sister and mother was challenging, knowing what I knew about Leah. I doubted they suspected anything. Leah leaned over the bar and kissed me. We raised our glasses to our wedding. It was bittersweet I still loved Leah deeply despite everything. Lydia and Leanne treated me like family, and it felt good. Our little party went on for hours, and by the time it was time to leave, we were all buzzed.

Our house was just a few blocks away. None of us were in a condition to drive, so I suggested we walk. Leah said she hadn't had much and offered to drive. We agreed and got in the car. The girls laughed and reminisced about childhood memories, especially when Leah and Lydia were little girls. Leanne seemed to enjoy it most.

When we arrived home, we all walked inside. Leah said, "Paul, I'm going to change   I'll be right out. Please get my mom and Lydia something to drink and meet me in the living room." I could tell the gathering wasn't over. Lydia and Leanne sat down while I went to the kitchen. "Is bourbon okay, ladies?" I asked. They both said yes, on ice. I poured and brought the drinks out. Leah and I drank our whiskey neat.

Leah came out in her sleeping attire. I always loved how she dressed for bed. I handed her the drink, and she sat down with us. We talked, and Leanne asked how I was feeling with the wedding so close. "A little nervous, but ready," I said.

Leanne smiled. "Paul, something you don't know about my girls is they're very protective of me." I nodded. "That's a good thing, right? They're always looking out for their mother. Admirable." Leanne's tone shifted. "Paul, can you guess what one thing neither of these beautiful daughters will stand for?" "No," I said. She continued, "They won't stand for deceit." "That's good too, right?" I asked. "Paul," Leanne said, "it's time you learned a bit about my girls' past."

Leah chimed in quickly, "Mother, not here. Not now!" I was stunned. Leanne stared at both Leah and Lydia with intensity. "Why not now? I think he should know," she insisted.

Lydia got up. "I'm going to change, I'll be right back. Mother, please don't start without me." I looked at Leah, unsure what to expect. We'd all been drinking, and the atmosphere felt tense. I wasn't sure I wanted to know.

When Lydia returned, she wore sleepwear similar to Leah's. Leanne smiled and looked at both girls, then at me. "Paul, have you ever seen two girls who look so alike?" "No, I haven't," I admitted.

Lydia asked me to play my new song, "We Still Had Something," for Leah. I hesitated   Lydia had warned me Leah might be upset, thinking the song was about Pam. Instead of saying that, I picked up the guitar and played.

Leah seemed surprised. Before I could explain, she asked, "Paul, why did you play it for Lydia and not tell me about it?" I said it was just an idea at first and I ran it by Lydia because she was home when I wrote it. Leanne asked, "What's the song about?" Leah asked, "Who's it about?" I answered honestly, "I don't know. It just came to me one night."

As we talked, I noticed Leanne starting to fall asleep. Lydia put her hand on her mother's shoulder and asked if she wanted to be taken to her room. Leanne nodded, and Lydia helped her up.

Leah asked me to play the song again. As I sang, Leah and Lydia watched, looking relaxed but tired from the drinks. After finishing, Leah said, "That was very good, Paul. I really liked it."

Lydia stood, said goodnight, and headed to her room. Leah and I sat quietly for a moment. Then Leah asked, "What did you expect to be asked?" "Paul, was that song about Pam?" she pressed. I said no, it wasn't intentionally about Pam, though some feelings from that time probably slipped in. It's just a song.

While speaking with Leah, my back was to the hallway. Suddenly, I felt the urge to turn around. When I did, no one was there. The strange feeling happened again   I felt watched. I turned once more; still, no one.

Leah noticed. "Paul, what's wrong? Why are you acting paranoid?" "Sorry," I said. "I don't know why I'm on edge."

We resumed talking about the song, and I ignored the feeling to look behind me. Leah pressed again if the song was about Pam. I told her some of it was inspired by my past with Pam, but it was just a song.

Leah then asked what Rick Simmons wanted. I guardedly said I wasn't sure   though I knew the truth.

Leah said softly, "Paul, I could have stood for almost anything. I really did love you." Shocked, I said, "Wait, did love me?"

"Yes," Leah said, "did. I'm sorry." "Sorry for what? You did nothing wrong," I said.

She looked deep into my eyes and said, "I'm sorry it has to end this way." Her eyes went soulless   like she'd undergone a dark transformation. The look was frightening.

Despite everything, I couldn't shake the paranoia gnawing at me. Something was off. I turned to look behind me again   and that's when it happened.

Leah whispered, "Paul, I did love you." Everything moved in slow motion, yet real time at once. I asked her what she meant.

She repeated, "I really did love you." Tears fell from her eyes. She stared into mine but seemed to look past me, behind me. The urge to look behind me surged again   but I focused on Leah.

Suddenly, sharp pain hit the side of my head, followed by a blow to my lower back. I tried to stand but saw Leah staring as Lydia swung a baseball bat, striking the side of my face.

In agony, I tried to escape but was hit again   to my left leg, right leg, then the back of my neck. I fell down but struggled to crawl away. Another sharp pain struck my right lower back.

Face down, blood everywhere, I knew I was badly hurt. Silence followed, broken only by muffled voices in the distance. Barely conscious, I felt myself being dragged.

I sensed stairs beneath me, each step thudding as I was pulled down into the cellar. I heard Leah crying, Lydia laughing, and maybe Leanne   but couldn't be sure.

The last sound was flesh hitting the concrete floor. Then I lost consciousness.

Even then, muffled voices spoke.

"He had it coming," one said.

"I knew he'd be unfaithful," another.

"He deserves this."

"Let's leave him down here tonight and deal with him in the morning."

"Leah, let's go. Paul's no different than the others. Same as your father and brother."

"It's time to let him go."

That was the last thing I heard before everything went black.

CHAPTER 28

I was awakened by the sound of muffled voices and a light shining into my face. I tried to open my eyes, but no matter how hard I tried, they wouldn't budge. I was aware of my surroundings because I could somehow see the light and hear the sounds, but I couldn't move not my arms, nor my legs. A numbness spread throughout my body, yet I remained strangely aware of the noises around me.

Then I heard a sound a door opening, I think. Footsteps followed, and then voices. I was still foggy, struggling to make sense not only of where I was but also of my inability to move or open my eyes.

"You girls, clean up the stairs and the living room. I'm going to untie him and take care of the areas around Paul," one voice said.

"Leah!" another voice screamed. "Get with it! Remember, he's just like your father, just like your brother, and just like Tony was. Now please, let's get this done. We can make it look like someone broke in and beat him to death."

Another voice chimed in, "Leah, when Paul doesn't show up for the wedding, they'll look for him."

"Mom is right. Let's go. Let's take care of this."

As they spoke, I gradually understood what was happening around me, but I remained unable to open my eyes or move. I couldn't feel anything, but I sensed I was being moved and repositioned. Even without sensation, I knew what was going on. I felt utterly helpless and vulnerable, unable to respond or speak.

Suddenly, I heard glass breaking nearby, shards scattering around me. Then a voice said, "Lydia, I need you to place something outside this window so no one can see it during the daytime."

Footsteps retreated, but someone remained near me I could hear breathing. Oddly, my sense of smell was still intact. The scent was familiar. It was Leah or at least, I thought it was.

Finally, someone spoke softly.

"Paul, I'm so sorry. I really did love you so much. My mother told me you kissed Lydia, and when I heard that song you wrote, I knew you still loved Pam. But I really loved you, Paul. I'll never forget you," Leah whispered.

I heard the faint sound of a kiss.

"I told Pam I would kill you. Pam wanted me to kill you. She hated you, Paul. Pam never loved you not like I did. Goodbye, my love."

I wasn't sure if Leah kissed me or blew me a kiss, but I knew she was saying goodbye.

At that moment, I was little more than a living, breathing mass of flesh able to hear, smell, and sense what was happening, but unable to react. It was deeply disturbing to be trapped in this condition.

I was certain I was being left in this cellar to die. As the voices and footsteps slowly faded and the light dimmed into darkness, I couldn't tell if I was alive or dead.

Having heard everything, somehow aware of my surroundings, I found no reason to hold on. What purpose did I have left? Each passing moment, I couldn't rationalize a reason to keep fighting.

So, I lay on the cold concrete floor, waiting to die.

Once again, I slipped in and out of consciousness, darkness and silence enveloping me. Somehow, I found the strength to pray to God. My whole life flashed before my eyes as I begged for help.

As I lay there in the cold cellar, visions appeared. I saw my boys at first shrouded in fog, but their shapes grew clearer as they approached me. A wave of serenity and comfort washed over me in that moment. Maybe I was on my way to be with Chris and Brian.

A warm sensation surrounded my body, an immense feeling of peace and love blanketed me. There was a bright light like those people describe when nearing the end of life.

Was this the end?

Drawn closer to the light, I reached out to touch it. But suddenly, a jerking sensation yanked my entire body away. I desperately wanted to grasp that amazing light, but it wasn't my time.

Then, I was thrust back into consciousness not awake, but aware of sounds around me.

It was still dark, I still felt nothing, but I could hear.

Muffled voices returned. I caught fragments of conversation, then multiple crashes glass breaking and a thunderous bang, like a door kicked in. Loud voices shouted, then a series of gunshots five or six rounds.

Rumbling followed, then screams.

I couldn't tell what was happening. It was hard to make sense of sounds alone, especially in my semi-conscious state.

Suddenly, silence.

Then the sound of a door opening and people coming down stairs.

Voices became clearer, but I still couldn't see or move. I couldn't respond, but I could hear everything.

One voice said, "I need an ambulance dispatched right away. One alive, three dead at #666 Deadwood Path."

Then two other voices I recognized immediately: Junior and Rick Simmons.

As they approached, I heard them exclaim, "Oh my God!"

They sounded rattled, but I couldn't tell them I was okay.

I heard crying next not sure who, but at that moment, I feared I might truly be dead.

But how? How could I still be aware? Why, God, could I still hear everything?

Then I felt myself being moved again.

Sounds of a radio crackled the kind you hear in police cars or ambulances.

Next came the sounds of a siren, followed by medics working on me.

Still able to hear and sense things around me, I had to surmise that I was indeed still alive. Everyone's voices sounded concerned as I seemed to be moving. Then, I heard the sound of automatic doors opening, followed by many background voices that quickly faded away. Most of the voices left, and I began to hear beeping perhaps from a heart monitor. There was also the sound of loud breathing. Could that be my own?

Still, I felt nothing. I could see some light and hear sounds, but I had no ability to move or feel. Slowly, the sounds grew faint and distant, and the light dimmed. Am I dying? God, what is happening to me?

As the sounds shifted from distant to near and the light brightened, I became aware of my surroundings once again. Voices I recognized filled the space. Though I still couldn't open my eyes or move, something about this awareness felt different more focused, closer.

Listening closely, I caught the conversation around me. The breathing remained steady, and in the background, voices whispered. Unlike before, I felt something like someone was holding my hand. Yet, no matter how hard I tried, I couldn't respond.

Can I still be alive, or is this something else?

I heard my friends Junior and Jayde speaking, mentioning how long it had been. Though I didn't fully understand, I listened intently. Then Jayde's voice came through clearly: "Paul, please wake up. We miss you. We know you're in there. Please, Paul, respond. Let us know you can hear us."

I felt compelled to respond. I tried to open my eyes, to move but failed. Trapped in this unconscious mental jail cell, I realized this might be the end. This could be my funeral.

Overcome with emotional pain, I felt tears start to well. I couldn't bear that they didn't know I was still here, still alive.

Then, Jayde called out, "Junior, come here! Come here! There are tears coming from Paul's eyes!" Junior yelled for a nurse. "Nurse! Nurse!"

It dawned on me I must be in a hospital. I must be dying or somewhere in between.

Suddenly, I sensed movement and noticed changes in the light. The breathing intensified. Bright beams of light shone intentionally into my head first on one side, then the other. This repeated several times.

After a few moments, the agitation and bright lights subsided, and other voices spoke. One said, "Junior, Jayde, this sometimes happens with coma patients. We shouldn't get our hopes up, but we also shouldn't give up."

Then, all voices stopped.

I felt as if I were back in a place that felt like nowhere. The light remained, the breathing constant and unending. Silence surrounded me.

In that moment of solitude, I felt pressure on my arm though I wasn't sure where. The pressure eased, and the light began to fade once again.

Suddenly, I was no longer in tune with my surroundings. Was I falling asleep? It was impossible to tell.

As the light and sounds faded, I slipped once more into darkness.

CHAPTER 29

Once again, I sensed activity around me. Light appeared, and voices filled the air. This time, there seemed to be more voices. I recognized some, but I began to doubt whether what was happening was real. I felt trapped in this place surrounded by light and voices but unable to engage.

Then I heard someone say, "Let her in." Several people discussed taking him off life support. Undoubtedly, that someone must be me. One voice asked if someone would sign some paperwork. I also heard crying, but I couldn't make out much more.

A man's voice said, "Before we take him off life support, do you want a moment alone with him?" A soft voice replied, "Yes, I would." Footsteps echoed, followed by a door closing, and then silence.

Then a voice said, "Junior, Jayde, please stay with me. I don't want to be alone when he goes." Next came a voice I knew: "Paul, I love you. I will never forget our life together. I will never forget you, Chris, or Brian. I know we haven't been close for some time, but I understand what happened, and I don't blame you. I blame Leah. I know you will be reunited with Chris and Brian. I know how much you loved our sons, and how much they loved you."

As I listened, memories surfaced. I saw Pam playing in the yard with the boys, recalled our walks along the Long Island Sound, and remembered kissing Pam goodnight. I realized Pam was speaking to me.

I screamed to God with all my being, "Please, God, let me wake up. Please!" Then I felt Pam's hand holding mine as she whispered, "I love you."

People entered the room again. A voice asked, "Are you ready?" I heard Pam reply, "Yes, I am." As I felt movement, the steady breathing I'd heard so long stopped. I tried to yell, scream, move anything but could not break through.

"Please let me live! Please, help me God. I want to wake up!"

Then the steady beeping I'd heard for so long ceased. Still unable to move, speak, or respond, I waited. I thought I was just waiting to die.

I heard Pam crying. It felt like she was still holding my hand. I wanted so badly to wake up, but I just couldn't break through.

Then something changed. I think I felt Pam kissing me warmth on my face and hair draped softly around me. I wasn't certain, but I truly felt something. I tried to squeeze Pam's hand and felt a response.

I heard nothing, but I felt wetness on my face and hand. My God I could feel!

With all my might, I tried to move, speak, scream, react and finally, after all this time, I screamed at the top of my lungs, "I am alive!"

But silence remained. No sounds, no voices just nothing.

Still, a warmth I couldn't explain filled me, undeniable and comforting.

I tried again this time, I tried to speak. When that failed, I tried to open my eyes. The sense of Pam's presence drove an unstoppable life force that refused to be denied. Over and over, I refused to relent because I wanted to be alive.

All I could feel was the strong desire to be with Pam. Although I knew she was there, it wasn't enough. I wanted to see her, hold her, and have one more chance at our life together.

These emotions surged through me, but I couldn't summon the strength to wake.

I didn't let each failure discourage me, knowing that if I didn't give up, God would see me through.

It was poetic irony asking God for help after all my years of denying His existence, after all the anger I'd felt toward Him for what happened.

During this time, thoughts ranged from the best moments of my life to the worst.

As I struggled to wake, the warmth grew stronger than before. I just knew that when I opened my eyes, Pam would be there.

Suddenly, the light I sensed became real. As I gazed through it, blurry images appeared. I heard crying and muffled voices. It was hard to make out what was being said.

Over minutes, the blurry vision sharpened, and muffled sounds became clearer.

I tried to move my hands, feet, and arms but couldn't.

I could, however, see Pam. She stood over me, crying. For a moment, I thought I had died.

Then Pam leaned in and kissed me. Her long hair blanketed my face, her tears wetting me everywhere.

In that moment, I fully understood I was alive.

All I could think was wanting to hug Pam.

As this unfolded, doctors and nurses came into focus, examining me. Pam stayed close, remaining in my vision throughout.

I still couldn't move, but for the first time in a long while, I could see, hear clearly, and feel.

I cannot describe what this feels like. Being there without really being there.

Understanding that God was with me and had helped me through, I now grasp what love and faith truly mean.

All I want is to work hard to show my gratitude to God for saving my life.

After the examination, the doctor asked if I could speak. I whispered, "Pam."

I repeated it, and Pam was still there. I saw a dozen or more people in the room watching me.

Still weak and unable to say much, I looked at Pam and found the strength to whisper, "I love you. Thank you."

At that moment, the doctor asked everyone to leave.

Pam kissed me on the cheek before leaving.

The nurses stayed behind and told me to rest. I couldn't reply, but if I could, I would have laughed and asked if they thought I'd had enough rest after all this time.

There may be a long road ahead, but I intend to heal
I want another chance at life.

I feel so grateful to still be alive.

As I lay there, I heard someone say, "It is a miracle

CHAPTER 30

The incredible series of events that brought me to where I am now cannot be fully explained. There is only one answer, and that answer is faith. Why God saved my life, I will never know, but I owe it to Him to show my deepest appreciation for this second chance.

A few months have passed since I woke up. I am now on a strict daily physical therapy regimen. They tell me that if I ever want to walk again, I have to work very hard to achieve that goal. Waking from this nightmare, I must catch up with everything. I couldn't even remember what happened to me.

Junior, Jayde, and Rick Simmons have visited frequently, slowly filling me in on all the events that led to my attack, my coma, and everything since I woke. Pam and I have spent quality time talking. She tiptoes around me, not wanting me to be emotionally stressed. We have discussed everything in great detail.

For me, recalling the past is difficult, but for the most part, Pam forgives me for how I abandoned her. I believe she understands that I didn't have all the right information. I never wanted to hurt her not ever.

Until now, I never realized what true love was. It's incredible how two people like Pam and me can endure so much adversity and still find their way back to a place where love can be rekindled. It's nothing short of a miracle.

Knowing my life will never be the same, I continue to work hard to salvage my physical abilities. The doctors say I might make a partial recovery, but they can't be sure if I'll regain all my physical or cognitive abilities. Both have been permanently affected.

They tell me that with hard work in therapy, I may improve physically and mentally. Every day, therapy is followed by Pam's visit.

Pam has explained all the legal matters that she is a free woman, Lydia and Leanne are dead, and Leah is in prison. So much has happened while I was in a coma. Leah was convicted of murder, and Pam has since been released.

Right now, I struggle to process all this. As we talk face to face, I often reflect on what we once had. I would give anything to have that back.

But for now, I'm just grateful to be alive and to have Pam with me.

Here we are talking, laughing, sometimes crying over what we had and lost. We share a bond forged by the tragedies we endured. We both have a future to look forward to and a past to keep us grounded.

Looking at Pam, I realize I'm still in love with her. She has grown harder around the edges; I think prison changed her. We are both very different from who we were all those years ago, but something inside us survived.

Something unspoken that initial spark that drew us together has brought us back. I'm thankful to God for this second chance.

Pam and I have gone through so much. Even when everything fell apart, we still had something: each other.

That something is a love stronger than ever a bond that can never be broken.

As I look ahead on this long, winding road of recovery, I look at Pam, the love of my life, and I know we will make the most of this second chance.

So tell me: What do you do when it all goes away? When there's nothing left to say? When it all falls down to nothing?

You recognize you still have something.

Pam and I still have something.

CHAPTER 31

Three years have passed, and looking back, it all feels like a blur. As far as my recovery goes, I've made a lot of progress, but unfortunately, I will never walk again. Living with this disability is hard, but Pam has been a tremendous help throughout my recovery. It's fortunate that her specialty is physical rehabilitation therapy she has been amazing.

We've both been through so much. Thinking about this moment, this second chance, fills me with a high level of excitement much like the very first time I met Pam back in school. I've been staying with her during my recovery. She's been there every step of the way. I've been surprised by how she's picked herself up and started over. We've truly started over from nothing.

Pam managed to find work at a facility in Sayville. New York State offers a program that helps ex-convicts find job opportunities. Pam took advantage of it and found a job in her field. We relocated from eastern Long Island to Oakdale, Long Island.

Throughout my recovery, I believed I would be able to work someday. I still hold onto that hope. I've made a commitment to myself, to God, and to Pam: I promised never to let a day go by without giving thanks for how blessed I am. I pledge never to question God's plan again. Being grateful for every experience that led me here is something I will always cherish.

Learning that God has a plan helped me get through so much loss.

Pam and I have talked about getting remarried. We're starting over, picking up where we left off, because right now, there's no other way to look at life. We're taking things one day at a time.

The doctors tell me I've sustained neuroglial damage and that my recovery has mostly stalled. The reality is, I may never walk again. Simple tasks I once took for granted like putting a sentence together or even putting on my shoes are now incredibly difficult. I've regained some speech, but I'm still far from how I used to speak. I honestly can barely get a sentence out; it takes me a long time.

Playing music is out of the question. The damage to my nervous system was so severe that, along with the inability to walk and speak, I also have no feeling in my fingers my arms and hands are numb.

These days mostly consist of watching television. Pam gets me set up each morning before work. I have to smoke medical marijuana several times a day to manage the pain from my injuries. Pam always leaves my marijuana cigarettes on the breakfast nook table so I can easily find them.

After breakfast, I just sit watching TV until lunchtime. I should mention I get around in a wheelchair.

I fantasize about better days. Sure, I'm grateful God spared my life, but I still struggle with my faith. It's much harder now. My disabilities are a constant reminder of my past.

Often, I wonder if there was a turning point a flashpoint where if I'd turned right instead of left, none of this would have happened to me or Pam.

Reflection can be valuable; it teaches us about ourselves by replaying our choices and experiences. But it's strange I still have fond memories of Leah. I suppose that's crazy, but then again, nothing in my life has made much sense lately.

I had a chance at happiness, and somehow, I blew it. Not only did I blow it, but I ended up here: a shadow of who I once was, wounded physically and mentally.

My emotions swing wildly from gratitude to God for sparing me, to bitterness and resentment over all I've endured and continue to endure.

I can't lie the thought of ending my own life has crossed my mind.

As I stare out the window, I drift off into daydreams. This happens often. My dreams blend past memories with fantasies of recovery. I dream of walking again, speaking again, playing my guitar again so many desires I long to fulfill.

Since leaving the hospital, the thrill of being alive has faded, replaced by a persistent depression.

I love being with Pam again, but the pain of not being able to truly be with her physically is deep.

I'm still attracted to her after all this time and everything that happened, but I'm no longer able to physically express that love. That hurts more than anything.

I would give anything to love Pam again the way I used to.

But here I am: a broken man, disabled, lonely, and very sad.

As tears well up, I realize there's one thing I can still do as before: cry. I cry several times a day.

The sadness is constant, and sometimes the feelings are overwhelming.

I keep praying tomorrow will be different, that better days will come. But day after day, night after night, nothing changes.

CHAPTER 32

Pam has the weekends off, which has been nice. She has so much to do around the house that sometimes the weekends fly by so fast, and we hardly feel like we've spent any time together. Since we moved out to Oakdale, we really haven't seen Junior, Jayde, or anyone else for that matter. People have moved on with their lives, leaving what happened in eastern Long Island and Pam and me behind. The concerned people who followed Pam's trial and then my near-death experience have all but disappeared.

I've become very reliant on medication and Pam's help just to get through each day. Pam has become somewhat of an introvert. She spends much of her time lost in thought. I often watch her as she seems to prefer being by herself. I wonder if this behavior developed during her time incarcerated.

Lately, Pam and I have little to say to one another. Because I have such a hard time speaking now, I'm reluctant to talk to her, so part of the blame for the silence lies with me. Sometimes she gets very impatient because I can't get the words out fast enough. My injuries are severe I sustained brain damage from the beating I took. It's very stressful for me, and it must be even harder for Pam, caring for me all the time.

Pam hasn't shared much about work or anything else. I just have this feeling something's off, something's wrong, and she's not telling me. It's just a feeling I can't shake. I'm not the man I used to be, and I can understand why Pam might be having second thoughts about taking me back into her home.

This afternoon was typical until late when I decided that at dinner, I would ask Pam to marry me again. I don't know why this feeling came over me it just did. Maybe asking Pam to marry me again will help us regain the love we once had so long ago.

Pam walked in the door looking preoccupied. Something was clearly on her mind, but I couldn't figure it out. Shortly after she came in, she said, "Paul, I'm making us a special dinner tonight." I smiled. For a moment, it felt like we were on the same page. As I sat watching Pam from my chair in the living room, I felt a flutter of excitement, rehearsing how I would ask her to marry me again. With my handicaps, I have a hard time putting a sentence together, but tonight, I was willing to give it everything I had.

Pam walked into the dining area, bringing me water and tea, and pouring herself some wine. She brought appetizers to the table, and we sat down to eat. Then Pam started talking to me something she hadn't done in a while.

As I sipped my tea, Pam began talking about the past. I was waiting for the right moment to ask her for her hand in marriage. She said, "Paul, Paul, Paul, what am I going to do with you?"

But Pam didn't sound like herself tonight. Her voice was different like someone else had taken over. The way she spoke was unlike anything I remembered, even her accent seemed off. I tried to respond, but I couldn't get the words out fast enough. I tried again, but Pam cut me off and smiled at me.

That smile wasn't warm or inviting it was cold, almost evil in some indescribable way. I tried to speak, but she cut me off again. Pam didn't seem to understand how hard it was for me to form a sentence. This time, she placed her open hand over my mouth and continued speaking.

"Paul," she said, "when we were married, it seemed good for a while, then it got boring for me. Paul, I don't blame you. Sometimes relationships are just like that. Ours was boring plain and simple. And you know what? I was willing to stick it out, to be with you no matter what. Then something happened."

Pam continued, "When you met Leah, I saw the way you looked at her. The day Tony and Leah moved into their house the look in your eyes said it all. You lusted for that girl. It was no secret. It was clear as day. At that moment, for me, our marriage was over. You just didn't know it yet. She went on, "I was really hurt by how captivated you were by Leah after I gave you my love and two children.

How could you even look at another woman? Yet you did."

"Paul, you did this to yourself. But I didn't let it get to me I had a plan. Two can play at that game. Tony had been hitting on me at work for a while. I liked it. I wanted to be with him, but I kept things at bay until the time was right."

"Leah was just his business partner. Tony and Leah were never anything more it was all about money. Once I knew that, I was with Tony often."

"Tony filled me in on what he and Leah did for money, and I wanted in. Leah, Lydia, and Leanne were all involved. Life became exciting. I discovered a side of me I never knew existed with Tony."

"As I listened, I still couldn't get a word in I was just sitting in my wheelchair, listening."

Pam went on: "I wanted in. Tony wanted me in. Leah and her family were willing to let me in because Tony wanted it."

"Leah and I became friends, and I asked her to keep you occupied while Tony and I spent time together."

Pam added, "You know the one thing I never thought would happen? Leah falling in love with you, Paul. Before I found out, Tony and I found something in common both of us enjoyed killing those people. Who knew? Once Tony introduced me to the thrill of taking a life, it turned me on. It gave me power. It made me feel dominant and alive a thrill I never felt before."

"It was a dark side of me I didn't know existed until Tony showed me."

"Leah knew what we were doing but wasn't involved in the killings just the fraud and money. Leanne and Lydia, however, were quite the devious duo."

"Paul, I just wanted out of our marriage and to change my life. I asked Leah to keep you occupied, and ironically, Leah fell in love with you."

"Lydia, Leah's sister, was supposed to kill you, Paul."

As Pam spoke, my eyes filled with tears. I fought back the pain what she was telling me was unimaginable. Why now?

Pam went on: "Somehow, Lydia mistakenly cut the brake lines on my sister's car because she thought it was yours. The two cars were the same model. The irony is cruel."

"Lydia killed my sons. That was supposed to be you. God, how I wish it was you," Pam said, tears falling.

Instead, she lost her two boys.

I sat there, feeling sad and hurt, as Pam kept talking.

"I wanted you dead, Paul."

"Then Leah turned on Tony and me. Leah was the weak link. Once she fell for you, she betrayed us all."

"She was the anonymous source who alerted the authorities and got Tony and me arrested."

"Paul, I bet you didn't know Leah made up the whole story about Tony beating her and you believed it!"

"Leah and I stayed friends during my trial. I wanted Leah, or Lydia, or any of them, to eliminate you."

I kept asking her to take care of you because I wanted her to kill you. I know you heard me ask Leah during my trial to, "take care of Paul," but Leah wanted to marry you. She really loved you, Paul. As I listened to Pam, what she was disclosing felt so unbelievable. I was starting to feel very tired, very numb. But Pam just kept talking. So, Paul; Pam said, "I want you to know two things. The first is that I truly am sorry you're going through this. Lydia was supposed to kill you, not maim you. In its own way, I find all this quite aggravating. Now I have to do this myself. It's so hard to get good help these days," Pam said, laughing out loud. "Second, I want you to know that I have poisoned you. That tea you're drinking will kill you in just a little while. I put a surprise in your tea. You know that heart medicine you take daily? Well, today you've taken too much. Oops! It should finish you off soon. So, Paul, I'm guessing all this comes as a surprise. It really shouldn't. You should be happy. You probably don't even want to live the way you are right now. Hell, I wouldn't. I'm going for a walk, Paul. When I come back, you should be dead. I want you to remember everything you put me through, Paul. It's a beautiful afternoon. I think I'll get some fresh air and enjoy the day."

As Pam walked out the door, I felt numb. It was clear the poison was starting to take effect. It was only a matter of time before I would succumb to the medication. As this realization settled in, all I could think about was Leah. Leah really loved me. She truly loved me. I felt that deep in my heart before everything happened. I knew, in my heart of hearts, that Leah loved me for real. Leah and I really had something. Suddenly, dying wasn't so intimidating. All I could think about was that Leah really loved me. As I was leaving this earth, that thought gave me so much peace. I really did love her, too. As my time with Leah flashed before my eyes, I felt grateful that I had known true love. I had it with Leah. As euphoria started to wash over me, it became clear my life was ending. I think Pam thought she was hurting me, but she actually made me ready for the end. I knew there was no way I was surviving this. I was confident I didn't want to live like this burdened by all these disabilities. I think Pam saw it the same way she was just putting me out of my misery. So, I remained here, waiting to die. Something told me Pam wasn't coming back. Something told me this was really the end.

I started to feel nauseous and had a sharp pain in my stomach that radiated to my chest. It was clear Pam wasn't lying or bluffing. Suddenly, I began salivating profusely and breathing heavily. I could actually hear and feel my heartbeat like it was about to explode from my chest cavity. My body started shaking, and sweat poured from me. Trying to stay in control, I struggled as racing thoughts flooded my mind. I felt dizzy and confused, overwhelmed by the sudden onset. Breathing became a struggle I just couldn't catch my breath. Numbness crept over me. I sat in my wheelchair, trying to withstand whatever Pam had poisoned me with. Over the next half hour, my heart rate slowed somewhat. Fatigue and weakness set in. Still sweating uncontrollably, I began to lose control of my bodily functions. Convulsions seized me, and breathing became harder. In the distance, I spotted the marijuana cigarette Pam had left for me on the table near the kitchen gas oven. The pain was overwhelming, but I summoned the strength to wheel myself over to the oven. I opened the door and turned the gas on full blast. Then, in agonizing pain, I wheeled back to the table, picked up the marijuana cigarette, and paused to confirm what I was doing. The pain was unbearable, so I lit the cigarette with a lighter and inhaled deeply. I held the smoke as I looked out the window.

For what felt like an eternity, I watched Pam walking away down the street. Suddenly, a loud explosion echoed. The pain vanished immediately. Instead of agony, I felt warmth and comfort. I saw my boys and an amazing light. Though I knew I should feel pain, I felt peace. I reached for the light, and my two sons reached out to me. I felt ready. I left my body, finally realizing it was real. I was going home. It was over.

In the end, after all the smoke cleared and the pain and heartache faded, I could say Leah and I really did find the love we desperately sought. It's a shame we didn't embrace it more when we had the chance. If you asked me to define what we had, I couldn't put it into words. All I could say was that we had something. After it all went away, when there was nothing left to say and everything fell to nothing we still had something.

The End

About The Author

Paul J. Magrone Jr. is a musician, songwriter turned author. Writing songs is a lot like telling stories. After all, a book is really just an extended set of lyrics. As a very creative individual, I spend a lot of time just thinking. Sometimes my thoughts are musically inspired while other times, my mind races. In this book, my mind was racing for most of the story. I decided to make it my signature approach as an author to write and record a song that comes out with each book that I write. I feel like combining the two definitely sets me apart from other authors and allows me to be different. After all, isn't that what we all want and even need? To stand out as who we believe we are. I am a happily married man approaching 60 years of age and have discovered that time may no longer be my ally. So, I do really hope that you enjoy this story. I also hope that you check out the song, "We Still Had Something" because it was written with this story in mind. Thank you for reading my work. I hope to bring many more books to the world of fiction stories. For now, I am just grateful for this opportunity to share my creation with all of you.

THANK YOU

I want to thank you for reading this book. It was enjoyable for me to create this story, and put it all together. As you know, this is my first ever fiction book. You taking the time to read this book, means so much to me. Thank you so much. There will be more to come.

Paul J. Magrone Jr.